ROBERT HEINLEIN MEMORIAL EDITION

Robert Heinlein was my friend. When he died I wanted to do something—no large or otherwise pretentious thing, but *something*—to, in effect, throw a flower on his grave. For that reason I approached his agent, Eleanor Wood, for permission to republish "The Notebooks of Lazarus Long" in *New Destinies*. Both Eleanor and Virginia Heinlein thought it was a fine idea.

Then it occurred to me that Robert had been very pleased with Spider Robinson's assessment of his work in "Rah Rah R.A.H!" So I called Spider. He was delighted, of course. Well, one thing led to another, as will happen when Robert is involved, and so was born the Robert Heinlein Memorial Edition of *New Destinies*. In addition to the "Notebooks" and "Rah Rah R.A.H!" it includes a eulogy by Jerry Pournelle and at Jerry's behest, and because it is central to the eulogy, Robert's story, "The Long Watch." It also includes "Farewell," by Robert's friends, Charles Sheffield and Yoji Kondo; Robert's own favorite story from all his oevre, "The Man Who Traveled in Elephants"; and best of all, two previously unpublished poems by Robert Heinlein on the subject that to him mattered more than anything else.

It is almost a matter of discomfort to me that my distributor thinks this issue of *New Destinies* will be in far greater demand than any before (and very probably any that will follow), but on reflection I'm sure that Mr. Heinlein would have been delighted.

Jim Baen
Publisher and Editor

JIM BAEN

THE PAPERBACK MAGAZINE OF SCIENCE FICTION AND SPECULATIVE FACT

VOLUME VI/WINTER 1988

This and every issue of *New Destinies* is dedicated to the memory of Robert A. Heinlein

NEW DESTINIES VOL. VI

A Baen Books Original

Baen Publishing Enterprises
260 Fifth Avenue
New York, N.Y. 10001

First printing, December 1988

ISBN: 0-671-69796-X

Cover art by David Cherry

Printed in the United States of America

Distributed by
SIMON & SCHUSTER
1230 Avenue of the Americas
New York, N.Y. 10020

CONTENTS

Acknowledgments

An address given at the annual Nebula Awards Ceremony of the Science Fiction Writers of America, Hollywood Roosevelt Hotel, Saturday, May 21, 1988.

IN APPRECIATION ROBERT A. HEINLEIN 7/7/1907—5/8/1988

Jerry Pournelle

On a high hill in Samoa there is a grave. Inscribed on the marker are these words:

> *"Under the wide and starry sky*
> *Dig the grave and let me lie.*
> *Glad did I live and gladly die*
> *And I laid me down with a will!*
>
> *"This be the verse you grave for me:*
> *'Here he lies where he longed to be,*
> *Home is the sailor, home from the sea,*
> *And the hunter home from the hill' ".*

These lines appear another place—scrawled on a shipping tag from a compressed-air container, and pinned to the ground with a knife.

That shipping tag is not yet on the Moon. It will be.

Some years ago when the United States flew spacecraft instead of endlessly re-designing them, I had the extraordinary fortune to be sitting with Robert A. Heinlein in the cafeteria at Cal Tech's Jet Propulsion Laboratory during the landing of the Viking probe to Mars. We were in the cafeteria because, while I had both press and VIP credentials, Mr. Heinlein did not. I had brought him to JPL because I thought he belonged there; but there hadn't been time to get him credentials, so the NASA authorities ordered him out of the Von Karman Center.

I was outraged, and wanted to make a scene, but Robert would have none of that. He trudged up the hill to the cafeteria.

There is sometimes justice in this world. At the moment our first spacecraft landed on Mars, most of the network news cameras were in the cafeteria trained on Mr. Heinlein, rather than down in the center recording what NASA's officialdom thought they should be watching.

On Sunday, May 8, Robert A. Heinlein died peacefully during a nap. Like one of his beloved cats, when it was time he left us without fuss. He was cremated and his ashes scattered at sea from a warship. If we want to take his ashes to the Moon, we will have to take a pint of seawater. I think he'd find that acceptable.

Mr. Heinlein began writing science fiction before World War II, at a time when most strategists thought that battleships would dominate naval warfare and the battleships's analog fire control system was the most advanced computer technology in the world; when the Norden bombsight was top secret technology. After the war, while Dr. Vannevar Bush was telling Congress that the US would never be threatened by intercontinental missiles, Robert Heinlein gave us *Space Cadet* and *Universe*.

He wrote the outline of his "future history" in 1940–41. He was ridiculed for predicting in that history that the first rocket to the Moon would fly as early as 1976—and that it would usher in a "false dawn" followed by a long hiatus in space travel during the "crazy years" of mass psychosis toward the end of the twentieth century. Alas, some of that is chillingly accurate.

Robert Heinlein had as much to do with creating our future as any man of this century. It was not remarkable that the science reporters for the networks chose to follow him to exile in the cafeteria. They, like most of JPL's scientists and engineers, would never have been there if his stories had not called them to study and learn so that they could make his dreams a reality. His stories have caused more young people to choose careers in science and engineering than all the formal recruitment pitches ever tried.

He created our future in other ways. His stories made us ready, convinced us that it could be done. Robert Heinlein was truly *The Man Who Sold The Moon*.

Twenty years ago, Robert Heinlein took the time to review the first novel of a young space scientist turned professor turned novelist. My novel. Five years later, he read the first draft of *The Mote In God's Eye* and sent us a 70 page single-spaced critique that has more about how to be a successful writer than all the creative writing courses ever taught.

I owe a great part of whatever success I've had as a writer to help and encouragement Robert Heinlein gave me over the past thirty years. I once asked him how I could pay him back. His answer was simple: "You can't. You pay it forward."

He changed our lives in many ways. His dreams prepared the way for space flight. We are all in his debt.

No debt was ever easier to pay. Indeed, it costs nothing, because we get back tenfold everything we invest.

We can pay Robert Heinlein forward by keeping the dream alive: A dream of an endless frontier where free people know no limits and knowledge has no bounds.

Ad Astra and Goodbye.

Introduction to "The Long Watch"

Jerry Pournelle's "In Appreciation" will serve better than any words of mine could do as the introduction for "The Long Watch." Read it before you read this story. This is not optional.

Robert A. Heinlein

"Nine ships blasted off from Moon Base. Once in space, eight of them formed a globe around the smallest. They held this formation all the way to Earth.

"The small ship displayed the insignia of an admiral—yet there was no living thing of any sort in her. She was not even a passenger ship, but a drone, a robot ship intended for radioactive cargo. This trip she carried nothing but a lead coffin—and a Geiger counter that was never quiet."

—from the editorial *After Ten Years*, film 38, 17 June 2009, Archives of the *N.Y. Times*

I

Johnny Dahlquist blew smoke at the Geiger counter. He grinned wryly and tried it again. His whole body was radioactive by now. Even his breath, the smoke from his cigarette, could make the Geiger counter scream.

How long had he been here? Time doesn't mean

much on the Moon. Two days? Three? A week? He let his mind run back: the last clearly marked time in his mind was when the Executive Officer had sent for him, right after breakfast—

"Lieutenant Dahlquist, reporting to the Executive Officer."

Colonel Towers looked up. "Ah, John Ezra. Sit down, Johnny. Cigarette?"

Johnny sat down, mystified but flattered. He admired Colonel Towers, for his brilliance, his ability to dominate, and for his battle record. Johnny had no battle record; he had been commissioned on completing his doctor's degree in nuclear physics and was now junior bomb officer of Moon Base.

The Colonel wanted to talk politics; Johnny was puzzled. Finally Towers had come to the point; it was not safe (so he said) to leave control of the world in political hands; power must be held by a scientifically selected group. In short—the Patrol.

Johnny was startled rather than shocked. As an abstract idea, Towers' notion sounded plausible. The League of Nations had folded up; what would keep the United Nations from breaking up, too, and thus lead to another World War. "And you know how bad such a war would be, Johnny."

Johnny agreed. Towers said he was glad that Johnny got the point. The senior bomb officer could handle the work, but it was better to have both specialists.

Johnny sat up with a jerk. "You are going to *do* something about it?" He had thought the Exec was just talking.

Towers smiled. "We're not politicians; we don't just talk. We act."

Johnny whistled. "When does this start?"

Towers flipped a switch. Johnny was startled to hear his own voice, then identified the recorded conversation as having taken place in the junior officers' mess-room. A political argument he remembered, which he had walked out on . . . a good thing, too! But being spied on annoyed him.

Towers switched it off. "We *have* acted," he said. "We know who is safe and who isn't. Take Kelly—" He waved at the loudspeaker. "Kelly is politically unreliable. You noticed he wasn't at breakfast?"

"Huh? I thought he was on watch."

"Kelly's watch-standing days are over. Oh, relax; he isn't hurt."

Johnny thought this over. "Which list am I on?" he asked. "Safe or unsafe?"

"Your name has a question mark after it. But I have said all along that you could be depended on." He grinned engagingly. "You won't make a liar of me, Johnny?"

Dahlquist didn't answer; Towers said sharply, "Come now—what do you think of it? Speak up."

"Well, if you ask me, you've bitten off more than you can chew. While it's true that Moon Base controls the Earth, Moon Base itself is a sitting duck for a ship. One bomb—*blooie!*"

Towers picked up a message form and handed it over; it read: I HAVE YOUR CLEAN LAUNDRY—ZACK. "That means every bomb in the *Trygve Lie* has been put out of commission. I have reports from every ship we need worry about." He stood up. "Think it over and see me after lunch. Major Morgan needs your help right away to change control frequencies on the bombs."

"The control frequencies?"

"Naturally. We don't want the bombs jammed before they reach their targets."

"What? You said the idea was to *prevent* war."

Towers brushed it aside. "There won't be a war—just a psychological demonstration, an unimportant town or two. A little bloodletting to save an all-out war. Simple arithmetic."

He put a hand on Johnny's shoulder. "You aren't squeamish, or you wouldn't be a bomb officer. Think of it as a surgical operation. And think of your family."

Johnny Dahlquist had been thinking of his family. "Please, sir, I want to see the Commanding Officer."

Towers frowned. "The Commodore is not available. As you know, I speak for him. See me again—after lunch."

The Commodore was decidedly not available; the Commodore was dead. But Johnny did not know that.

Dahlquist walked back to the messroom, bought cigarettes, sat down and had a smoke. He got up, crushed out the butt, and headed for the Base's west airlock. There he got into his space suit and went to the lockmaster. "Open her up, Smitty."

The marine looked surprised. "Can't let anyone out on the surface without word from Colonel Towers, sir. Hadn't you heard?"

"Oh, yes! Give me your order book." Dahlquist took it, wrote a pass for himself, and signed it "by direction of Colonel Towers." He added, "Better call the Executive Officer and check it."

The lockmaster read it and stuck the book in his pocket. "Oh, no, Lieutenant. Your word's good."

"Hate to disturb the Executive Officer, eh? Don't blame you." He stepped in, closed the inner door, and waited for the air to be sucked out.

Out on the Moon's surface he blinked at the light and hurried to the track-rocket terminus; a car was waiting. He squeezed in, pulled down the hood, and punched the starting button. The rocket car flung itself at the hills, dived through and came out on a plain studded with projectile rockets, like candles on a cake. Quickly it dived into a second tunnel through more hills. There was a stomach-wrenching deceleration and the car stopped at the underground atom-bomb armory.

As Dahlquist climbed out he switched on his walkie-talkie. The space-suited guard at the entrance came to port-arms. Dahlquist said, "Morning, Lopez," and walked by him to the airlock. He pulled it open.

The guard motioned him back. "Hey! Nobody goes in without the Executive Officer's say-so." He shifted his gun, fumbled in his pouch and got out a paper. "Read it, Lieutenant."

Dahlquist waved it away. "I drafted that order myself. *You* read it; you've misinterpreted it."

"I don't see how, Lieutenant."

Dahlquist snatched the paper, glanced at it, then pointed to a line. "See? '—except persons specifically designated by the Executive Officer.' That's the bomb officers, Major Morgan and me."

The guard looked worried. Dahlquist said, "Damn it, look up 'specifically designated'—it's under '*Bomb Room, Security, Procedure for,*' in your standing orders. Don't tell me you left them in the barracks!"

"Oh, no, sir! I've got 'em." The guard reached into his pouch. Dahlquist gave him back the sheet; the guard took it, hesitated, then leaned his weapon against his hip, shifted the paper to his left hand, and dug into his pouch with his right.

Dahlquist grabbed the gun, shoved it between the guard's legs, and jerked. He threw the weapon away and ducked into the airlock. As he slammed the door he saw the guard struggling to his feet and reaching for his side arm. He dogged the outer door shut and felt a tingle in his fingers as a slug struck the door.

He flung himself at the inner door, jerked the spill lever, rushed back to the outer door and hung his weight on the handle. At once he could feel it stir. The guard was lifting up; the lieutenant was pulling down, with only his low Moon weight to anchor him. Slowly the handle raised before his eyes.

Air from the bomb room rushed into the lock through the spill valve. Dahlquist felt his space suit settle on his body as the pressure in the lock began to equal the pressure in the suit. He quit straining and let the guard raise the handle. It did not matter; thirteen tons of air pressure now held the door closed.

He latched open the inner door to the bomb room, so that it could not swing shut. As long as it was open, the airlock could not operate; no one could enter.

Before him in the room, one for each projectile rocket,

were the atom bombs, spaced in rows far enough apart to defeat any faint possibility of spontaneous chain reaction. They were the deadliest things in the known universe, but they were his babies. He had placed himself between them and anyone who would misuse them.

But, now that he was here, he had no plan to use his temporary advantage.

The speaker on the wall sputtered into life. "Hey! Lieutenant! What goes on here? You gone crazy?" Dahlquist did not answer. Let Lopez stay confused—it would take him that much longer to make up his mind what to do. And Johnny Dahlquist needed as many minutes as he could squeeze. Lopez went on protesting. Finally he shut up.

Johnny had followed a blind urge not to let the bombs—*his* bombs!—be used for "demonstrations on unimportant towns." But what to do next? Well, Towers couldn't get through the lock. Johnny would sit tight until hell froze over.

Don't kid yourself, John Ezra! Towers could get in. Some high explosive against the outer door—then the air would whoosh out, our boy Johnny would drown in blood from his burst lungs—and the bombs would be sitting there, unhurt. They were built to stand the jump from Moon to Earth; vacuum would not hurt them at all.

He decided to stay in his space suit; explosive decompression didn't appeal to him. Come to think about it, death from old age was his choice.

Or they could drill a hole, let out the air, and open the door without wrecking the lock. Or Towers might even have a new airlock built outside the old. Not likely, Johnny thought; a *coup d'état* depended on speed. Towers was almost sure to take the quickest way—blasting. And Lopez was probably calling the Base right now. Fifteen minutes for Towers to suit up and get here, maybe a short dicker—then *whoosh!* the party is over.

Fifteen minutes—

In fifteen minutes the bombs might fall back into the hands of the conspirators; in fifteen minutes he must make the bombs unusable.

An atom bomb is just two or more pieces of fissionable metal, such as plutonium. Separated, they are no more explosive than a pound of butter; slapped together, they explode. The complications lie in the gadgets and circuits and gun used to slap them together in the exact way and at the exact time and place required.

These circuits, the bomb's "brain," are easily destroyed—but the bomb itself is hard to destroy because of its very simplicity. Johnny decided to smash the "brains"—and quickly!

The only tools at hand were simple ones used in handling the bombs. Aside from a Geiger counter, the speaker on the walkie-talkie circuit, a television rig to the base, and the bombs themselves, the room was bare. A bomb to be worked on was taken elsewhere—not through fear of explosion, but to reduce radiation exposure for personnel. The radioactive material in a bomb is buried in a "tamper"—in these bombs, gold. Gold stops alpha, beta, and much of the deadly gamma radiation—but not neutrons.

The slippery, poisonous neutrons which plutonium gives off had to escape, or a chain reaction—explosion! —would result. The room was bathed in an invisible, almost undetectable rain of neutrons. The place was unhealthy; regulations called for staying in it as short a time as possible.

The Geiger counter clicked off the "background" radiation, cosmic rays, the trace of radioactivity in the Moon's crust, and secondary radioactivity set up all through the room by neutrons. Free neutrons have the nasty trait of infecting what they strike, making it radioactive, whether it be concrete wall or human body. In time the room would have to be abandoned.

Dahlquist twisted a knob on the Geiger counter; the instrument stopped clicking. He had used a suppressor circuit to cut out noise of "background" radiation at the level then present. It reminded him uncomfortably of the danger of staying here. He took out the radiation exposure film all radiation personnel carry; it was a direct-response type and had been fresh when he arrived. The most sensitive end was faintly darkened already. Halfway down the film a red line crossed it. Theoretically, if the wearer was exposed to enough radioactivity in a week to darken the film to that line, he was, as Johnny reminded himself, a "dead duck."

Off came the cumbersome space suit; what he needed was speed. Do the job and surrender—better to be a prisoner than to linger in a place as "hot" as this.

He grabbed a ball hammer from the tool rack and got busy, pausing only to switch off the television pick-up. The first bomb bothered him. He started to smash the cover plate of the "brain," then stopped, filled with reluctance. All his life he had prized fine apparatus.

He nerved himself and swung; glass tinkled, metal creaked. His mood changed; he began to feel a shameful pleasure in destruction. He pushed on with enthusiasm, swinging, smashing, destroying!

So intent was he that he did not at first hear his name called. "Dahlquist! Answer me! Are you there?"

He wiped sweat and looked at the TV screen. Towers' perturbed features stared out.

Johnny was shocked to find that he had wrecked only six bombs. Was he going to be caught before he could finish? Oh, no! He *had* to finish. Stall, son, stall! "Yes, Colonel? You called me?"

"I certainly did! What's the meaning of this?"

"I'm sorry, Colonel."

Towers' expression relaxed a little. "Turn on your pick-up, Johnny, I can't see you. What was that noise?"

"The pick-up is on," Johnny lied. "It must be out of order. That noise—uh, to tell the truth, Colonel, I was fixing things so that nobody could get in here."

Towers hesitated, then said firmly, "I'm going to assume that you are sick and send you to the Medical Officer. But I want you to come out of there, right away. That's an order, Johnny."

Johnny answered slowly. "I can't just yet, Colonel. I

came here to make up my mind and I haven't quite made it up. You said to see you after lunch."

"I meant you to stay in your quarters."

"Yes, sir. But I thought I ought to stand watch on the bombs, in case I decided you were wrong."

"It's not for you to decide, Johnny. I'm your superior officer. You are sworn to obey me."

"Yes, sir." This was wasting time; the old fox might have a squad on the way now. "But I swore to keep the peace, too. Could you come out here and talk it over with me? I don't want to do the wrong thing."

Towers smiled. "A good idea, Johnny. You wait there. I'm sure you'll see the light." He switched off.

"There," said Johnny. "I hope you're convinced that I'm a half-wit—you slimy mistake!" He picked up the hammer, ready to use the minutes gained.

He stopped almost at once; it dawned on him that wrecking the "brains" was not enough. There were no spare "brains," but there was a well-stocked electronics shop. Morgan could jury-rig control circuits for bombs. Why, he could himself—not a neat job, but one that would work. Damnation! He would have to wreck the bombs themselves—and in the next ten minutes.

But a bomb was solid chunks of metal, encased in a heavy tamper, all tied in with a big steel gun. It couldn't be done—not in ten minutes.

Damn!

Of course, there was one way. He knew the control circuits; he also knew how to beat them. Take this bomb: if he took out the safety bar, unhooked the proximity circuit, shorted the delay circuit, and cut in the arming circuit by hand—then unscrewed *that* and reached in *there*, he could, with just a long stiff wire, set the bomb off.

Blowing the other bombs and the valley itself to Kingdom come.

Also Johnny Dahlquist. That was the rub.

All this time he was doing what he had thought out, up to the step of actually setting off the bomb. Ready to go, the bomb seemed to threaten, as if crouching to spring. He stood up, sweating.

He wondered if he had the courage. He did not want to funk—and hoped that he would. He dug into his jacket and took out a picture of Edith and the baby. "Honeychile," he said, "if I get out of this, I'll never even try to beat a red light." He kissed the picture and put it back. There was nothing to do but wait.

What was keeping Towers? Johnny wanted to make sure that Towers was in blast range. What a joke on the jerk! Me—sitting here, ready to throw the switch on him. The idea tickled him; it led to a better: why blow himself up—alive?

There was another way to rig it—a "dead man" control. Jigger up some way so that the last step, the one that set off the bomb, would not happen as long as he kept his hand on a switch or a lever or something. Then, if they blew open the door, or shot him, or anything—up goes the balloon!

Better still, if he could hold them off with the threat of it, sooner or later help would come—Johnny was sure that most of the Patrol was not in this stinking conspiracy—and then: Johnny comes marching home! What a reunion! He'd resign and get a teaching job; he'd stood his watch.

All the while, he was working. Electrical? No, too little time. Make it a simple mechanical linkage. He had it doped out but had hardly begun to build it when the loudspeaker called him. "Johnny?"

"That you, Colonel?" His hands kept busy.

"Let me in."

"Well, now, Colonel, that wasn't in the agreement." Where in blue blazes was something to use as a long lever?

"I'll come in alone, Johnny, I give you my word. We'll talk face to face."

His word! "We can talk over the speaker, Colonel." Hey, that was it—a yardstick, hanging on the tool rack.

"Johnny, I'm warning you. Let me in, or I'll blow the door off."

A wire—he needed a wire, fairly long and stiff. He tore the antenna from his suit. "You wouldn't do that, Colonel. It would ruin the bombs."

"Vacuum won't hurt the bombs. Quit stalling."

"Better check with Major Morgan. Vacuum won't hurt them; explosive decompression would wreck every circuit." The Colonel was not a bomb specialist; he shut up for several minutes. Johnny went on working.

"Dahlquist," Towers resumed, "that was a clumsy lie. I checked with Morgan. You have sixty seconds to get into your suit, if you aren't already. I'm going to blast the door."

"No, you won't," said Johnny. "Ever hear of a 'dead man' switch?" Now for a counterweight—and a sling.

"Eh? What do you mean?"

"I've rigged number seventeen to set off by hand. But I put in a gimmick. It won't blow while I hang on to a strap I've got in my hand. But if anything happens to me—*up she goes!* You are about fifty feet from the blast center. Think it over."

There was a short silence. "I don't believe you."

"No? Ask Morgan. He'll believe me. He can inspect it, over the TV pick-up." Johnny lashed the belt of his space suit to the end of the yardstick.

"You said the pick-up was out of order."

"So I lied. This time I'll prove it. Have Morgan call me."

Presently Major Morogan's face appeared. "Lieutenant Dahlquist?"

"Hi, Stinky. Wait a sec." With great care Dahlquist made one last connection while holding down the end of the yardstick. Still careful, he shifted his grip to the belt, sat down on the floor, stretched an arm and switched on the TV pick-up. "Can you see me, Stinky?"

"I can see you," Morgan answered stiffly. "What is this nonsense?"

"A little surprise I whipped up." He explained it—what circuits he had cut out, what ones had been shorted, just how the jury-rigged mechanical sequence fitted in.

Morgan nodded. "But you're bluffing, Dahlquist. I

feel sure that you haven't disconnected the 'K' circuit. You don't have the guts to blow yourself up."

Johnny chuckled. "I sure haven't. But that's the beauty of it. It can't go off, *so long as I am alive*. If your greasy boss, ex-Colonel Towers, blasts the door, then I'm dead and the bomb goes off. It won't matter to me, but it will to him. Better tell him." He switched off.

Towers came on over the speaker shortly. "Dahlquist?"

"I hear you."

"There's no need to throw away your life. Come out and you will be retired on full pay. You can go home to your family. That's a promise."

Johnny got mad. "You keep my family out of this!"

"Think of them, man."

"Shut up. Get back to your hole. I feel a need to scratch and this whole shebang might just explode in your lap."

II

Johnny sat up with a start. He had dozed, his hand hadn't let go the sling, but he had the shakes when he thought about it.

Maybe he should disarm the bomb and depend on their not daring to dig him out? But Towers' neck was already in hock for treason; Towers might risk it. If he did and the bomb were disarmed, Johnny would be dead and Towers would have the bombs. No, he had gone this far, he wouldn't let his baby girl grow up in a dictatorship just to catch some sleep.

He heard the Geiger counter clicking and remembered having used the suppressor circuit. The radioactivity in the room must be increasing, perhaps from scattering the "brain" circuits—the circuits were sure to be infected; they had lived too long too close to plutonium. He dug out his film.

The dark area was spreading toward the red line.

He put it back and said, "Pal, better break this deadlock or you are going to shine like a watch dial."

It was a figure of speech; infected animal tissue does not glow—it simply dies, slowly.

The TV screen lit up; Towers' face appeared. "Dahlquist? I want to talk to you."

"Go fly a kite."

"Let's admit you have us inconvenienced."

"Inconvenienced, hell—I've got you stopped."

"For the moment. I'm arranging to get more bombs—"

"Liar."

"—but you are slowing us up. I have a proposition."

"Not interested."

"Wait. When this is over I will be chief of the world government. If you cooperate, even now, I will make you my administrative head."

Johnny told him what to do with it. Towers said, "Don't be stupid. What do you gain by dying?"

Johnny grunted. "Towers, what a prime stinker you are. You spoke of my family. I'd rather see them dead than living under a two-bit Napoleon like you. Now go away—I've got some thinking to do."

Towers switched off.

Johnny got out his film again. It seemed no darker but it reminded him forcibly that time was running out. He was hungry and thirsty—and he could not stay awake forever. It took four days to get a ship up from Earth; he could not expect rescue any sooner. And he wouldn't last four days—once the darkening spread past the red line he was a goner.

His only chance was to wreck the bombs beyond repair, and get out—before that film got much darker.

He thought about ways, then got busy. He hung a weight on the sling, tied a line to it. If Towers blasted the door, he hoped to jerk the rig loose before he died.

There was a simple, though arduous, way to wreck the bombs beyond any capacity of Moon Base to repair them. The heart of each was two hemispheres of plutonium, their flat surface polished smooth to permit perfect contact when slapped together. Anything less would prevent the chain reaction on which atomic explosion depended.

Johnny started taking apart one of the bombs.

He had to bash off four lugs, then break the glass envelope around the inner assembly. Aside from that the bomb came apart easily. At last he had in front of him two gleaming, mirror-perfect half globes.

A blow with the hammer—and one was no longer perfect. Another blow and the second cracked like glass; he had trapped its crystalline structure just right.

Hours later, dead tired, he went back to the armed bomb. Forcing himself to steady down, with extreme care he disarmed it. Shortly its silvery hemispheres too were useless. There was no longer a usable bomb in the room—but huge fortunes in the most valuable, most poisonous, and most deadly metal in the known world were spread around the floor.

Johnny looked at the deadly stuff. "Into your suit and out of here, son," he said aloud. "I wonder what Towers will say?"

He walked toward the rack, intending to hang up the hammer. As he passed, the Geiger counter chattered wildly.

Plutonium hardy affects a Geiger counter; secondary infection from plutonium does. Johnny looked at the hammer, then held it closer to the Geiger counter. The counter screamed.

Johnny tossed it hastily away and started back toward his suit.

As he passed the counter it chattered again. He stopped short.

He pushed one hand close to the counter. It's clicking picked up to a steady roar. Without moving he reached into his pocket and took out his exposure film.

It was dead black from end to end.

III

Plutonium taken into the body moves quickly to bone marrow. Nothing can be done; the victim is finished. Neutrons from it smash through the body ionizing tissue, transmuting atoms into radioactive isotopes, destroying and killing. The fatal dose is unbelievably small; a mass a tenth the size of a grain of table salt is more than enough—a dose small enough to enter through the tiniest scratch. During the historic "Manhattan Project" immediate high amputation was considered the only possible first-aid measure.

Johnny knew all this but it no longer disturbed him. He sat on the floor, smoking a hoarded cigarette, and thinking. The events of his long watch were running through his mind.

He blew a puff of smoke at the Geiger counter and smiled without humor to hear it chatter more loudly. By now even his breath was "hot"—carbon-14, he supposed, exhaled from his blood stream as carbon dioxide. It did not matter.

There was no longer any point in surrendering, nor would he give Towers the satisfaction—he would finish out this watch right here. Besides, by keeping up the bluff that one bomb was ready to blow, he could stop them from capturing the raw material from which bombs were made. That might be important in the long run.

He accepted, without surprise, the fact that he was not unhappy. There was a sweetness about having no further worries of any sort. He did not hurt, he was not uncomfortable, he was no longer even hungry. Physically he still felt fine and his mind was at peace. He was dead—he knew that he was dead; yet for a time he was able to walk and breathe and see and feel.

He was not even lonesome. He was not alone, there were comrades with him—the boy with his finger in the dike, Colonel Bowie, too ill to move but insisting that he be carried across the line, the dying Captain of the *Chesapeake* still with deathless challenge on his lips, Rodger Young peering into the gloom. They gathered about him in the dusky bomb room.

And of course there was Edith. She was the only one he was aware of. Johnny wished that he could see her face more clearly. Was she angry? Or proud and happy?

Proud though unhappy—he could see her better now and even feel her hand. He held very still.

Presently his cigarette burned down to his fingers. He took a final puff, blew it at the Geiger counter, and put it out. It was his last. He gathered several butts and fashioned a roll-your-own with a bit of paper found in a pocket. He lit it carefully and settled back to wait for Edith to show up again. He was very happy.

He was still propped against the bomb case, the last of his salvaged cigarettes cold at his side, when the speaker called out again, "Johnny? Hey, Johnny. Can you hear me? This is Kelly. It's all over. The *Lafayette* landed and Towers blew his brains out. Johnny? *Answer me.*"

When they opened the outer door, the first man in carried a Geiger counter in front of him on the end of a long pole. He stopped at the threshold and backed out hastily. "Hey, chief!" he called. "Better get some handling equipment—uh, and a lead coffin, too."

"Four days it took the little ship and her escort to reach Earth. Four days while all of Earth's people awaited her arrival. For ninety-eight hours all commercial programs were off television; instead there was an endless dirge—the Dead March *from* Saul, *the* Valhalla *theme,* Going Home, *the Patrols' own* Landing Orbit.

"The nine ships landed at Chicago Port. A drone tractor removed the casket from the small ship; the ship was then refueled and blasted off in an escape trajectory, thrown away into outer space, never again to be used for a lesser purpose.

"The tractor progressed to the Illinois town where Lieutenant Dahlquist had been born, while the dirge continued. There it placed the casket on a pedestal, inside a barrier marking the distance of safe approach. Space marines, arms reversed and heads bowed, stood

guard around it; the crowds stayed outside this circle. And still the dirge continued.

"When enough time had passed, long, long after the heaped flowers had withered, the lead casket was enclosed in marble, just as you see it today."

Introduction

Virginia Heinlein has graciously arranged for our publication of this and another poem placed later in this volume. Except for material incorporated in his fiction they are Robert's first published poetry. Mrs. Heinlein has requested that they be published without further comment. So be it.

DANCE SESSION

The squeegeed ice in the great dim hall
Was clean and blue and fit for the ball;
So the music sounded and the lights glared out
And the cruel steel blades went swirling about
In flight fantastic and fancy free,
In crisp, clean spins, with gutsy glee—
Etching the ice with outre art,
While the cruel bright blades
  sliced sharp in my heart

Out of the leaping rushing spate
A voice sang out for a three-lobed eight;
The ice fauns paired with their elfin sprites
To start their intricate woven rites.
In complex, structured demonstration
They captured Art in one equation;
In sweet incredible enthymeme
They proved the logic of cold Moon beam.

Out form the pattern of Killian and Blues
Emerged the sprite whom the Ice Gods choose
To show us weary earth-bound creatures
The cool, sweet lines of Beauty's features.
Rosy her long limbs, snow white were her gants,
Rime blue was her jerkin, and merry her glance—
Hoyden her hair bow, among the gallants.
Ice fairy Virginia, First in the Dance!

(Oh, great was the shock of the sudden stop
When the music ceased and the patterns broke
And fairyland melted in cigarette smoke
In the warm dull light of a coffee shop!)

RAH, June 1946

Concerning "Rah Rah R.A.H.!":

When Jim Baen left Galaxy, *shortly before I did, it was to become sf editor of Ace Books. Ace promptly became the largest publisher of sf in the world, printing more titles in 1977 than any other house.*

Suddenly Jim found himself in custody of a great many cheese sandwiches.

So he built the magazine he had always wanted Galaxy *to be and couldn't afford to make it, and he named it* Destinies. *It was a quarterly paperback bookazine from Ace, a book filled with fiction and speculative fact and artwork and all the little extras that make up a magazine, and it was the most consistently satisfying and thought-provoking periodical that came into my house, not excluding* Omni *and the* Scientific American. *I did review columns for the first five issues, dropping out for reasons that in retrospect seem dumb.*

So one day shortly after I quit writing reviews for Destinies, *Jim called and offered me a proposition: he would send me a xerox of the newest Robert Heinlein manuscript,* months *in advance of publication, if I would use the book as a springboard for a full-length essay on the lifework of Heinlein, for* Destinies. *The new book was* Expanded Universe, *which by now you will almost certainly have seen and therefore own; let me tell you, it blew me away.*

The following is what came spilling out of me when I was done reading Expanded Universe*—and when I used it as my Guest of Honor speech at Bosklone, the 1980 Boston sf convention, it was received with loud and vociferous applause. Perhaps I overestimated the amount of attention people pay to critics. Perhaps the essay was unnecessary.*

But oooh *it was fun!*

Rah Rah R.A.H.!

Spider Robinson

A swarm of petulant blind men are gathered around an elephant, searching him inch by inch for something at which to sneer. What they resent is not so much that he towers over them, and can see farther than they can imagine. Nor is it that he has been trying for nearly half a century to warn them of the tigers approaching through the distant grasses downwind. They do resent these things, but what they really, bitterly resent is his damnable contention that they are not blind, *his insistent claim that they can open up their eyes any time they acquire the courage to do so.*

Unforgivable.

How shall we repay our debt to Robert Anson Heinlein?

I am tempted to say that it can't be done. The sheer size of the debt is staggering. He virtually invented modern science fiction, and did not attempt to patent it. He opened up a great many of sf's frontiers, produced the first reliable maps of most of its principal territories, and did not complain when each of those frontiers filled up with hordes of johnny-come-latelies, who the moment they got off the boat began to complain about the climate, the scenery and the employment opportunities. I don't believe there can be more than a handful of science fiction stories published in the last forty years that do not show his influence one way or another. He has written the definitive time-travel stories ("All You Zombies—" and "By His Bootstraps"), the definitive longevity books (*Methuselah's Children* and *Time Enough for Love*), the definitive theocracy novel (*Revolt In 2100*), heroic fantasy/sf novel (*Glory Road*), revolution novel (*The Moon Is A Harsh Mistress*), transplant novel (*I Will Fear No Evil*), alien invasion novel (*The Puppet Masters*), technocracy story ("The Roads Must Roll"), arms race story ("Solution Unsatisfactory"), technodisaster story ("Blowups Happen"), and about a dozen of the finest science fiction juveniles ever published. These last alone have done more for the field than any other dozen books. And perhaps as important, he broke sf out of the pulps, opened up "respectable" and lucrative markets, broached the wall of the ghetto. He continued to work for the good of the entire genre: his most recent book sale was a precedent-setting event, representing the first-ever SFWA Model Contract signing. (The Science Fiction Writers of America has drawn up a hypothetical ideal contract, from the sf writer's point of view—but until "*The Number of the Beast—*" no such contract had ever been signed.) Note that Heinlein did not do this for his own benefit: the moment the contract was signed it was renegotiated *upward*.

You *can't* copyright ideas; you can only copyright specific arrangements of words. If you could copyright ideas, every living sf writer would be paying a substantial royalty to Robert Heinlein.

So would a lot of other people. In his spare time Heinlein invented the waldo and the waterbed (and God knows what else), and he didn't patent them either. (The first waldos were built by Nathan Woodruff at Brookhaven National laboratories in 1945, three years after Heinlein described them for a few cents a word.

As to the waterbed, see *Expanded Universe.*) In addition he helped design the spacesuit as we now know it.

Above all Heinlein is better educated, more widely read and traveled than anyone I have ever heard of, and has consistently shared the Good Parts with us. He has learned prodigiously, and passed on the most interesting things he's learned to us, and in the process passed on some of his love of learning to us. Surely that is a mighty gift. When I was five years old he began to teach me to love learning, and to be skeptical about what I was taught, and he did the same for a great many of us, directly or indirectly.

How then shall we repay him?

Certainly not with dollars. Signet claims 11.5 million Heinlein books in print. Berkley claims 12 million. Del Rey figures are not available, but they have at least a dozen titles. His latest novel fetched a record price. Extend those figures worldwide, and it starts to look as though Heinlein is very well repaid with dollars. But consider at today's prices you could own all 42 of his books for about a hundred dollars plus sales tax. Robert Heinlein has given me more than a C-note's worth of entertainment, knowledge and challenging skullsweat, more by several orders of magnitude. His books do *not* cost five times the price of Philip Roth's latest drool; hence they are drastically underpriced.

We can't repay him with awards, nor with honors, nor with prestige. He has a shelf-full of Hugos (voted by his readers), the first-ever GrandMaster Nebula for Lifetime Contribution to Science Fiction (voted by his fellow writers), he is an Encyclopedia Britanica authority, he is the only man ever to be a World Science Fiction Convention Guest of Honor three times—it's not as though he needs any more flattery.

We can't even thank him by writing to say thanks—we'd only make more work for his remarkable wife Virginia, who handles his correspondence these days. There are, as noted, *millions* of us (possibly hundreds of millions)—a quick thank-you apiece would cause the U.S. Snail to finally and forever collapse—and if they were actually delivered they would make it difficult for Heinlein to get any work done.

I can think of only two things we could do to thank Robert Heinlein.

First, give blood, now and as often as you can spare a half hour and a half pint. It pleases him; blood donors have saved his life on several occasions. (Do you know the *I Will Fear No Evil* story? The plot of that book hinged on a character having a rare blood type; routine [for him] research led Heinlein to discover the National Rare Blood Club; he went out of his way to put a commercial for them in the forematter of the novel. After it was published he suffered a medical emergency, requiring transfusion. Surprise: Heinlein has a rare blood type. His life was saved by Rare Blood Club members. There is a persistent rumor, which I am unable to either verify or disprove, that at least one of those donors had joined because they read the blurb in *I will Fear No Evil.*)

The second suggestion also has to do with helping to ensure Heinlein's personal survival—surely the sincerest form of flattery. Simply put, we can all do the best we personally can to assure that the country Robert Heinlein lives in is not ruined. I think he would take it kindly if we were all to refrain from abandoning civilization as a failed experiment that requires too much hard work. (I think he'll make out okay even if we don't—but he'd be a lot less comfortable.) I think he would be pleased if we abandoned the silly delusion that there are any passengers on Starship Earth, and took up our responsibilities as crewmen—as he has.

Which occasionally involves giving the Admiral your respectful attention. Even when the old fart's informed opinions conflict with your own ignorant prejudices.

The very size of the debt we all owe Heinlein has a lot to do with the savagery of the recent critical assaults on him. As Jubal Harshaw once noted, gratitude often translates as resentment. Sf critics, parasitic on a field which would not exist in anything like its present form or size without Heinlein, feel compelled to bite the hand that feeds them. Constitutionally unable to respect anything insofar as it resembles themselves, some critics are compelled to publicly display disrespect for a talent of which not one of them can claim the tenth part.

And some of us pay them money to do this.

Look, Robert Heinlein is not a god, not even an angel. He is "merely" a good and great man, and a good and great writer, no small achievements. But there seems to be a dark human compulsion to take the best man around, declare him a god, and then scrutinize him like a hawk for the sign of human weakness that will allow us to slay him. Something in us likes to watch the mighty topple, and most especially the good mighty. If someone wrote a book alleging that Mother Theresa once committed a venial sin, it would sell a million copies.

And some of the cracks made about Robert Heinlein have been pretty personal. Though the critics swear that their concern is with criticizing literature, few of them can resist the urge to criticize Heinlein the man.

Alexei Panshin, for instance, in *Heinlein In Dimension*, asserts as a biographical fact, without disclaimer of hearsay, that Heinlein "cannot stand to be disagreed with, even to the point of discarding friendships." I have heard this allegation quoted several times in the twelve years since Panshin committed it to print. Last week I received a review copy of Philip K. Dick's new short story collection, *The Golden Man* (Berkley); I quote from its introduction:

> I consider Heinlein to be my spiritual father, even though our political ideologies are totally at variance. Several years ago, when I was ill, Heinlein offered his help, anything he could do, and we had never met; he would phone me to cheer me up and see how I was doing. He wanted to buy me an electric typewriter, God bless him—one of the few true gentlemen in this world. *I don't agree with any ideas he*

> *puts forth in his writing, but that is neither here nor there*. One time when I owed the IRS a lot of money and couldn't raise it, Heinlein loaned the money to me. . . . he knows I'm a flipped-out freak and still he helped me and my wife when we were in trouble. That is the best in humanity, there; that is who and what I love.
>
> (italics mine—SR)

Full disclosure here: Robert Heinlein has given me, personally, an autograph, a few gracious words, and a couple of hours of conversation. Directly. But when I was five he taught me, with the first and weakest of his juveniles, three essential things: to make up my own mind, always; to think it through *before* doing so; to get the facts *before* thinking. Perhaps someone else would have taught me those things sooner or later; that's irrelevant: it was Heinlein who did it. That is who and what *I* love.

Free speech gives people the right to knock who and what I love; it also gives me the right to rebut.

Not to "defend." As to the work, there it stands, invulnerable to noise made about it. As to the man, he once said that "It is impossible to insult a man who is not unsure of himself." Fleas can't bite him. Nor is there any need to defend his literary reputation; people who read what critics tell them to deserve what they get.

No, I accepted this commission because I'm personally annoyed. I grow weary of hearing someone I love slandered; I have wasted too many hours at convention parties arguing with loud nits, seen one too many alleged "reference books" take time out to criticize Heinlein's alleged political views and literary sins, heard one too many talentless writers make speeches that take potshots at the man who made it possible for them to avoid honest work. At the next convention party I want to be able to simply hand that loud nit a copy of *Destinies* and go back to having fun.

So let us consider the most common charges made against Heinlein. I arrange these in order of intelligence, with the most brainless first.

I. PERSONAL LAPSES

(Note: all these are most-brainless, as not one of the critics is in any position to know anything about Heinlein the man. The man they attack is the one they infer from his fiction: a mug's game.)

(1) "*Heinlein is a fascist.*" This is the most popular Heinlein shibboleth in fandom, particularly among the young—and, of course, exclusively among the ignorant. I seldom bother to reply, but in this instance I am being paid. Dear sir or madam: kindly go to the library, look up the dictionary definition of fascism. For good measure, read the history of fascism, asking the librarian to help you with any big words. Then read the works of Robert Heinlein, as you have plainly not done yet. If out of 42 books you can produce one shred of evidence that Heinlein—or any of his protagonists—is a fascist, I'll eat my copy of *Heinlein In Dimension*.

(2) "*Heinlein is a male chauvinist.*" This is the second most common charge these days. That's right, Heinlein populates his books with dumb, weak, incompetent women. Like Sister Maggie in "If This Goes On—"; Dr. Mary Lou Martin in "Let There Be Light"; Mary Sperling in *Methuselah's Children*; Grace Cormet in "—We Also Walk Dogs"; Longcourt Phyllis in *Beyond This Horizon*; Cynthia Craig in "The Unpleasant Profession of Jonathan Hoag"; Karen in "Gulf"; Gloria McNye in "Delilah And the Space-Rigger"; Allucquere in *The Puppet Masters*; Hazel and Edith Stone in *The Rolling Stones*; Betty in *The Star Beast*; all the women in *Tunnel In the Sky*; Penny in *Double Star*; Pee Wee and the Mother Thing in *Have Spacesuit—Will Travel*; Jill Boardman, Becky Vesant, Patty Paiwonski, Anne, Miriam and Dorcas in *Stranger In A Strange Land*; Star, the Empress of Twenty Universes, in *Glory Road*; Wyoh, Mimi, Sidris and Gospazha Michelle Holmes in *The Moon*

Is A Harsh Mistress; Eunice and Joan Eunice in *I Will Fear No Evil*; Ishtar, Tamara, Minerva, Hamadryad, Dora, Helen Mayberry, Llita, Laz, Lor and Maureen Smith in *Time Enough For Love*; and Dejah Thoris, Hilda Corners, Gay Deceiver and Elizabeth Long in "*The Number of the Beast—*".*

Brainless cupcakes all, eh? (Virtually every one of them is a world-class expert in at least one demanding and competitive field; the exceptions plainly will be as soon as they grow up. Madame Curie would have enjoyed chatting with any one of them.) Helpless housewives! (Any one of them could take Wonder Woman three falls out of three, and polish off Jirel of Joiry for dessert.)

I think one could perhaps make an excellent case for Heinlein as a *female* chauvinist. He has repeatedly insisted that women average smarter, more practical and more courageous than men. He consistently underscores their biological and emotional superiority. He married a woman he proudly described to me as "smarter, better educated and more sensible than I am." In his latest book, *Expanded Universe*—the immediate occasion for this article—he suggests without the slightest visible trace of irony that the franchise be taken away from men and given exclusively to women. He consistently created strong, intelligent, capable, independent, sexually aggressive women characters for a quarter of a century *before* it was made a requirement, right down to his supporting casts.

Clearly we are still in the area of delusions which can be cured simply by reading Heinlein while awake.

(3) "*Heinlein is a closet fag*." Now, this one I have only run into twice, but I include it here because of its truly awesome silliness, and because one of its proponents is Thomas Disch, himself an excellent writer. In a speech aptly titled, "The Embarrassments of Science Fiction," reprinted in Peter Nicholls' *Explorations of the Marvelous*, Disch asserts, with the most specious arguments imagin-

*An incomplete list, off the top of my head.

able, that there is an unconscious homosexual theme in *Starship Troopers*. He apparently feels (a) that everyone in the book is an obvious fag (because they all act so macho, and we all know that all macho men are really fags, right? Besides, some of them wear jewelry, as *real* men have never done in all history.); (b) that Heinlein is clearly unaware of this (because he never overtly raises the issue of the sex habits of infantry in a book intended for children and published in 1962), and (c) that (a) and (b), stipulated and taken together, would constitute some kind of successful slap at Heinlein or his book or soldiers . . . or something. Disch's sneers at "swaggering leather boys" (I can find no instance in the book of anyone wearing leather) simply mystify me.

The second proponent of this theory was a young woman at an sf convention party, ill-smelling and as ugly as she could make herself, who insisted that *Time Enough For Love* proved that Heinlein wanted to fuck himself. I urged her to give it a try, and went to another party.

(4) "*Heinlein is right wing.*" This is not *always* a semantic confusion similar to the "fascist" babble cited above; occasionally the loud nit in question actually has some idea of what "right wing" means, and is able to stretch the definition to fit a man who bitterly opposes military conscription, supports consensual sexual freedom and women's ownership of their bellies, delights in unconventional marriage customs, champions massive expenditures for scientific research, suggests radical experiments in government; and has written with apparent approval of anarchists, communists, socialists, technocrats, limited-franchise-republicans, emperors and empresses, capitalists, dictators, thieves, whores, charlatans and even career civil servants (Mr. Kiku in *The Star Beast*). If this indeed be conservatism, then Teddy Kennedy is a liberal, and I am Marie of Roumania.

And if there *were* anything to the allegation, when exactly was it that the conservative viewpoint was proven unfit for literary consumption? I missed it.

(5) "*Heinlein is an authoritarian.*" To be sure, re-

spect for law and order is one of Lazarus Long's most noticeable characteristics. Likewise Jubal Harshaw, Deety Burroughs, Fader McGee, Noisy Rhysling, John Lyle, Jim Marlowe, Wyoming Knott, Manual Garcia O'Kelly-Davis, Prof de la Paz and Dak Broadbent. In his latest novel, "*The Number of the Beast—*," Heinlein seems to reveal himself authoritarian to the extent that he suggests a lifeboat can have only one captain at a time. He also suggests that the captain be elected, by unanimous vote.

(6) "*Heinlein is a libertarian.*" Horrors, no! How dreadful. Myself, I'm a serf.*

(7) "*Heinlein is an elitist.*" Well, now. If by that you mean that he believes some people are of more value to their species than others, I'm inclined to agree—with you and with him. If you mean he believes a learned man's opinion is likely to be worth more than that of an ignoramus, again I'll go along. If by "elitist" you mean that Heinlein believes the strong should rule the weak, I strongly *dis*agree. (Remember frail old Professor de la Paz, and Waldo, and recall that Heinlein himself was declared "permanently and totally disabled" in 1934.) If you mean he believes the wealthy should exploit the poor, I refer you to *The Moon Is A Harsh Mistress* and *I Will Fear No Evil*. If you mean he believes the wise should rule the foolish and the competent rule the incompetent, again I plead guilty to the same offense. *Somebody's* got to drive—should it not be the best driver?

How do you *pick* the best driver? Well, Heinlein has given us a multiplicity of interesting and mutually exclusive suggestions; why not examine them?

(8) "*Heinlein is a militarist.*" Bearing in mind that he abhors the draft, this is indeed one of his proudest boasts. Can there really be people so naive as to think that their way of life would survive the magic disappearance of their armed forces by as much as a month? Evidently; I meet 'em all over.

*I know it sounds crazy, but I've heard "libertarian" used as a pejorative a few times lately.

(9) *"Heinlein is a patriot."* (Actually, they always say "superpatriot." To them there is no other kind of patriot.) Anyone who sneers at patriotism—and continues to *live* in the society whose supporters he scorns—is a parasite, a fraud, or a fool. Often all three.

Patriotism does not mean that you think your country is perfect, or blameless, or even particularly likeable on balance; nor does it mean that you serve it blindly, go where it tells you to go and kill whom it tells you to kill. It means that you are committed to keeping it alive and making it better, that you will do whatever seems necessary (up to and including dying) to protect it whenever you, personally, perceive a mortal threat to it, military or otherwise. This is something to be ashamed of? I think Heinlein has made it abundantly clear that in any hypothetical showdown between species patriotism and national patriotism the former, for him, would win hands down.

(10) *"Heinlein is an atheist,"* or *"agnostic,"* or *"solipsist,"* or *"closet fundamentalist,"* or *"hedonistic Calvinist,"* or . . . Robert Heinlein has consistently refused to discuss his personal religious beliefs; in one of his stories a character convincingly argues that it is *impossible* to do so meaningfully. Yet everyone is sure they know where he stands. *I* sure don't. The one thing I've *never* heard him called (yet) is a closet Catholic (nor am I suggesting it for a moment), but in my new anthology, *The Best of All Possible Worlds* (Ace Books), you will find a story Heinlein selected as one of his personal all-time favorites, a deeply religious tale by Anatole France (himself generally labeled an agnostic) called "Our Lady's Juggler," which I first heard in Our Lady of Refuge grammar school in the Bronx, so long ago that I'd forgotten it until Heinlein jogged my memory.

In any event his theology is none of anybody's damned business. God knows it's not a valid reason to criticize his fiction.

(11) *"Heinlein is opinionated."* Of course, I can't speak for him, but I suspect he would be willing to accept this compliment. The people who offer it as an insult are

always, of course, as free of opinions themselves as a newborn chicken.

Enough of personal lapses. What are the indictments that have been handed down against Heinlein's *work*, his failures as a science fiction writer? Again, we shall consider the most bone-headed charges first.

II. LITERARY LAPSES

(1) *"Heinlein uses slang."* Sorry. Flat wrong. It is *very* seldom that one of his *characters* uses slang or argot; he in authorial voice never does. What he uses that is *miscalled* "slang" are idiom and colloquialism. I won't argue the (to me self-evident) point that a writer is *supposed* to preserve them—not at this time, anyway. I'll simply note that you can't very well criticize a man's use of a language whose terminology you don't know yourself.

(2) *"Heinlein can't create believable women characters."* There's an easy way to support this claim: simply disbelieve in all Heinlein's female characters, and maintain that all those who believe them are gullible. You'll have a problem, though: several of Heinlein's women bear a striking resemblance to his wife Virginia, you'll have to disbelieve in her, too—which could get you killed if your paths cross. Also, there's a lady I once lived with for a long time, who used to haunt the magazine stores when *I Will Fear No Evil* was being serialized in *Galaxy*, because she could not wait to read the further adventures of the "unbelievable" character with whom she identified so strongly—you'll have to disbelieve in her, too.

Oddly, this complaint comes most often from radical feminists. Examination shows that Heinlein's female characters are almost invariably highly intelligent, educated, competent, practical, resourceful, courageous, independent, sexually aggressive and sufficiently personally secure to be able to stroke their men's egos as often as their own get stroked. I will—reluctantly—concede that this does *not* sound like the average woman as I have known her, but I am bemused to find myself in the position of trying to convince *feminists* that such women can in fact exist.

I think I know what enrages the radicals: two universal characteristics of Heinlein heroines that I left out of the above list. They are always beautiful and proud of it (regardless of whether they happen to be pretty), and they are often strongly interested in having babies. *None* of them bitterly regrets and resents having been born female—which of course makes them not only traitors to their exploited sex, but unbelievable.

(3) *"Heinlein's male characters are all him."* I understand this notion was first put forward by James Blish in an essay titled, "Heinlein, Son of Heinlein," which I have not seen. But the notion was developed in detail by Panshin. As he sees it, there are three basic male personae Heinlein uses over and over again, the so-called Three-Stage Heinlein Individual. The first and youngest stage is the bright but naive youth; the second is the middle-aged man who knows how the world works; the third is the old man who knows how it works and why it works, knows how it got that way. All three, Panshin asserts, are really Heinlein in the thinnest of disguises. (Sounds like the average intelligent man to me.)

No one ever does explain what, if anything, is *wrong* with this, but the implication seems to be that Heinlein is unable to get into the head of anyone who does not think like him. An interesting theory—if you overlook Dr. Ftaeml, Dr. Mahmoud, Memtok, David McKinnon, Andy Libby, all the characters in "Magic, Inc." and "And He Built a Crooked House," Noisy Rhysling, the couple in "It's Great To Be Back," Lorenzo Smythe, The Man Who Traveled in Elephants, Bill Lermer, Hugh Farnham, Jake Salomon, *all* the extremely aged characters in *Time Enough For Love*, all the extremely young characters in *Tunnel In the Sky* except Rod Walker, and all four protagonists of *"The Number of the*

Beast—" (among many others). Major characters all, and none of them fits on the three-stage age/wisdom chart. (Neither, by the way, does *Heinlein*—who was displaying third-stage wisdom and insight in his early thirties.)

If all the male Heinlein characters that *can* be forced into those three pigeonholes are Heinlein in thin disguise, why is it that I have no slightest difficulty in distinguishing (say) Juan Rico from Thorby, or Rufo from Dak Broadbent, or Waldo from Andy Libby, or Jubal Harshaw from Johann Smith? If Heinlein writes in characterizational monotone, why don't I confuse Colonel Dubois, Colonel Baslim and Colonel Manning? Which of the four protagonists of "*The Number of the Beast—*" is the *real* Heinlein, and how do you know?

To be sure, some generalizations can be made of the majority of Heinlein's heroes—he seems fascinated by competence, for example, whereas writers like Pohl and Sheckley seem fascinated by incompetence. Is this a flaw in *any* of these three writers? If habitual use of a certain type of character *is* a literary sin, should we not apply the same standard to Alfred Bester, Kurt Vonnegut, Phil Dick, Larry Niven, Philip Roth, Raymond Chandler, P.G. Wodehouse, J.P. Donleavy and a thousand others?

(4) "*Heinlein doesn't describe his protagonists physically*." After I have rattled off from memory extensive physical descriptions of Lazarus and Dora and Minerva Long, Scar Gordon, Jubal Harshaw and Eunice Branca, complainers of this type usually add, "unless the mechanics of the story require it." Thus amended, I'll chop it—as evidence of the subtlety of Heinlein's genius. A maximum number of his readers can identify with his characters.

What these types are usually complaining about is the absence of any *poetry* about physical appearance, stuff like, "Questing eyes like dwarf hazelnuts brooded above a strong yet amiable nose, from which depended twin parentheses framing a mouth like a pink Eskimo Pie. Magenta was his weskit, and his hair was the color of mild abstraction on a winter's morning in Antigonish." In Heinlein's brand of fiction, a picture is seldom worth a thousand words—least of all a portrait.

But I have to admit that Alexei Panshin put his finger on the fly in the ointment on p. 128 of *Heinlein In Dimension:* ". . . while the reader doesn't notice the lack of description while he reads, afterwards individual characters aren't likely to stand out in the mind." In other words, if you leave anything to the reader's imagination, you've lost better than half the critics right there. Which may be the best thing to do with them.

(5) "*Heinlein can't plot.*" One of my favorite parts of *Heinlein In Dimension* is the section on plot. On p. 153 Panshin argues that Heinlein's earliest works are flawed because "they aren't told crisply. They begin with an end in mind and eventually get there, but the route they take is a wandering one." On the *very next page* Panshin criticizes Heinlein's later work for *not* wandering, for telling him only those details necessary to the story.

> In "Gulf," for instance, Heinlein spends one day in time and 36 pages in enrolling an agent. He then spends six months, skimmed over in another 30-odd pages, in training the agent. Then, just to end the story, he kills his agent off in a job that takes him one day, buzzed over in a mere 4 pages. The gradual loss of control is obvious.

Presumably the significant and interesting parts of Panshin's life come at steady, average speed. Or else he wanted the boring and irrelevant parts of Joe's life thrown in to balance some imaginary set of scales. (Oh, and just to get the record straight, it is clearly stated in "Gulf" that Joe's final mission takes him many days.)

All written criticism I have seen of Heinlein's plotting comes down to this same outraged plaint: that if you sit down and make an outline of the sequence of events in a Heinlein story, it will most likely not come out symmetrical and balanced. Right you are: it won't. It will just *seem* to sort of ramble along, just like life does, and at the end, when you have reached the place where the author wanted you to go, you will look back at your tracks and fail to discern in them any mathematical pattern or regular geometric shape. If you keep looking, though, you'll notice that they got you there in the shortest possible distance, as straightforwardly as the terrain allowed. And that you hurried.

That they cannot be described by any simple equation is a sign of Heinlein's excellence, not his weakness.

(6) "*Heinlein can't write sex scenes.*" This one usually kicks off an entertaining hour defining a "good sex scene." Everybody disagrees with everybody on this, but most people I talk to can live with the following four requirements: a "good" sex scene should be believable, consensual (all parties consenting), a natural development of the story rather than a pasted-on attention-getter, and, hopefully, sexually arousing.

In order: Heinlein has never described *any* sexual activity that would cause either Masters or Johnson even mild surprise. In forty-two books I can recall only one scene of even attempted rape (unsuccessful, fatally so) and two depictions of extremely mild spanking. I have found *no* instances of gratuitous sex, tacked on to make a dull story interesting, and I defy anyone to name one.

As to the last point, if you have spent any time at all in a pornshop (and if you haven't, why not? Aren't you at all curious about people?) you'll have noticed that *none* of the clientele is aroused by more than 5–10% of the available material. Yet it all sells or it wouldn't be there. One man's meat is another man's person. Heinlein's characters may not behave in bed the way you do—so what?

It has been argued by some that "Heinlein suddenly started writing about sex after ignoring it for years . . ." They complain that all of Heinlein's early heroes, at least, are Boy Scouts. Please examine any reasonably complete bibliography of early Heinlein—the one in the back of *Heinlein In Dimension* will do fine. Now: if you exclude from consideration (a) juvenile novels, in which Heinlein *could not* have written a sex scene, any more than any juvenile-novelist could have in the forties and fifties; (b) stories sold to John Campbell, from which Kay Tarrant cut all sex no matter who the author; (c) stories aimed at and sold to "respectable," slick, non-sf markets which were already breaking enough taboos by buying science fiction at all; (d) tales in which no sex subplot was appropriate to the story; and (e) stories for *Boy's Life* whose protagonists were *supposed* to be Boy Scouts; what you are left with as of 1961 is two novels and two short stories, all rife with sex. Don't take *my* word, go look it up. In 1961, with the publication of *Stranger In A Strange Land*, Heinlein became one of the first sf writers to openly discuss sex at any length, and he has continued to do so since. (Note to historians: I know Farmer's "The Lovers" came nine years earlier—but note that the story did not appear in book form until 1961, the same year as *Stranger* and a year after Sturgeon's *Venus Plus X*.) I know vanishingly few septuagenarians whose view of sex is half so liberal and enlightened as Heinlein's—damn few people of *any* age, more's the pity.

(7) "*Heinlein is preachy*." "preachy: inclined to preach." "preach: to expound upon in writing or speech; especially, to urge acceptance of or compliance with (specified religious or moral principles)."

Look: the classic task of fiction is to create a character or characters, give he-she-or-them a problem or problems, and then show his-her-their struggle to find a solution or solutions. If it doesn't do that, comparatively few people will pay cash for the privilege of reading it. (Rail if you will about "archaic rules stifling creative freedom": that's the way readers are wired up, and *we* exist for *their* benefit.) Now: if the solution proposed does not involve a moral principle (extremely difficult to pull off), you have a cook-book, a how-to manual, Spaceship Repair for the Compleat Idiot. If no optimal solution is suggested, if the problem is left unsolved, there are three possibilities: either the writer is propounding the *moral principle* that some problems have no optimal solutions (e.g. "Solution Unsatisfactory" by R.A.H.), or the writer is suggesting that *some*body should find a solution to this dilemma because it beats the hell out of him, or the writer has simply been telling you a series of pointless and depressing anecdotes, speaking at great length without saying anything (e.g. most of modern mainstream litracha). Perhaps this is an enviable skill, for a politician, say, but is it really a requirement of good fiction?

Exclude the above cases and what you have left is a majority of all the fiction ever written, and the overwhelming majority of the good fiction.

But one of the oddities of humans is that while we all want our fiction to propose solutions to moral dilemmas, we do not want to admit it. Our writers are *supposed* to answer the question, "What is moral behavior?"—but they'd better not let us catch them palming that card. (Actually, Orson and I are just good friends.) The pill must be heavily sugar-coated if we are to swallow it. (I am not putting down people. *I'm* a people. That bald apes can be cajoled into moral speculation by any means at all is a miracle, God's blessing on us all. Literature is the antithesis of authoritarianism and of most organized religions—which seek to replace moral speculation with laws—and in that cause we should all be happy to plunge our arms up to the shoulders in sugar.)

And so, when I've finished explaining that "preachy" is a *complimentary* thing to call a writer, the people who made the charge usually backpedal and say that what they *meant* was

(8) "*Heinlein lectures at the expense of his fiction.*" Here, at last, we come to something a little more than noise. This, if proved, would seem a genuine and serious literary indictment.

Robert Heinlein himself said in 1950:

> A science fiction writer may have, and often does have, other motivations in *addition to* pursuit of profit. He may wish to create "art for art's sake," he may want to warn the world against a course he feels disastrous (Orwell's *1984*, Huxley's *Brave New World*—but please note that each is intensely entertaining, and that each made stacks of money), he may wish to urge the human race toward a course which he con-

siders desirable (Bellamy's *Looking Backwards*, Wells' *Men Like Gods*), he may wish to instruct, to uplift, or even to dazzle. But the science fiction writer—any fiction writer—must keep entertainment consciously in mind as his prime purpose . . . or he may find himself back dragging that old cotton sack.

(from "Pandora's Box," reprinted in *Expanded Universe*)

The change is that in his most recent works, Robert Heinlein has subordinated entertainment to preaching, that he has, as Theodore Sturgeon once said of H.G. Wells' later work, "sold his birthright for a pot of message." In evidence the prosecution adduces *I Will Fear No Evil, Time Enough For Love,* the second and third most recent Heinlein novels, and when *"The Number of the Beast—"* becomes generally available, they'll probably add that one too.

Look: nobody wants to be lectured to, right? That is, no one wants to be lectured to by some jerk who doesn't know any more than they do. But do not good people, responsible people, enlightened citizens, *want* to be lectured to by someone who knows more than they do? Have we really been following Heinlein for forty years because he does great card tricks? Only?

Defense is willing to stipulate that, proportionately speaking, all three of People's Exhibits tend to be—*by comparison with early Heinlein*—rather long on talk and short on action (*Time Enough For Love* perhaps least so of the three). Defense wishes to know, however, what if anything is wrong with that, and offers for consideration *Venus Plus X, Triton, Camp Concentration* and *The Thurb Revolution*.

I Will Fear No Evil concerns a man whose brain is transplanted into the body of a healthy and horny woman; to his shock, he learns that the body's original personality, its soul, is still present in his new skull (or perhaps, as Heinlein is careful not to rule out, he has a sustained and complex hallucination to that effect). She teaches him about how to be female, and in the process learns something of what it's like to be male. Is there any conceivable way to handle this theme *without* lots of internal dialogue, lots of sharing of opinions and experiences, and a minimum of fast-paced action? Or is the theme itself somehow illegitimate for sf?

Time Enough For Love concerns the oldest man in the Galaxy (by a wide margin), who has lived *so* long that he no longer longs to live. But his descendants (and by inescapable mathematical logic most of the humans living by that point *are* his descendants) will not let him die, and seek to restore his zest for living by three perfectly reasonable means: they encourage him to talk about the Old Days, they find him something *new* to do, and they smother him with love and respect. Do not all of these involve a lot of conversation? As I mentioned above, this book *has* action aplenty, when Lazarus gets around to reminiscing (and lying); that attempted-rape scene, for instance, is a small masterpiece, almost a textbook course in how to handle a fight scene.

But who says that ideas are not as entertaining as fast-paced action?

"*The Number of the Beast—*" (I know, on the cover of the book it says *The Number of the Beast*, without quotes or dash; that is the publishers' title. I prefer Heinlein's.) I hesitate to discuss this book as it is unlikely you can have read it by now and I don't want to spoil any surprises (of which there are many). But I will note that there is more action here than in the last two books put together, and—since all four protagonists are extraordinarily educated people, who love to argue—a whole lot of lively and spirited dialogue. I also note that its basic premise is utterly, delightfully preposterous—and that I do not believe it can be disproved. (Maybe Heinlein and Phil Dick aren't *that* far apart after all.) It held my attention most firmly right up to the last page, and indeed holds it yet.

Let me offer some more bits of evidence.

One: According to a press release which chanced to land on my desk last week, three of Berkley Publishing Company's top ten all-time best-selling sf titles are

Stranger In A Strange Land, Time Enough For Love, and *I Will Fear No Evil.*

Two: In the six years since it appeared in paperback, *Time Enough For Love* has gone through thirteen printings—a feat it took both *Stranger In A Strange Land* and *The Moon Is A Harsh Mistress* ten years apiece to achieve.

Three: Gregg Press, a highly selective publishing house which brings out quality hardcover editions of what it considers to be the finest in sf, has already printed an edition of *I Will Fear No Evil,* designed to survive a thousand readings. It is one of the youngest books on the Gregg List.

Four: *The Notebooks Of Lazarus Long,* a 62-page excerpt from *Time Enough For Love* comprising absolutely *nothing but opinions,* without a shred of action, narrative or drama, is selling quite briskly in a five-dollar paperback edition, partially hand-lettered by D.F. Vassallo. I know of no parallel to this in all sf (unless you consider Tolkien "sf").

Five: Heinlein's latest novel, "*The Number of the Beast*—," purchased by editors who, you can assume, knew quite well the dollars-and-cents track record of Heinlein's last few books, fetched an all-time genre-record-breaking half a million dollars.

Plainly the old man has lost his touch, eh? Mobs of customers, outraged at his failure to entertain them, are attempting to drown him in dollars.

What's that? You there in the back row, speak up. You say *you* aren't entertained, and that proves Heinlein isn't entertaining? Say, aren't you the same person I saw trying to convince that guy from the *New York Times* that sf is not juvenile brainless adventure but the literature of ideas? Social relevance and all that?

What that fellow in the back row means is not that ideas and opinions do not belong in a science fiction novel. He means he disagrees with some of Heinlein's opinions. (Even that isn't strictly accurate. From the noise and heat he generates in venting his disagreement, it's obvious that he hates and bitterly resents Heinlein's opinions.)

I know of many cases in which critics have disagreed with, or vilified, or forcefully attacked Robert Heinlein's opinions. A few were even able to accurately identify those opinions.* I know of none who has succeeded in *disproving*, demonstrating to be false, a single one of them. I'm sure it could happen, but I'm still waiting to see it.

Defense's arms are weary from hauling exhibits up to the bench; perhaps this is the point at which Defense should rest.

Instead I will reverse myself, plead guilty with an explanation, and throw myself on the mercy of the court. I declare that I *do* think the sugar-coating on Heinlein's last few books is (comparatively) thin, and not by accident or by failure of craft. I believe there is a good reason *why* the plots of the last three books allow and require their protagonists to preach at length. Moral, spiritual, political and historical lessons which he once would have spent at least a novelette developing are lately fired off at the approximate rate of a half dozen per conversation. That his books do *not* therefore fall apart the way Wells' last books did is only because Heinlein is incapable of writing dull. Over four decades it has become increasingly evident that he is not the "pure entertainment" song and dance man he has always claimed to be, that he has sermons to preach—and the customers keep coming by the carload. Furthermore, with the passing of those four decades, the urgency of his message has grown.

And so now, with his very latest publication, *Expanded Universe*, Heinlein has finally blown his cover altogether. I think that makes *Expanded Universe*, despite a significant number of flaws, the single most important and valuable Heinlein book ever published.

Let me tell you a little about the book. It is built around a previously available but long out of print Heinlein collection, *The Worlds of Robert A. Heinlein*, but it has been expanded by about 160%, with approximately 125,000 words of new material, for a total of about 202,500 words. Some of the new stuff is fiction, although little of

*—As distinct from the opinions of his protagonists.

it is science fiction (about 17,500 words). But the bulk of the new material, about 84,000 words, is non-fiction. Taken together it's as close as Heinlein is ever going to get to writing his memoirs, and it forms his ultimate personal statement to date. In ten essays, a polemic, one and a half speeches and extensive forewords and afterwords for most of thirteen stories, Heinlein lets us further inside his head then he ever has before. And hey, you know what? He doesn't resemble Lazarus Long much at all.

For instance, although he is plainly capable of imaging and appreciating it, Heinlein is not himself able to sustain Lazarus's magnificent ingrained indifference to the fate of any society. Unlike Lazarus, Heinlein loves the United States of America. He'll tell you why, quite specifically, in this book. Logical, pragmatic reasons why. He will tell you, for instance, of his travels in the Soviet Union, and what he saw and heard there. If, after you've heard him out, you still don't think that for all its warts (hell, running sores), the United States is the planet's best hope for an enlightened future, there's no sense in us talking further; you'll be wanting to pack. (Hey, have you heard? The current government of the People's Republic of China [half-life unknown] has allowed as how limited freedom of thought will be permitted this year. Provisionally.)* You know, the redneck clowns who chanted "America—love it or leave it!" while they stomped me back in the sixties didn't have a *bad* slogan. The only problem was that they got to define "love of America," and they limited its meaning to "blind worship of America." In addition they limited the definition of America to "the man in the White House."

These mistakes Heinlein certainly does not make. (Relevant quote from *Expanded Universe:* "Brethren and Sistren, have you ever stopped to think that *there has not been one rational decision out of the Oval Office for fifty years?*"—[italics his—SR]). In this book he identifies clearly, vividly and concisely the specific brands of rot that are eating out America's heart. He

*At press time, they have given every sign of having changed their minds.—SR.

outlines each of the deadly perils that face the nation, and predicts their consequences. As credentials, he offers a series of fairly specific predictions he made in 1950 for the year 2000, updated in 1965, and adds 1980 updates supporting a claim of a 66% success rate—enormously higher than that of, say Jeanne Dixon. He pronounces himself dismayed not only by political events of the last few decades, but by the terrifying decay of education and growth of irrationalism in America. (Aside: in my own opinion, one of the best exemplars of this latter trend is Stephen King's current runaway bestseller *The Stand*, a brilliantly entertaining parable in praise of ignorance, superstition, reliance on dreams, and the sociological insights of feeble-minded old Ned Lud.)

It is worth noting in this connection that while Heinlein has many scathing things to say about the U.S. in *Expanded Universe*, he has prohibited publication of the book in any other country.* We don't wash family linen with strangers present. I don't know of any other case in which an sf writer deliberately (and drastically) limited his royalties out of patriotism, or for that matter any moral or ethical principle. I applaud.

Friends, one of the best educated and widely-traveled men in America has looked into the future, and he is not especially optimistic.

It cannot be said that he despairs. He makes *many* positive, practical suggestions—for real cures rather than bandaids. He outlines specifically how to achieve the necessary perspective and insight to form intelligent extrapolations of world events, explains in detail how to get a decent education (by the delightful device of explaining how *not* to get one), badly names the three pillars of wisdom, and reminds us that "Last to come out of Pandora's Box was a gleaming, beautiful thing—eternal Hope."

But the last section of the book is a matched pair of mutually exclusive prophecies, together called "The Happy Days Ahead." The first is a gloomy scenario of

*—at presstime I learn that the book can be obtained in Canada. I follow the logic; the two countries are Siamese Twins.

doom, the second an optimistic scenario. He says, "I can risk great gloom in the first because I'll play you out with music at the end."

But I have to admit that the happy scenario, *Over The Rainbow*, strikes me as preposterously unlikely.

In fact, the only thing I can imagine that would increase its probability would be the massive widespread reading of *Expanded Universe*.

Which brings me to what I said at the beginning of this essay: if you want to thank Robert A. Heinlein, do what you can to see to it that the country he loves, the culture he loves, the magnificent ideal he loves, is not destroyed. If you have the wit to see that this old man has a genuine handle on the way the world wags, kindly stop complaining that his literary virtues are not classical and go back to doing what you used to do when sf was a ghetto-literature scorned by all the world: force copies of Heinlein on all your friends. Unlike most teachers, Heinlein has been successfully competing with television for forty years now. Anyone that *he* cannot convert to rationalism is purely unreachable, and you know, there are a hell of a lot of people on the fence these days.

I do not worship Robert Heinlein. I do not agree with everything he says. There are a number of his opinions concerning which I have serious reservations, and perhaps two with which I flat-out disagree (none of which I have the slightest intention of washing with strangers present). But all of these tend to keep me awake nights, because the only arguments I can assemble to refute him are based on "my thirty years of experience," of a very limited number of Americans and Canadians—and I'm painfully aware of just how poorly that stacks up against his seventy-three years of intensive study of the entire population and the entire history of the planet.

And I repeat: if there is anything that can divert the land of my birth from its current stampede into the Stone Age, it is the widespread dissemination of the thoughts and perceptions that Robert Heinlein has been selling as entertainment since 1939. You can thank him, not by buying his book, but by *loaning out* the copy you buy to as many people as will sit still for it, until it falls apart from overreading. (Be sure and loan *Expanded Universe* only to fellow citizens.) Time is short: it is no accident that his latest novel devotes a good deal of attention to the subject of lifeboat rules. Nor that *Expanded Universe* contains a quick but thorough course in how to survive the aftermath of a nuclear attack. (When Heinlein said in his Guest of Honor speech at MidAmeriCon that "there will be nuclear war on Earth in your lifetime," some people booed, and some were unconvinced. But it chanced that there was a thunderstorm over the hotel next morning—and I woke up three feet in the air, covered with sweat.) Emergencies require emergency measures, so drastic that it will be hard to persuade people of their utter necessity.

If you want to thank Robert Heinlein, open your eyes and look around you—and begin loudly demanding that your neighbors do likewise.

Or—at the very least—please stop loudly insisting that the elephant is merely a kind of inferior snake, or tree, or large barrel of leather, or oversized harpoon, or flexible trombone, or . . .

(When I read the above as my Guest of Honor speech at the New England Science Fiction Association's annual regional convention, Boskone, I took Heinlein's advice about playing them out with music literally, and closed with a song. I append it here as well. It is the second filksong I've ever written, and it is set to the tune of* Old Man River, *as arranged by Marty Paich on Ray Charles's* Ingredients In a Recipe For Soul. *[If you're not familiar with that arrangement, the scansion will appear to limp at the end.] Guitar chords are provided for would-be filksingers, but* copyright is reserved *for recording or publishing royalties, etc.)*

*A filksong is not a typo, but a generic term for any song or song-parody sung by or for sf fans.

Ol' Man Heinlein
(lyrics by Spider Robinson)

D G7 D G7
Ol' man Heinlein That ol' man Heinlein
D A7 Bm E7
He must know somethin' His heart keeps pumpin'
A Asus A A+ D
He just keep writin' And lately writin' 'em long

D G7 D G7
He don't write for critics Cause that stuff's rotten
D A7 Bm E7
And them that writes it Is soon forgotten
A Asus A A+ D
But ol' man Heinlein keeps speculatin' along

F#m C#7 F#m C#7 F#m C#7 F#m C#7
You and me Sit and think Heads all empty except for drink
F#m C#7 F#m C#7 F#m F#m Em A7
Tote that pen Jog that brain Get a little check in the mail from Baen

D G7 D G7
I get bleary And feel like shirkin'
D A7 Bm E7
I'm tired of writin' But scared of workin'
A Asus A A+ D
But ol' man Heinlin He keeps on rollin' along

Abm Eb7 Abm Eb7 Abm Eb7 Abm Eb7
You and me Read his stuff Never can seem to get enough
Abm Eb7 Abm Eb7 Abm Eb7 Abm F#m B7
Turn that page Dig them chops Hope the old gentleman never stops

E A7 E A7
So raise your glasses It's only fittin'
E B C#m F#7
The best sf that was ever written
E E+ E6 Am E C#m F#7 B7 E
Is Old Man Heinlein May he live as long as Lazarus Long!

Introduction

Knowing full well that he was one of the Great Ones, Robert Heinlein was nonetheless a man remarkably free of hubris. I really don't think his attitude toward those he allowed into his life would have been very different had he stayed a sailor or become a shopkeeper. And though this attitude of his was deeply warming to those who knew him well, in a way it's too bad: he never really believed that there were millions and millions of us who wanted not just his stories, but his wisdom.

Alas, now we must settle for the wisdom of Lazarus, who, it is well known, was a rascal, and not always to be trusted.

Excerpts from the Notebooks of Lazarus Long

Robert A. Heinlein

Always store beer in a dark place.

*

By the data to date, there is only one animal in the Galaxy dangerous to man—man himself. So he must supply his own indispensable competition. He has no enemy to help him.

*

Men are more sentimental than women. It blurs their thinking.

*

Certainly the game is rigged. Don't let that stop you; if you don't bet, you can't win.

*

Any priest or shaman must be presumed guilty until proved innocent.

*

Always listen to experts. They'll tell you what can't be done, and why. Then do it.

*

Get a shot off *fast*. This upsets him long enough to let you make your second shot perfect.

*

There is no conclusive evidence of life after death. But there is no evidence of any sort against it. Soon enough you will *know*. So why fret about it?

*

If it can't be expressed in figures, it is not science; it is opinion.

*

It has long been known that one horse can run faster than another—but *which one?* Differences are crucial.

*

A fake fortuneteller can be tolerated. But an authentic soothsayer should be shot on sight. Cassandra did not get half the kicking around she deserved.

*

Delusions are often functional. A mother's opinions about her children's beauty, intelligence, goodness, et cetera ad nauseam, keep her from drowning them at birth.

*

Most "scientists" are bottle washers and button sorters.

*

A "pacifist male" is a contradiction in terms. Most self-described "pacifists" are not pacific; they simply assume false colors. When the wind changes, they hoist the Jolly Roger.

*

Nursing does not diminish the beauty of a woman's breasts; it enhances their charm by making them look lived in and happy.

*

A generation which ignores history has no past—and no future.

*

A poet who reads his verse in public may have other nasty habits.

*

What a wonderful world it is that has girls in it!

*

Small change can often be found under seat cushions.

*

History does not record anywhere at any time a religion that has any rational basis. Religion is a crutch for people not strong enough to stand up to the unknown without help. But, like dandruff, most people do have a religion and spend time and money on it and seem to derive considerable pleasure from fiddling with it.

*

It's amazing how much "mature wisdom" resembles being too tired.

*

If you don't like yourself, you *can't* like other people.

*

Your enemy is never a villain in his own eyes. Keep this in mind; it may offer a way to make him your friend. If not, you can kill him without hate—and quickly.

*

A motion to adjourn is always in order.

*

No state has an inherent right to survive through conscript troops and, in the long run, no state ever has. Roman matrons used to say to their sons: "Come back with your shield, or on it." Later on, this custom declined. So did Rome.

*

Of all the strange "crimes" that human beings have legislated out of nothing, "blasphemy" is the most amazing—with "obscenity" and "indecent exposure" fighting it out for second and third place.

*

Cheops' Law: Nothing *ever* gets built on schedule or within budget.

*

It is better to copulate than never.

*

All societies are based on rules to protect pregnant women and young children. All else is surplusage, excrescence, adornment, luxury, or folly which can—and must—be dumped in emergency to preserve this prime function. As racial survival is the *only* universal morality, no other basic is possible. Attempts to formulate a "perfect society" on any foundation other than "Women and children first!" is not only witless, it is automatically genocidal. Nevertheless, starry-eyed idealists (all of them male) have tried endlessly—and no doubt will keep on trying.

*

All men are created unequal.

*

Money is a powerful aphrodisiac. But flowers work almost as well.

*

A brute kills for pleasure. A fool kills from hate.

*

There is only one way to console a widow. But remember the risk.

*

When the need arises—and it does—you must be able to shoot your own dog. Don't farm it out—that doesn't make it nicer, it makes it worse.

*

Everything in excess! To enjoy the flavor of life, take big bites. Moderation is for monks.

*

It may be better to be a live jackal than a dead lion, but it is better still to be a live lion. And usually easier.

*

One man's theology is another man's belly laugh.

*

Sex should be friendly. Otherwise stick to mechanical toys; it's more sanitary.

*

Men rarely (if ever) manage to dream up a god superior to themselves. Most gods have the manners and morals of a spoiled child.

*

Never appeal to a man's "better nature." He may not have one. Invoking his self-interest gives you more leverage.

*

Little girls, like butterflies, need no excuse.

*

You can have peace. Or you can have freedom. Don't ever count on having both at once.

*

Avoid making irrevocable decisions while tired or hungry. N.B.: Circumstances can force your hand. So think ahead!

*

Place your clothes and weapons where you can find them in the dark.

*

An elephant: A mouse built to government specifications.

*

Throughout history, poverty is the normal condition of man. Advances which permit this norm to be exceeded—here and there, now and then—are the work of an extremely small minority, frequently despised, often condemned, and almost always opposed by all right-thinking people. Whenever this tiny minority is kept from creating, or (as sometimes happens) is driven out of a society, the people then slip back into abject poverty.

This is known as "bad luck."

*

In a mature society, "civil servant" is semantically equal to "civil *master*."

*

When a place gets crowded enough to require ID's, social collapse is not far away. It is time to go elsewhere. The best thing about space travel is that it made it possible to go elsewhere.

*

A woman is not property, and husbands who think otherwise are living in a dreamworld.

*

The second best thing about space travel is that the distances involved make war very difficult, usually impractical, and almost always unnecessary. This is probably a loss for most people, since war is our race's most popular diversion, one which gives purpose and color to dull and stupid lives. But it is a great boon to the intelligent man who fights only when he must—never for sport.

*

A zygote is a gamete's way of producing more gametes. This may be the purpose of the universe.

*

There are hidden contradictions in the minds of people who "love Nature" while deploring the "artificialities" with which "Man has spoiled 'Nature.'" The obvious contradiction lies in their choice of words, which imply that Man and his artifacts are *not* part of "Nature"—but beavers and their dams *are*. But the contradictions go deeper than this prima-facie absurdity. In declaring his love for a beaver dam (erected by beavers for beavers' purposes) and his hatred for dams erected by men (for the purposes of men) the "Naturist" reveals his hatred for his own race—i.e., his own self-hatred.

In the case of "Naturists" such self-hatred is understandable; they are such a sorry lot. But hatred is too strong an emotion to feel toward them; pity and contempt are the most they rate.

As for me, willy-nilly I am a man, not a beaver, and H. sapiens is the only race I have or can have. Fortunately for me, I *like* being part of a race made up of men and women—it strikes me as a fine arrangement and perfectly "natural."

Believe it or not, there were "Naturists" who opposed the first flight to old Earth's Moon as being "unnatural" and a "despoiling of Nature."

*

"No man is an island—" Much as we may feel and act as individuals, our race is a single organism, always growing and branching—which must be pruned regularly to be healthy. This necessity need not be argued; anyone with eyes can see that any organism which grows without limit always dies in its own poisons. The only rational question is whether pruning is best done before or after birth.

Being an incurable sentimentalist I favor the former of these methods—killing makes me queasy, even when it's a case of "He's dead and I'm alive and that's the way I wanted it to be."

But this may be a matter of taste. Some shamans think that it is better to be killed in a war, or to die in childbirth, or to starve in misery, than never to have lived at all. They may be right.

But I don't have to like it—and I don't.

*

Democracy is based on the assumption that a million men are wiser than one man. How's that again? I missed something.

*

Autocracy is based on the assumption that one man is wiser than a million men. Let's play that over again, too. Who decides?

*

Any government will work if authority and responsibility are equal and coordinate. This does not insure "good" government; it simply insures that it will work. But such governments are rare—most people want to run things but want no part of the blame. This used to be called the "backseat-driver syndrome."

*

What are the facts? Again and again and again—what are the *facts?* Shun wishful thinking, ignore divine revelation, forget what "the stars foretell," avoid opinion, care not what the neighbors think, never mind the unguessable "verdict of history"—what are the facts, and to how many decimal places? You pilot always into an unknown future; facts are your single clue. Get the facts!

*

Stupidity cannot be cured with money, or through education, or by legislation. Stupidity is not a sin, the victim can't help being stupid. But stupidity is the only universal capital crime; the sentence is death, there is no appeal, and execution is carried out automatically and without pity.

*

God is omnipotent, omniscient, and omnibenevolent—it says so right here on the label. If you have a mind capable of believing all three of these divine attributes simultaneously, I have a wonderful bargain for you. No checks, please. Cash and in small bills.

*

Courage is the complement of fear. A man who is fearless cannot be courageous. (He is also a fool.)

*

The two highest achievements of the human mind are the twin concepts of "loyalty" and "duty." Whenever these twin concepts fall into disrepute—get out of there fast! You may possibly save yourself, but it is too late to save that society. It is doomed.

*

People who go broke in a big way never miss any meals. It is the poor jerk who is shy a half slug who must tighten his belt.

*

The truth of a proposition has nothing to do with its credibility. And vice versa.

*

Anyone who cannot cope with mathematics is not fully human. At best he is a tolerable subhuman who has learned to wear shoes, bathe, and not make messes in the house.

*

Moving parts in rubbing contact require lubrication to avoid excessive wear. Honorifics and formal politeness provide lubrication where people rub together. Often the very young, the untraveled, the naïve, the unsophisticated deplore these formalities as "empty," "meaningless," or "dishonest," and scorn to use them. No matter how "pure" their motives, they thereby throw sand into machinery that does not work too well at best.

*

A human being should be able to change a diaper, plan an invasion, butcher a hog, conn a ship, design a building, write a sonnet, balance accounts, build a wall, set a bone, comfort the dying, take orders, give orders, cooperate, act alone, solve equations, analyze a new problem, pitch manure, program a computer, cook a tasty meal, fight efficiently, die gallantly. Specialization is for insects.

*

The more you love, the more you *can* love—and the more intensely you love. Nor is there any limit on how *many* you can love. If a person had time enough, he could love all of that majority who are decent and just.

*

Masturbation is cheap, clean, convenient, and free of any possibility of wrongdoing—and you don't have to go home in the cold. But it's *lonely*.

*

Beware of altruism. It is based on self-deception, the root of all evil.

*

If tempted by something that feels "altruistic," examine your motives and root out that self-deception. Then, if you still want to do it, wallow in it!

*

The most preposterous notion that H. sapiens has ever dreamed up is that the Lord God of Creation, Shaper and Ruler of all the Universes, wants the saccharine adoration of His creatures, can be swayed by their prayers, and becomes petulant if He does not receive this flattery. Yet this absurd fantasy, without a shred of evidence to bolster it, pays all the expenses of the oldest, largest, and least productive industry in all history.

*

The second most preposterous notion is that copulation is inherently sinful.

*

Writing is not necessarily something to be ashamed of—but do it in private and wash your hands afterwards.

*

$100 placed at 7 percent interest compounded quarterly for 200 years will increase to more than $100,000,000—by which time it will be worth nothing.

*

Dear, don't bore him with trivia or burden him with your past mistakes. The happiest way to deal with a man is never to tell him anything he does not need to know.

*

Darling, a true lady takes off her dignity with her clothes and does her whorish best. At other times you can be as modest and dignified as your *persona* requires.

*

Everybody lies about sex.

*

If men were the automatons that behaviorists claim they are, the behaviorist psychologists could not have invented the amazing nonsense called "behaviorist psychology." So they are wrong from scratch—as clever and as wrong as phlogiston chemists.

*

The shamans are forever yacking about their snake-oil "miracles." I prefer the Real McCoy—a pregnant woman.

*

If the universe has any purpose more important than topping a woman you love and making a baby with her hearty help, I've never heard of it.

*

Thou shalt remember the Eleventh Commandment and keep it Wholly.

*

A touchstone to determine the actual worth of an "intellectual"—find out how he feels about astrology.

*

Taxes are not levied for the benefit of the taxed.

*

There is no such thing as "social gambling." Either you are there to cut the other bloke's heart out and eat it—or you're a sucker. If you don't like this choice—don't gamble.

*

When the ship lifts, all bills are paid. No regrets.

*

The first time I was a drill instructor I was too inexperienced for the job—the things I taught those lads must have got some of them killed. War is too serious a matter to be taught by the inexperienced.

*

A competent and self-confident person is incapable of jealousy in anything. Jealousy is invariably a symptom of neurotic insecurity.

*

Money is the sincerest of all flattery.
Women love to be flattered.
So do men.

*

You live and learn. Or you don't live long.

*

Whenever women have insisted on absolute equality with men, they have invariably wound up with the dirty end of the stick. What they are and what they can do makes them superior to men, and their proper tactic is to demand special privileges, all the traffic will bear. They should never settle merely for equality. For women, "equality" is a disaster.

*

Peace is an extension of war by political means. Plenty of elbowroom is pleasanter—and much safer.

*

One man's "magic" is another man's engineering. "Supernatural" is a null word.

*

The phrase "we (I) (you) simply *must*—" designates something that need not be done. "That goes without saying" is a red warning. "Of course" means you had best check it yourself. These small-change clichés and others like them, when read correctly, are reliable channel markers.

*

Do not handicap your children by making their lives easy.

*

Rub her feet.

*

If you happen to be one of the fretful minority who can do creative work, never force an idea; you'll abort it if you do. Be patient and you'll give birth to it when the time is ripe. Learn to wait.

*

Never crowd youngsters about their private affairs—sex especially. When they are growing up, they are nerve ends all over, and resent (quite properly) any invasion of their privacy. Oh, sure, they'll make mistakes—but that's *their* business, not yours. (You made your own mistakes, did you not?)

*

Never underestimate the power of human stupidity.

Introduction

In 1986, at a meeting of the Citizens' Advisory Council on Space, Robert Heinlein and a few others were addressing the question of the Challenger *crash. It was proposed that a memorial to The Seven be established at the earliest possible date—at the center of the first permanent lunar settlement.*

For a while after Robert's death, I considered proposing a modification to that proposal: that the memorial be to the Challenger astronauts—and to Robert Heinlein. But in reality Robert Heinlein's memorial is independent of any mass of stone and metal with which we might wish to console ourselves. More than any other man or woman, he gave us The Dream. That is his memorial.

Robert Heinlein and The Coming Age of Space

Rick Cook

"These are the times that try men's souls."
Thomas Paine

I'm writing this in June. The Space Shuttle is grounded and Robert Heinlein is dead.

Symbolically those are not unconnected. Heinlein probably did more than anyone to push us toward space. He wasn't a politician like John Kennedy, he wasn't a rocket engineer like Werner von Braun, he wasn't an astronaut like John Glenn or the *Challenger* crew. Heinlein was something more important. He was a dreamer of a particularly contagious sort. He spent most of his life writing propaganda for space. And he did so cleverly he infected millions of us with his dream.

For more than forty years he wrote stories. Good,

entertaining stories, that people read and loved for their own sakes. And nearly all of them expanded our horizons. They called us up and away from the world and pushed us out beyond the sky.

Heinlein didn't preach. He was far too good a craftsman for that. He simply showed us what we could be. By doing that he made the dream live for an entire generation and he turned thousands of us toward space.

Some of what he wrote is dated now, outmoded by the very forces Heinlein helped to set in motion. We know that Willis and the Old Ones don't frolic in the strange forests of Mars. Sir Isaac Newton and his fellow dragons don't waddle through the oily swamps of Venus. But somehow that doesn't matter. The urge is still there. It still sings in our blood, those of us whom Heinlein infected with the dream. The urge to push on, to roll out beyond this ball of earth and its thin skin of air. That is still there and that is what matters.

What matters too is that we aren't doing it. The Space Shuttle *Challenger* is gone and with it seven brave men and women, part of the price we always knew space would extract. The Space Station that was supposed to be our stepping stone to other worlds is receding further and further into the future and becoming capable of less and less as it goes.

Today the only nation on Earth with an active space program (as distinct from launching a few communications satellites) is the Soviet Union. Already the Russians have not one but two working space stations and a heavy lift booster bigger than anything the world has seen since the Saturn moon rockets. By the time you read this their own space shuttle should be flying as well. While our Galileo mission to Jupiter is years behind schedule and will be less capable than what we originally planned, the Soviets have launched an elaborate mission to the moons of Mars. A manned Mars mission is supposed to follow sometime after the year 2000.

Putting it all together, it could hardly be worse for Heinlein's dream.

And yet, and yet . . .

Riding The Roller Coaster

There is a very old trick, well known to the designers of roller coasters, that is guaranteed to scare the bejeesus out of anyone.

It starts with a long, steep climb. The roller coaster inches its way up and up the incline until the world drops away beneath the car and you grow dizzy with the height. Ahead the summit looms ominously. As the car approaches the top of the climb you suck in your breath and grab the safety bar until your knuckles turn white. Your stomach is already doing anticipatory flip-flops as you edge over the top.

Then nothing. Instead of the paralyzing drop you knew was waiting, there is only a gentle slope. As the car glides forward you instinctively relax, exhale and slack your aching fingers off the bar.

Then the bottom drops out.

The gentle slope is just long enough to get you relaxed. Then you reach the top of a gentle rise and suddenly you're pitched over in the closest thing to falling free this side of a parachute jump.

And that is essentially what is happening to us in space.

The universe isn't deliberately out to scare us to death, (I don't think!) but the same principle applies. We are most sensitive to what we see immediately ahead of us and we tend to extrapolate our future from that.

In the case of space development, there are excellent reasons to believe we are at the absolute low point in our efforts. What we are seeing is not a long decline but a hiatus. But the gentle, narrow slope in front of us is deceptive.

This isn't to deny we have problems. Things are undeniably bad and there doesn't seem to be much hope that our original grand scheme for getting into space is ever going to work. But that doesn't mean that we are permanently stalled.

Over the next decade we are going to see almost

imperceptible progress. Then sometime before the end of the century we are going to break out in an explosion that will carry us throughout the inner solar system in two decades or less.

In all probability this is the last hiatus in our efforts. Once that explosion hits we will have enough momentum to carry us well past the point of no return.

This is an old pattern. First comes a grand achievement, a major milestone in history. Then, little or nothing for twenty to thirty years as what was once seen as an area of high promise seems to stagnate.

Then something occurs. Some event sets off an avalanche. Major events come thick and fast and when things finally slow down twenty or thirty years later, the face of the world is forever changed.

We saw this happen in the Age of Exploration that opened the world to Europe. It happened in the development of the New World. It happened with commercial flight and it has happened in many other fields.

The Lesson of History

The last great Age of Exploration is usually held to have begun in 1418 when Prince Henry of Portugal, called The Navigator, determined to push exploration down the coast of Africa and find a way around the Moslem states to the riches of the Orient.

This was the fifteenth century equivalent of the space program. To realize his dream, Henry built a complex at the southern Portuguese village of Sagres that included a shipyard, an arsenal and a school of navigation. There pilots were trained and maps were made as new voyages added to the store of knowledge. Henry spent lavishly, rewarded his captains generously and sent them south with orders to find their way around Africa.

At that time no European had been further than 800 miles into the Atlantic or further south than Cape Bojador on the African coast. You can find Cape Bojador on a globe, but you will have to look for it. It is an insignificant hump of land just south of the Canary Islands and not even marked on most modern maps. In theory, Henry's captains should have breezed past it easily. In fact it was 1434 before one of one of Henry's squires, his ears still burning from the dressing down his master had given him for a previous failure, made it around the cape.

Even after that progress was painfully slow. It wasn't until 1436 that the first cargo, of seal skins, was brought back from the African reaches and not until 1441, nearly twenty years after Henry began his great endeavor, that contact was made with the natives below Cape Bojador.

To someone obsessed with the riches of the East, as Henry was, the rate of progress must have been maddening. After twenty years of effort by one of the major nations of Europe, after a massive research and development program, after spending lavishly on the best ships that could be built, the West's knowledge of the route to the Orient stopped a few hundred miles down the African coast, a distance a modern sailboat can make in a couple of weeks.

Prince Henry the Navigator died in 1460, impoverished by 40 years of effort which had seen his ships go only as far as Cape Palmas, what is now the Ivory Coast.

But even by the time of Henry's death the pace of exploration was picking up. In 1469 King Alfonso of Portugal made an agreement with a Lisbon merchant calling for him to explore 400 miles of coast a year for five years in return for trading privileges. The contract was fulfilled and by 1482 Portuguese ships had reached Walvis Bay on the coast of South West Africa.

From there milestones came thick and fast. In 1487 Bartolomeu Diaz rounded the Cape of Good Hope on the southern tip of Africa. In 1498 Vasco da Gama finally reached India and Prince Henry's dream was fulfilled. Finally in 1522, just over a century after Henry started his quest, a leaky, worm-eaten and weatherbeaten little ship named *Victoria* limped into the port of Sanlucar de Barrameda in southern Spain. Ferdinand Magellan had died along the way, but his expedition had circumnavigated the planet.

The point of this recitation is not inspiration, although it is certainly inspiring enough. The point is that once Henry launched his great project, very little happened for fifteen years and it was more than twenty before progress became self-sustaining.

Again, everyone knows that columbus discovered the New World in 1492. What most people don't know is that for about twenty years it didn't amount to a hill of beans. There were voyages of exploration, and a few settlements, but things moved very slowly until Cortez' conquest of Mexico about 1520.

These are not isolated instances. In general, there is a twenty to thirty year hiatus after the initial push into a new area. We tend to miss it because our history naturally skips from high point to high point. If you don't pay close attention to the dates it seems that we have had an unbroken curve of progress from initial discovery to triumphant flowering. It was no such thing, of course, but that tends to get lost in the shuffle and the romanticism.

Yet it is very real, that hiatus—and the reasons for it have a direct bearing on what we can expect in space.

Reviewing The Situation

Today our basic problem is simple. Access to space is limited and hideously expensive. We can't get there from here, at least not cost-effectively.

The thing that drives space advocates nuts is that we have done the hard part; the equivalent of that long, steep roller coaster climb. We know how to get into space. We know how to live there. But we aren't doing it.

Today getting into space is just a matter of straightforward engineering. The days of "solving the re-entry problem" and other arcane technical challenges are long gone.

The first artificial satellite was launched more than

thirty years ago. We had men on the Moon twenty years ago. A decade ago we had the Skylab space station. The engineers and scientists who got us to the Moon have either retired or are on the verge of retirement. Most of today's college graduates weren't even born when we started putting men in space.

We know how to do it. We have multiple design studies for most of the equipment gathering dust on the shelves in aerospace companies. We know pretty much what it would cost to go into space. (Expensive to medium-expensive.) We know what the payback would be. (Enormous.) But we won't make the flipping effort!

And that is the true frustration.

The Silver Lining

Although the *Challenger* explosion was a disaster for the space program, not all its effects were negative. In the two-and-a-half years since we lost the *Challenger* we have made some fundamental changes in our space effort and those changes are having an important positive effect on our future in space.

Notice I did not say "changes in our space program." There have been changes there all right, but they have been mostly negative. Some important items were fixed on the Shuttle and NASA's management was shaken up and those are probably both to the good. But the basic problems facing our space program—notably a lack of money and commitment from Congress and the Administration—have not changed and probably won't change.

There has been the Ride Commission Report urging a bold program of space exploration including a Moon colony, and there has been a movement for a joint expedition to Mars with the Soviets, but neither of those is likely to lead to anything. Implementing the resolutions in the Ride Report will take money, and we're in this mess because we cannot get the money for existing programs, never mind pie in the sky.

The Air Force and NASA have started work on a heavy-lift booster designed to cut the cost of getting payload to orbit. But that project is intimately tied up with Strategic Defense Initiative and is unlikely to survive the budget and political battles over Strategic Defense Initiative in the next three or four years.

Still, there have been some positive changes. One of the most important positive results has been that the government was finally driven to realize that it could not serve as the principal launch provider for the free world's satellites. When the Shuttle starts flying again it will be on a much-reduced schedule. Only fourteen flights a year are planned, compared to twenty-four per year before the accident. There is a backlog of military and important scientific payloads that will soak up most Shuttle capacity for years to come.

Currently there are between sixty and one hundred satellites either sitting in storage or under construction. They have to be launched somehow and that presents an opportunity for private launch companies.

Last year the government announced a new policy on commercial satellite launches. Instead of being used to launch everything, almost no commercial satellites will fly on the Shuttle. The companies must make deals with private launch facilities to get their birds into orbit.

Further, the government will generally stop buying rockets. Instead it will contract for launch services. The private companies will own the rockets and they and not NASA will launch them from government facilities.

The impact of all this is to get NASA out of a business it was never set up to handle well and to encourage people who can do it better to take over. NASA was set up as a research agency, not a transportation business. It is still very good at research, but it has always been at best mediocre at transportation. Private companies say they can shave millions of dollars off the cost of launching a satellite if they are allowed to do it their way—even using the same launch vehicles from the same facilities and operating under fairly close government supervision.

The government also sat down and made its first

major effort to work out a unified commercial space policy. What emerged wasn't terribly exciting, but it was extremely significant.

The essence of the policy is to encourage private development in space in a stable environment. In other words, as much work as possible will be done by private companies and the government would try to avoid the kind of policy shifts that had left companies hanging out to dry.

It's too early to know how well all this will work in practice, but the early signs are encouraging.

For one thing, it has revitalized the commercial launch business. When the government decided that most commercial satellites would not fly on the Shuttle, it opened the door to the booster companies to go after the business. They have done so with a vengeance.

The traditional booster manufacturers, General Dynamics, Martin Marietta and McDonnell Douglas are all producing boosters. General Dynamics' program is especially interesting because the company started building a series of 18 Atlas *Centaur* launchers on speculation. It had no customers for most of them when it announced the program. Since then it has sold several and may have sold all of them by the time you read this.

This is not just an American phenomenon. The French *Ariane* booster is launching payloads again and the French have started work on larger follow-on derivatives, including one that will carry a small two-man shuttle called the *Hermes*. The Chinese are seeking customers for their *Long March* booster. Even the Russians have checked into the game, offering their *Proton* launcher.

Perhaps more significantly, the Japanese are becoming active. The Japanese recently announced they were starting work on a space program that would include a manned spaceplane. This is significant because it means there may be four manned space programs by the turn of the century: Soviet, American (probably), European (possibly) and Japanese. The Europeans have a worse record for completing high tech projects than the Americans do, but the Japanese do things very differently. When they start something they almost always finish it.

Meanwhile, the new policy, combined with the shortage of launchers, has revitalized the small entrepreneurial companies who are trying to build new launchers from the ground up. Companies like American Rocket (AmRoc) and Space Services Inc. (SSI) have designed small launch vehicles that can put a few hundred pounds into low Earth orbit. None of them has launched as this is written, but that may change by the time you read this.

In addition, the government is developing a new air-launched booster called the Pegasus which is supposed to put 600 to 900 pounds into low earth orbit. The booster is carried aloft by a B-52 (the same one used for the X-15 program, as a matter of fact) and is expected to make its first flight by the end of next year.

All of these efforts are in response to market demand. In addition to the satellites already waiting launches, there are a number of others that have been held up short of firm commitments by the lack of launch vehicles. They include more communications satellites to replace the aging ones in orbit, global positioning satellites and other innovative satellites for geosynchronous orbits, and reconnaissance and remote imaging satellites.

What is perhaps more interesting are the number of missions needed for low earth orbit in addition to the conventional recon and imaging satellites. The Defense Department has begun pushing a "lightsat" program using small special purpose satellites to supplement the larger ones for reconnaissance and communication. More interesting yet are a number of companies who want small satellites or even sub-orbital flights for materials processing experiments.

Materials processing was perhaps the hardest hit of all the space technologies by the *Challenger* accident and the Space Station stretchout. Making things in space is best done in a man-tended environment. Several experiments had flown in the Shuttle and one of the main jobs of the Space Station is supposed to be materials experiments.

Our initial experiments have been very encouraging, but they are also very preliminary. The last experiment 3M flew, for instance, involved a red dye commonly used in Tupperware. What companies are trying to do now is to find out how materials react in microgravity. That is a long way from producing commercial products, but it is an important first step.

Although some companies, notably Boeing Aerospace and 3M, are still committed to flying experiments on the Shuttle, others have decided not to wait. They are designing experiments that can be flown in small unmanned rockets. Some of the packages will be returned to Earth for examination. Others will just send back data. This isn't as neat as doing a manned experiment in space, but it gets the work done a lot faster.

Although satellite launches and major experiments are going to be severely curtailed, experiments that fly in the Shuttle's cabin are not nearly as affected. There are a number of materials experiments planned for the Shuttle and they should help us build our database on space materials processing.

Even the Russians are helping in their own way. The Soviets are regularly conducting materials experiments in space. While they aren't exactly open with the results, the general outlines are getting out. Even this much information is a help at this stage.

All this activity is going to continue and expand over the next few years. As the Space Station struggles, and the Shuttle flies its reduced schedule, private companies are going to be building rockets and launching payloads with increasing frequency. In the process they will be gaining experience and preparing us for the next major step: The big breakout.

The Magic InGREEDient

Active launch companies may be encouraging, but it is hardly a substitute for space development. You don't build Moon colonies with ancient ICBM designs.

This is undeniable. But the important point is that in spite of the mess in our space program, there is still a lot of work being done on space development. That work is the first step.

The second, and crucial, step will come sometime in the next five to fifteen years. That is the thing that will trigger the boom comparable to the one that marked the last Age of Exploration. It is the step that will move us out into space in a big way. Essentially it will be the same thing that made the Portuguese exploration of Africa self-sustaining well before prince Henry's death, or the thing that opened up the New World.

Simply put, someone will find a way to make a whole lot of money in space.

The thing that has always turned exploring from an expensive hobby for princes and nations into a self-sustaining, accelerating process has been economic return. Exploring is a risky business, so it takes the potential for an enormous return to bring people flocking to it. Africa exploration became hot for Portugal when the explorers started bringing back gold, ivory and slaves. The New World became a magnet for explorers when Cortez started shipping back gold by the galleon load. Space will become equally active when we come up with something that pays off equivalently.

How? If I knew that I'd be taking out a second mortgage and calling my broker. As it is, I have some pretty good ideas, but I don't know the details.

My guess is that it will be some kind of product manufactured in microgravity. It may be a pharmaceutical or biological that can be separated on a large scale by electrophoresis in low gravity. Perhaps it will be a new kind of high-temperature super conductor. Maybe a semiconductor material composed of elements that won't mix on Earth. What it is is unimportant. The important thing is it will be something that can only be made or done in space.

Note that whatever this thing is, it has to be very valuable. We're not just talking about a twenty or thirty percent return on investment, but a 300 or 1,000 percent return. Historically those are the kinds of returns that have led to an explosion of effort. The traders of the Age of Exploration could probably have shown a reasonable profit in commerce with the Orient on the basis of hides, mahogany and brassware, but it was gold and spices that sent their ships beating around the Cape of Good Hope. What we need to trigger the explosion is the 20th century equivalent of gold and spices.

There is very little doubt that there are a lot of things like that to be had. Space offers a novel environment that we can't duplicate on Earth, notably microgravity. Experience teaches us that any time we get a situation like that we can develop new things and some of them are worth plenty.

The discoverer of this wonder substance doesn't have to be an American. Things being what they are he or she is more likely to be a Russian or a Japanese. That doesn't really matter. All that matters is that it is found.

Sometime in the next few years we will find the equivalent of gold, pepper and nutmeg and at that point the whole world changes.

Today our basic problem is not that we can't get into space in a big way, it is that the people who can afford to pay the bills don't want it badly enough (the Russians excepted). If people see that they can make a lot of money in space, they will be lining up ten deep to pay for it.

The History Of The Future

Now you can argue that such a human explosion into space is inevitable, but that American participation in it is not. (Indeed, it has been argued. That is how this article came to be written.)

The fact is that Americans still have the strongest capital markets and the most finely honed entrepreneurial skills of any country on Earth—at least for now. Given a whiff of a bonanza, the entrepreneurs will be circling like hungry sharks.

The very nice thing about the American capital markets is that they can raise huge amounts of capital for new ventures very quickly. Nobody else in the world can match us at that. We may not develop the technology and we may not discover the products, at least not initially, but we will probably surge rapidly in this phase. One result is that the United States comes roaring back in the space business.

One of the peculiar and very attractive things about this process is that it isn't necessary for everyone to make a profit, or even stay in the business. In fact, in a boom it is entirely possible for an industry as a whole to lose money and for most of the participants to be selling at or below cost. Historically most of the entrepreneurs who venture into a new area go broke. How many personal computer companies succeeded, after all?

More to the point, most of the investments in the New World were abject failures, economically. But in space as in America, just a few companies striking it rich will keep a boom going for some time.

Once we have our product, the consequences are fairly predictable. First comes the mad scramble as everyone tries to cash in and then the situation settles down for a long, steady haul.

The first phase will be a desperate push to get something, anything, that can get into space. If the product turns out to be a material made in space, a lot of the first activity will center on small automated facilities that can be sent up in unmanned rockets. Everyone will be working madly to build manned facilities, but that will take time.

Initially the companies with launch vehicles in production will be in the catbird seat. But all our present vehicles are expensive. We talk about "production lines," but they are virtually handmade. They aren't cheap and they can't be made cheap.

Other companies will try to develop and sell vehicles with a lower cost to orbit. There are plenty of these designs sitting around. They range all the way from the Big Dumb Booster types, which are simply very large solid or liquid fuel rockets built as simply and as cheaply as possible, to exotics like Gary Hudson's Phoenix Single Stage To Orbit (SSTO) plug-nozzle design. Even further out, but technically quite feasible, are the mass drivers and laser launchers for putting small amounts of cargo in orbit at rock-bottom prices.

Most of the companies are not likely to mix cargo and passengers, so there will be surge of interest in space planes as well as cargo launchers. These will be two-to-four person vehicles designed to get people into LEO with a minimum of expense and reasonable safety.

There will be plenty of investors for all these schemes and a number of them will undoubtedly make it to launch.

At this point several things start happening. The first is that the price of a pound to orbit takes a swan dive. That will expand the market for space products by making the existing ones cheaper and opening the door to new ventures.

It is in the nature of booms to overextend. A few years after the bonanza starts we will have too much launch capacity, so companies will start cutting prices to try to stay in business. That will make it even cheaper to launch and encourage even more uses for space.

Another thing that happens is that industries of all sorts will start thinking of space as a place to do business. There are probably a great many things we are already making on Earth which would be better made in space. But we don't have the necessary data on how to make things there and everyone "knows" space is a terribly expensive and utterly alien environment. Once we start working in space, people's attitude toward space will change. Space will be as accepted as ordinary and necessary as personal computers are today and the implications of that change are profound.

Finally, recall that getting free of the Earth's gravity is the energy equivalent of getting halfway to anywhere in the solar system. Once we have cheap transportation to low Earth orbit, we can break free of Earth completely fairly inexpensively. From there the only limit on how far we go is how good our life support systems are and how much isolation our crews can stand.

We don't know the details, but the outline is pretty clear. Somewhere out in space there is a mother lode waiting to be tapped. We don't know what it is and we certainly can't prove its existence to the MBA types with their calculators and their net present value formulas. But everything we have seen in history, everything we know about space tells us it is there. If it is there, someone—Communist or capitalist, Russian or American or European—will stumble over it. Five years after that happens the face of space and the course of human history will be irretrievably altered.

And somewhere, off beyond the sunset, Robert Heinlein will be grinning his head off.

Introduction

One of the more profound and surprising aspects of the march of technology has been its effect on the relationship of the sexes. As on deeper and deeper levels it becomes clear that masculine surge-strength really doesn't matter anymore, who does what to/with/for whom is ever more up for grabs, so to speak. Alas, we can't talk about the technical aspects of this story without violating Spider's right to surprise you. Let's just say that it takes place under the sign of the RAM.

Copyright Violation

Spider Robinson

I was singing along with John Lennon when she crowned me from behind: that's how the rape began.

I don't often sing along with jukeboxes; a fellow like me can get hurt that way. It's not just that I can't carry a tune. I seem to have one of those faces that stevedores and bikers and truckers—even the odd minister in his cups—love to punch, just on general principles, I guess, so I tend to avoid drawing attention to myself when I'm in a bar.

No, I'll be more honest than that. I *can* be honest, you see—because it's *my* choice. I'll metaphorically strip myself for you, and then you'll see that it wasn't because she raped my body that I wanted to kill her, or even my mind, but because she raped my soul.

So, being honest: it isn't just for fear of getting punched that I make myself inconspicuous in bars. Contrary to what you may have heard, there aren't that many real bullies in the world; most men looking for a fight will leave me alone, the way a hunter with an elephant gun will walk past a gerbil. What I'm really avoiding when I make myself inconspicuous is pity.

I mean, look at me. Most of the people who ever

have, failed to see me at all—the eye tends to subtract me—but those who do notice me usually feel sorry for me. My chin and my Adam's Apple are like twin brothers in bunk beds. I got this nose. My dad used to say that my ears made me look like a taxicab coming down the street with the doors open. My glasses weigh more than my shoes, and my shoes weigh more than the rest of me.

I mean, I'll bet you think a prostitute will take anybody, that any man with enough money can get laid. It may be true. *I've* never had enough money. Oh, once I got a woman to agree, for three times the going rate . . . but the way she went about it, I just couldn't do it—to her total lack of surprise. I've never really given up hope since, in my adolescence, I first heard the term "mercy hump"—but so far, I haven't found that much mercy in the world.

So when the jukebox clicked, and John Lennon began to tell me that he was a loser, I just naturally chimed in on the second, "I'm a l-o-o-oser."

And felt something circular and weighty being pressed down over my head—and heard the most beautiful voice in the world, right behind my ear, sing the next line of the song—and spun quickly around and saw her.

Oh my, it hurt to look at her. You're a normal man, friend, no doubt you've won some and lost some—but didn't you ever see one that you just *knew* on sight you'd trade your home and wife and children and hope of immortality and twenty years of your mortal life for ten minutes in bed with—and knew just as clearly that you'd never ever get her, even at that price? God, it's a sweet pain, that is, and I know a lot more about it than you do. Every man has in his mind an ideal of the Perfectly Beautiful Woman—and she was better-looking than that, and better dressed.

"Forgive me, sir," she said.

I guess I should remember that those were the first words she said to me—if you don't count the song lyric. At the time I remember thinking that I was prepared to forgive her anything whatsoever. It shows you how wrong you can be.

To my gratified surprise, my voice worked. "Forgive you?"

"I just couldn't help myself."

With an effort I tore my attention from a close examination of her parts and perimeters, and tried to imagine why she could possibly feel a need to apologize to me. Oh yes—she had put something heavy on my head. I felt it with my fingertips. It felt like a crown. Reluctantly I took my eyes away from her and looked in the mirror behind the bar.

Yep, that was a crown on my head, all right. A simple, inch-wide band of gold around my forehead, elaborately chased but otherwise unadorned. It was so heavy, it had to be real gold or gilded lead.

Alongside the twin miracles of her existence and the fact that she was speaking to me (and calling me "sir"!), nothing was strange. "That's perfectly all right," I said, quite as though preternaturally beautiful women put thousands of dollars worth of gold on my brow every third Thursday, and I were becoming resigned to it. System crash of the brain.

She did something with her face that I don't have a word for. Deep in the shielded core of my heart, graphite rods slid up out of the fuel mass, and the pile temperature began climbing toward meltdown point. "It was unforgivable of me to intrude upon your privacy."

She had a faint, indefinable accent; I guessed Middle European of some kind. She was . . . well, I'd say she was beaming at me, but you'd think I only meant she was smiling. I mean she was *beaming* at me, the way an airport beams at an approaching plane to guide it. I realized with a start that she was looking at me just exactly the same way I was looking at her. Captivated, wistful, yearning—no, outright hungering and thirsting. I'd seen the look before, in movies starring Marilyn Chambers.

I ask you to believe that I am not a complete idiot. My first thought was that it had to be a mistake. But the light in the bar wasn't bad enough. So my second thought was that it had to be a trick, a trap of some kind.

That was absolutely fine with me. I tried to visualize the worst possible outcome. Say that, in exchange for being allowed to touch her, to put my hand somewhere on her skin—her shoulder, say—I were to be beaten, robbed and killed. Okay, fair enough; no problem there. A weird little phrase ran through my head: *I'll be her sucker if she'll be my succor*. (I seem now to hear a phantom Kingfish saying, "Boy, you is de suck*ee*.") Male black widow spiders obviously think they have a good deal going for them.

"It's uncanny," she repeated, and touched my hand. With hers.

"It certainly is," I said, referring to the astonishing discovery that knuckles can be erogenous zones.

"Would you mind standing up, sir?"

That kicked off an ambiguous reaction. If I stood up, the bulge in my trousers would become visible. Even more embarrassing, it might not become visible *enough*. Conflicting imperatives paralyzed me.

"I'm sorry," she said. "I'm being rude again. It's just that I dreamt about you last night. It was a *very* pleasant dream."

"I've dreamed about you all my life," I said, "and it has always been pleasant. You're very beautiful." A happy feeling was growing in me. First, because I had finally managed to say something intelligent and gallant. And second, because she had just named a barely plausible reason why a woman like her could be interested in a guy like me.

I mean, you have to understand that my father always insisted I wasn't his—until my sixteenth birthday, when he gave up and apologized to my mother. "It has to be some kind of mutation," he admitted. "You would *never* have cheated on me with someone who looked like that."

But anything can happen in a dream. Lord, who knows better than I? For the first time I was willing to—tentatively—believe that her obvious attraction signals might just be genuine. The possibilities were staggering.

"My mother was," she answered, dimpling, "the most beautiful Queen that Ragovia ever had."

"You're a princess." Well, of course. Dream logic.

"Only by courtesy. I'll never be Queen—Ragovia became a democracy a few years ago."

"I'm *terribly* sorry to hear that."

"Oh, it was a bloodless coup. A telegram to our summer place in Barbados, and that was essentially it. Father moped for a week."

"Well, naturally."

"I can't get over how much you look like the man in my dream. He was wearing Father's crown. That's why I just had to put it on your head—to see if the resemblance could possibly be as complete as it seemed."

I threw caution to the winds and stood up. "And is it?"

Her eyes went down and then up me. On the way down they paused just where I had hoped/feared they would. When her eyes got back up to mine, she was smiling. "The resemblance is exact."

"Princess—uh—"

"Oh, forgive me again. My name is Marga."

"My name is Fleming, Princess Marga."

"Please, 'Marga' alone is sufficient." And without the slightest hesitation or change of voice or manner, she went on, "Fleming, do you know of some quiet, private place nearby where we could be alone together?"

A man next to me made an odd swallowing sound. I dug a finger into my ear. "Too much noise in here. I could have sworn that you just asked me . . ." I could not repeat what I thought I had heard.

"I asked you if you have a place where we can be alone together. As we were in my dream last night."

I drew in a deep breath, and then could not remember what to do with it. "Why?" I croaked.

"So that I can screw you into a coma."

Exhale. That was what you did with deep breaths.

No, too late now: I was paralyzed. That breath was going to have to last me the rest of my life.

"—," I said.

"If you have no place near," she went on, "we could find an alley. Or we could lock ourselves in the toilet here. But I am mad with lust for you and must have you as soon as possible."

People had been surreptitiously watching ever since Marga had sat down next to me, and now there were two small, musical explosions as the customers on either side of us dropped their drinks.

I decided that, while this was a splendid moment to die, even better ones might lie in the future; with an effort I got my breathing reflex started again.

"The feeling is mutual. That is, I hope it will be. That is—yes, I have a place near here."

"Let's *hurry*! In my dream we were *wonderful* together!"

A lot of people were watching now. I glanced around as I took her hand, the way I've seen it done in movies, and nothing in my life had ever tasted as good as the sight of all those gaping faces.

Understand, I knew perfectly well that something was going to go wrong. I would never get her to my place, or she'd change her mind, or I wouldn't get it up, or I wouldn't get it in, or I'd get in and it'd be disappointing, or she'd have A.I.D.S., or a bonebreaker boyfriend—the exact nature of the doom was as yet unknown, but I knew in my heart that *some*thing was going to go wrong. (And of course, I was mistaken about that.) But I didn't care. The thrill of seeing all those stunned faces watching *her* leave with *me*, rubbing up against me like a cat who's just heard the can-opener, was—I firmly believed—worth any disappointment. (And you know, perhaps I was nearly right about that.) As we reached the door, she opened it for me with her left hand, and her right hand settled firmly and unmistakably on my ass to guide me out into the night. There was an audible collective gasp from behind us.

Once we were on the sidewalk I flung up my arm to hail a cab. Now, cabs *never* stop for me, even when I wave large bills at them. I was operating on dream logic.

And a cab pulled up with a squeal of brakes, and the cabbie jumped out and *opened the door for us.*

It was her, of course, not me. I knew just how the cabbie felt. I could sense his astonishment that she was with me, and I agreed with him, and gave him a smile that tried to say, "It's a dream, pal, go with it. For God's sake, go with it!"

When he got back behind the wheel, he adjusted the rearview mirror and I met his baffled gaze. I gave my address, Marga added "—and *hurry*!" in a voice thick with lust, and his eyes widened even further. We started up with a roar and a lurch, and the moment we were up to speed she opened my fly.

The cab seemed to lock its brakes on ice, spin wildly and smash into a gasoline truck. She made a small sound of contentment and continued what she was doing. The phantom flames roared . . .

The cabdriver was so profoundly shocked he was actually driving at a safe legal speed, and took us to my place by the shortest, most direct route. Marga appeared to be totally engrossed in what she was doing, and God knows I was, but she sensed when we were approaching our destination somehow, and had me zipped back up as the cab came to a halt. She paid the driver before he or I could think of it. I had just enough presence of mind to hold the door for her as she got out. A group of leathered teens were monopolizing the stoop of my brownstone, as usual. They turned to brown stone at the sight of us, and did not even turn to watch as we walked up past them and into the building.

As the elevator door closed behind us, she shut off the light, leaned back against the wall and pulled me against her. She tucked my face against her neck and hugged me so tightly, with both arms and one leg, that I could move only a single muscle. But she seemed to be under no such constraint: she *rippled*, in several directions at once, and if I lived one floor higher I'd have disgraced myself. But the elevator door slid back and light burst in on us, and reluctantly she released me.

Standing outside the elevator, waiting to board, was Hal Grimsby, the slickest stud in my building, a jock-type who had been bringing home a different girl every night for the four years I'd been living there, each girl prettier than the last. He was making no move to get on the elevator. You could have put one of his handballs into his mouth without touching his lips.

Marga straightarmed him out of the way and led me past him. "Hurry, darling," she said clearly. "I'm *dripping*."

Behind us, Hal made a faint gargling sound. The elevator closed and left without him.

And *still* it wasn't perfect yet. As we approached my apartment, the door across the hall opened and Mary Zanfardino stepped out.

For the past four years, Mary Zanfardino had been the leading lady in an endless series of fantasies much like the one I was now living—save that I didn't have this good an imagination. I had never succeeded in starting a conversation with her, but I knew that she was perfectly aware of my attraction to her, and deeply revolted by it. Now she was thunderstruck. I'd never seen pupils that large.

I turned to look at Marga. I found the sight of her as devastating as everyone else did. Her hair was disheveled. Her nipples were prominent beneath her silk dress. Her eyes were heavy-lidded, and her smile would have looked just like the Mona Lisa's except for the smeared lipstick . . .

I turned back to Mary, former girl of my dreams, and she looked like a mud simulacrum of a woman, fashioned by a competent primitive and dressed by a small child.

This was no time for introductions. I nodded curtly to Mary, brushed past her, and unlocked my door. As Marga came toward me (utterly ignoring Mary) she was unbuttoning her dress, and before I could get the door closed behind me she was out of it entirely. I caught one last flash-glimpse of Mary that made me want to giggle, but I knew intuitively that if I started I might never stop, and this once in my life I did not want to remind myself of Jerry Lewis. Then the latch slid home and Marga and I were alone. I knew that my bedroom was a mess, but I also knew we were not going to get that far.

I can see it in my mind, even now, but I can't describe it. Just say that, even displayed to the best possible advantage—that is, even if Marga were wearing it—there is nothing in the Frederick's of Hollywood catalogue that could ever look half as lovely, as provocative, as inflammatory, as what Marga was wearing under that dress. Enchanted elves had made it. My mouth had gone drier than a user's manual, and I knew why: some helpful internal resource-dispatcher was rerouting all the moisture in my body to where it was most needed.

"Which one of us shall undress you, my king?" she asked.

We took turns. She left the crown on my head and I didn't argue.

* * * * * * * * * * * * * * *

No, I'm not going to cheat you; that was not a discreet fade to black. Those asterisks are there because what she and I did deserves to be set off by itself. It merits special ceremony.

I will admit that part of me wants to take refuge in those asterisks, to leave the lurid details in the limbo which is symbolized by the six-pointed star. I never learned to enjoy locker-room boasting; it never came up, so to speak. But if I don't tell you just how it was, you'll never understand how I felt afterward.

Besides, it won't be a *real* invasion of my privacy. I mean, it's only me *telling* you, and telling you *my* version of things, and only the parts that can be fit into words at that. Not even all of them. I'm trying to make the point that what she did to me was *worse* than anything I could do to myself.

So you want to know, was it good, eh friend?

* * * * * * * * * * * * * * * *

As I've said, I *knew* going in that it would be a fiasco of some kind; we'd be interrupted, or I'd Fail To Perform and nothing would happen. Probably that's what you're expecting, and I can't blame you.

But then to my vast astonishment our clothes seemed to melt away and we were naked and touching and she was warm and slippery and it was just sort of happening. No: it was not sort of anything. It was most emphatically happening.

And happening.

The Physical Aspect:

I have no frame of reference except for what I've read, and the accounts all conflict. You tell me: is it normal for a twenty-five-year-old male losing his virginity to experience eight orgasms in the space of four hours, without ever completely losing the original erection? Does a woman's tenth orgasm in half an hour usually trigger an hour-long continuous climax? I'd always assumed those *Penthouse* letters were fantasy. And is it always that *noisy*? And wet? And glorious?

For the record, we did everything I've ever heard of that can be done without additional cast or esoteric equipment and doesn't involve former food, former people, or animals. We *did* make use, from time to time, of candles, neckties, scarves, shoelaces, a little water-color paintbrush, her hairbrush, butter, whipped cream, strawberry jam, Johnson's Baby Oil, my Swedish hand vibrator, a fascinating bead necklace she had, miscellaneous other common household items, and every molecule of flesh that was exposed to the air or could be located with strenuous search.

The Mental Aspect:

So that's what it's like to feel virile! Fascinating. Heady. As sweet as it's cracked up to be. Potentially addictive. Primitively stirring. Part of me wanted to go punch some son of a bitch—in a little while . . .

Part of me wanted to dedicate my remaining life to thanking her, even though—perhaps *because*—she was making it clear that she wanted no more thanks than she was getting. Hyperalert for pretense as only a virgin can be, I was certain I was genuinely pleasing her.

We *knew* each other, in more than the purely Biblical sense. At least, I seemed to come to know her more intimately, more quickly, than *I* have ever known anyone, not excepting my parents, and she, being more experienced than I, surely learned more than I did. She learned things about me that no one else had ever cared to, things that I didn't know. My grandmother's heirloom rocking chair collapsed under us and we howled with laughter together.

We *touched* each other.

The Spiritual Aspect:

Oh my God I'm not alone anymore! Even if I never see her again after tonight, I'm not alone anymore. Trillions of my cells, stamped with my identity, have left my shores and established colonies in another being—and it doesn't even matter *if all the colonies end up as dead as Jamestown or Jonestown: I'm not alone anymore! This isn't another test shot, another dummy run targeted for a handful of Kleenex, this is a genuine launch. My sperm have achieved spaceflight.* God, *they cry, dying on Mars,* we made it!

Thank you, God, for this crazy stranger, for granting me these memories to cherish; I never really believed in You before . . .

* * * * * * * * * * * * * * * *

And inevitably there was an ending. I think that in my last round I finally lost the last shred of fear—the subconscious suspicion that any minute I was going to wake up from coma or a jealous husband was going to kick in the door or some other slapstick disaster would spoil it—and was able to fully relax and enjoy myself. To lose myself, to throw myself away, to expand to the size of the universe and trust that there would still be someone to be when I recondensed.

Perhaps, indeed, I became someone else in that timeless time—or perhaps it was the glorious hours that led up to it which worked some kind of change on me, developing, or maybe only tapping, wells of unsuspected strength.

Because I'm fairly sure the man I had been when I'd walked into that apartment would have concluded such stupefying carnal excess with a deep sleep of hours, if not days . . .

Whereas I returned to something resembling normal consciousness, to a vastly-changed but basically recognizable reality, only a few minutes after the last generation ship left the launch pad. I waited until my breathing slowed, and lifted myself up onto an elbow which was missing considerable skin, and said, "Tell me about yourself, Marga; what do you do with your life?"

Something infinitely subtle changed in her face, and even without my glasses I sensed she was unhappy with the question. The man I had been would have sprained his tongue changing the subject. I waited, forcing her to make some reply, and the wait was just long enough for me to notice that the silly crown she had insisted I leave on was heavy enough to strain my neck; I reached up to remove it.

"Don't!" she blurted. "It's still saving—"

There was no pause at all; I'm breaking the sentence only to indicate a barely perceptible alteration in the tone of her voice as she finished, "—the sweat from running into your eyes, my love."

A moment before I'd have been prepared to cut my throat if she wished it. But she herself had recently and repeatedly wakened in me the primitive male essence, the killer-ape ancestry I had always thought to be purely theoretical. The old ape is paranoid.

I removed the crown.

"Darling," she said, her lighthearted tone perfectly plausible, "don't spoil it, now. You look so handsome with it on—come, let me put it back on and I'll tell you anything about me you want to know. How I lost my virginity, perhaps . . . ?"

As she reached coyly for it I pulled it away and sat up. "Just a second, Marga." I switched on the table lamp—we were on the floor at the time—and turned fractionally away from her to study the crown. She made a grab for my elbow, aborted it quickly.

The light was just a little better than it had been in the bar. I held the crown close to my eyes, tilted it so the light picked out a portion of its interior surface in high relief. Most of the intricate engraving was unfamiliar to me, seemingly purely artistic in design, like the elaborate chasings on the outer surface, but a portion of it I recognized. Rotating the crown slightly I made out another such portion, extrapolated a total of three. It reminded me of a mouse I knew . . .

"I was afraid the sweat might be tarnishing the gold. It is pure gold, isn't it?"

"Yes, Fleming, but it's sealed against corrosion. Please put it back on? To please me?" She sat up beside me and tugged playfully at one of my nipples.

I pondered for a half second. "Anything to please you, Marga." I swept back my damp hair and put the crown back on my head, allowed her to adjust its position slightly. "Now if you'll excuse me for just one second, my . . . bladder is bursting."

I got up and padded toward the bathroom. Everybody has some cliché they use: my back teeth are floating, or, my eyes are turning yellow, or, my cup runneth over. My own customary euphemism is, "my buffer needs purging," and I was glad I had caught myself. It might have warned her.

I have never been a decisive, quick-thinking quick-responding kind of guy. It's easy to play practical jokes on me; I'm slow to catch on and even slower—days slower, usually—to figure out what to do about it. Maybe a dozen times in my life I've had one of those flashes of satori, those moments of insight in which a whole long logic-chain appears at once before the mind's eye—and each time it came in my work rather than my social life.

So maybe it helped that this one was work-related. Maybe it helped that I had just had the best confidence boosting of my life. Maybe there is a kind of preternatural clarity of thought that comes with total physical satisfaction . . . and how in Hell would *I* know?

It just seemed so simple, so obvious. So inescapable—

"Don't bang your elbow on that chair behind you, darling," I called back over my shoulder, and as she turned to look I bent down.

Just as I had guessed, the time machine was in her purse. It wasn't hard to recognize. It looked like a bulky watch with no band. I was interested to find that there was a weapon along with it, an unfamiliar but unmistakable handgun. I spun and leaped, whipping my head to shake off the crown, and the distance was short; as she was turning back toward me I cannoned into her and we went over in a heap, my cheek against hers and my arms tight around her. For perhaps a second she mistook it for clumsy erotic play, and that was enough time in the lamplight for me to read the little word *Quit* and thumbnail the tiny recessed button which it labeled on her "watch."

The light changed drastically, became laboratory bright. Appropriate, as we were now in a laboratory.

So was an astonished man in a white smock of odd design, and a shorter, weasel-faced man in red high heels, pink patterned stockings, and a loudly-clashing maroon kilt. Marga and I looked down on them slightly from a railing-encircled platform whose height must have been calibrated to a high degree of precision.

Weasel-face was the loudest of the pair in more ways than one, and slowest on the uptake; as the other man gaped, he was booming cheerily, "Welcome back, pixel, did you get a good—*crash*, Marga! What did you bring the mark *back* for?" His face curled reflexively on itself. "The frotter wants points, eh?"

"*Jimby, help!*" Marga screamed, and he stepped back a pace, high heels clattering on the lab floor. She tried to break my embrace, and should have succeeded, but now I was as strong as a normal man. I not only held her, I got my thumbnail back on that button.

The lights dimmed again suddenly, and my rug prickled once again on my bare skin. I let her go and rolled convulsively clear, sprang to my feet clutching her time machine. She started to rise too. Halfway up she saw her gun in my other hand, and sank back down. I must have been holding it correctly.

I knew that if I said anything my voice would crack, so I waited until I was sure I had control.

"Did you ever think to wonder," I asked at last, "what a guy like me would do for a living?"

"Do you want me to guess?" she asked sullenly. "All right. A janitor? An accountant? A fast-food cook? A painter? A writer?"

I nodded. "You wouldn't know, would you? This is too good an apartment for any of those. But that aside, even in those professions you have to be . . . more impressive-looking than I am."

"I can believe it," she said. "All right, surprise me."

"I write software, for a mouse-driven computer called the Macintosh. Independents can't make a lot at it, but no one ever has to see your face."

"Frot," she said. It was some kind of obscenity where she came from.

"You may have heard of hackers. A vanguard subculture of today, like the beatniks and the hippies of earlier days. Just like with them, some expressions that will be common idiom in another ten or twenty years are familiar to me now. When you said the word 'save,' I heard it the way you would."

"Frot," she said again, a little more forcefully.

"Yeah. As in 'saving the changes to disk.' The inside

of that crown thing looks a lot like the ball-cavity of the mouse on my Mac, two little phototransistors and a reference point. Yours wouldn't be optical, though, would they? Other than that, the analogy is pretty good: you . . . 'turn the head around,' and the sensors translate it into data. That's ROM circuitry around the sensors, sure as hell. The rest of the crown is RAM storage space, right? Hell's own data capacity, from the size.

"So the rest was logic. The only thing you could possibly be recording from my head that required that kind of byte room was . . . my memories, my *thoughts*. My feelings. That told me you had to be from the future: even the Japanese don't have brain interface *yet*. You had to have a way to get back to your own time, and I was certain you were not wearing it, externally or internally. But you wouldn't go far from it, so it had to be in the purse. The only thing I don't understand is why your magical brain-robbing Peeping ROM takes so infernally long to write the data."

She looked up at me. There was none of the new respect in her eyes that I had earned. "Fool. We cannot get at *short*-term memory; Heisenberg effect. If we could we'd have effective telepathy, wouldn't we?"

I was feeling telepathic. I sensed her thinking about trying to take the time machine from me; with great pleasure I felt her decide against it. "And mind-control," I agreed. "I'd never have reached the purse. You have to wait for the memories to seep from short-term to long-term storage—and I came out of the fog too soon." I grinned. "Taking off that crown must have been like yanking a disk out of the drive while it's spinning, huh?"

Her eyes flashed. "I could have killed you. After all I did for you—"

Give me this much credit. I did not kill her then.

When I had myself back in control, I spoke very softly. "Recorded memories must have beat out most other artforms and recreations. I'll bet the pornography is sensational by my standards. But even my primitive pornography has taught me something interesting, and you confirmed it earlier tonight: *there is a finite limit to the possibilities*. There are only so many ways to do it for the camera: at some point even you people must get jaded. So you'll pay extra for the candid-camera kick, for the memories of someone who *doesn't know you're watching*, somebody with no copy-protection on his head.

"More: for recordings of someone who's given up all hope of ecstasy, falling suddenly into the middle of his wildest wet dreams. For recordings of the ending of despair, the ending of a solitude such as none of you must ever have known. Heightened dramatic effect. Casanova may be happy, skillfully plundering his hundreth willing wench, but not a fraction as happy as I was tonight. Your world must not have pain like mine any more—you had to come back here to find it."

I shifted my weight, and my foot touched something cold. I glanced down and saw the crown.

Suddenly I was roaring in a voice I had never known I had. "Do you know that the moment a pain is first relieved is the moment you learn how large it truly was? Agony is *defined* by relief! I learned tonight just what a horrible joke my life has been and will be—*and I didn't even mind*! I was *grateful* to you for calibrating my misery! For showing me *exactly* what I'd been missing!"

I crouched and came up with my ultimate wet dream in my fist. I was dimly astonished to realize that I was not crying. Rage had always made me cry. "This *is* solid gold you've got here," I said, brandishing the crown. "You're very good at what you do. Not hard, I suppose, when you can rent—or more likely, copy—all the tricks there are."

She scowled.

I looked at it for awhile. "Can this thing play back by itself," I asked huskily, "or do you need other equipment?"

She looked me in the eye. For the first time since I'd gotten up to pee, a smile touched the corners of her mouth. "There's a thumbnail toggle inside. Once to stop, twice to rewind, three times to play back. You'll get the whole thing in six seconds of realtime."

"Slick."

I tore my eyes from the crown, and made a small gasping sound. In the soft lamplight, without my glasses, her naked body was the most beautiful thing I had ever seen. Even more beautiful, perhaps, than that same body had been four hours ago. She did that thing that women have been able to do since Eve. There are no discernible gross muscle movements, but the whole body seems to rearrange itself . . . to *beckon* to you, somehow.

I didn't want to ask. The words were torn out of me. "It was all faked, wasn't it, Marga?"

"In the sense that all performance art is faked."

A graceful out. I wouldn't take it. "You know what I mean. As the cliché goes . . . *was it good for you, too*?"

I saw a flicker of pity in her eyes. I know that one real well, and I saw it die in the instant it was born. She knew I couldn't be conned any more. She glanced down briefly to my groin, and back up. "You notice I didn't wear a crown myself," she muttered.

Again I didn't kill her. I didn't do anything at all, as far as I know. I'm sure I stopped breathing, I remember hearing the fan in the next room in the sudden silence. How long did I stare at her in the stillness, feeling the metal crown cool against one palm, the time machine and gun faintly warm against the other? My medulla kicked in finally, and I sucked in a deep breath.

And she said, clear as a bell and twice as pretty, "But you *were* sweet, and you're taking it like a man. All right: nine percent of the net, my final offer. Jimby will be furious: that's a point over the going rate."

In that instant I became, not merely a functional male animal, but a man.

I put the time machine gently down on the couch. "All right," I said, "you got me good. I guess the joke's on me. And as long as you're prepared to give me a whore's usual cut, I guess I really have no kick coming, have I? Oh, I admit, I'm tempted to give you a good spanking—"

Her eyes showed genuine interest for the first time.

"—but why give you more good material for free? Tell you what: make my end *ten* percent—why should I pay an agent's commission?—and you can have your time machine and gun and crown back."

She relaxed. "Fleming, you're a sport."

"Damn right." I smiled. "A contact sport, as clumsy and laughable as professional wrestling. But at least I'm well paid."

And I gave her back her time machine and gun and crown, and she went back home to her boss Jimby. I'm still waiting to hear back from her, but I assume the check is in the mail.

Perhaps the delay has something to do with what I did *before* I gave her back her things. While I still held the gun trained on her lovely face, I took that crown and crushed it flat in my hands, and ripped it into pieces, and hammered the pieces into gold leaves with a ball peen hammer, and made multiple passes over each leaf with my tape-head demagnetizer, and scrubbed them with steel wool, and heated them just to melting point with a blowtorch, and I really *had* had to pee for quite some time so I cooled the pieces the way they used to temper swords, and finally I wrapped the damp and sizzling shards up in her dress and handed her the whole bundle with my compliments—

—yes, now that I come to think of it, I *do* seem to recall a rather unhappy expression on her face as she winked out of existence for the last time.

I don't see why. I let her live . . .

There was a whole lot of tedious low comedy then, which lasted several days. Too many people had the vivid memory of Marga coming home on my arm indelibly engraved on their brains, in persuasive detail; too many neighbors had heard our frenzied athletics and shouted quarrel and the sound of repeated hammering; no one had seen her leave. No clothing or ID was found. I had not cleaned up the suggestive clutter in the apartment. I flatly refused to hear any questions whatsoever concerning her, let alone answer them. I declined a lawyer. I ignored the third-degree treatment, the good-cop/bad-cop and the threats and all that.

What kept it from mattering was that they lacked a corpse and they lacked a missing person from which to infer one. All witnesses were unanimous and emphatic in describing the kind of woman who could not conceivably disappear from the world (by any means known) without being missed. There was no Marga missing. The bartender and two patrons remembered the name "Ragovia," and of course there is no such country. The only people who were *certain* where she had gone had, in all likelihood, not been born yet. The police, growing more indifferent as they sensed a conviction receding out of probability, finally stopped bothering me.

Mary Zanfardino knocked on my door a few days after that, and a few days later she became my girlfriend. She has never once asked me about Marga, and she has no complaints about my lovemaking, and all things considered we are reasonably happy. One of these days perhaps we'll come to know each other so well that we'll be inside each other's skull—and since she'll be there *by invitation,* I don't plan to charge her.

I know *exactly* how happy we are, and exactly how happy we are not. And she and I are the only persons anywhere in space and time who know that . . . and that suits me fine.

Introduction

Vernor Vinge has a heck of a problem for a science fiction writer: he doesn't believe in the future, at least not in any future we on the nearside of the coming Singularity can conceive. According to Vernor, the imminent appearance of Artificial Intelligence and total, instantaneous information access make all our past tomorrows non-starters in the race for reality.

Consider just one aspect of the computer revolution that is yet to be: artificial awarenesses that are vastly more intelligent and knowledgeable than any human who has ever lived; everyone will own a couple—and can mind-link with them. What price standard-issue Galactic Empire then?

But Vernor likes *galactic derring do. ("Put down that blaster, Bat Durston!") And thus was born a rather remarkable universe (our own) wherein the computer revolution is heading for some major snags.*

THE BLABBER

Vernor Vinge

Some dreams take a long time in dying. Some get a last minute reprieve . . . and that can be even worse.

It was just over two klicks from the Elvis revival to the center of campus. Hamid Thompson took the long way, across the Barker's stubbly fields and through the Old Subdivision. Certainly the Blabber preferred that route. She raced this way and that across Ham's path, rooting at roach holes, and covertly watching the birds that swooped close on her seductive calls. As usual, her stalking was more for fun than food. When a bird came within striking distance, the Blab's head would flick up, touching the bird with her nose, blasting it with a peal of human laughter. The Blab hadn't taken this way in some time; all the birds in her regular haunts had wised up, and were no fun anymore.

When they reached the rock bluffs behind the subdivision, there weren't any more roach holes, and the birds had become cautious. Now the Blab walked companionably beside him, humming in her own way: scraps of Elvis overlaid with months-old news commentary. She went a minute or two in silence . . . listening? Contrary to what her detractors might say, she could be both awake and silent for hours at a time—but even then Hamid felt an occasional buzzing in his head, or a flash of pain. The Blab's tympana could emit across a two hundred kiloherz band, which meant that most of her mimicry was lost on human ears.

They were at the crest of the bluff. "Sit down, Blab. I want to catch my breath." *And look at the view. . . . And decide what in heaven's name I should do with you and with me.*

The bluffs were the highest natural viewpoints in New Michigan province. The flatlands that spread around them were pocked with ponds, laced with creeks and rivers, the best farmland on the continent. From orbit, the original colonists could find no better. Water landings would have been easier, but they wanted the best odds on long term survival. Thirty klicks away, half hidden by gray mist, Hamid could see the glassy streaks that marked the landing zone. The history books said it took three years to bring down the people and all the salvage from the greatship. Even now the glass was faintly radioactive, one cause for the migration across the isthmus to Westland.

Except for the forest around those landing strips, and the old university town just below the bluff, most everything in this direction was farmland, unending squares of brown and black and gray. The year was well into autumn and the last of the Earth trees had given up their colored leaves. The wind blowing across the plains was chill, leaving a crispness in his nose that promised snow someday soon. Halloween was next week. Halloween indeed. *I wonder if in Man's thirty thousand years, there has ever been a celebration of that holiday like we'll be seeing next week.* Hamid resisted the impulse to look back at Marquette. Ordinarily it was one of his favorite places: the planetary capital, population four hundred thousand, a real city. As a child, visiting Marquette had been like a trip to some far star system. But now reality had come, and the stars were so *close*. . . . Without turning, he knew the position of every one of the Tourist barges. They floated like colored balloons above the city, yet none massed less than a thousand tonnes. And those were their *shuttles*. After the Elvis revival, Halloween was the last big event on the Marquette leg of the Tour. Then they would be off to Westland, for more semi-fraudulent peeks at Americana.

Hamid crunched back in the dry moss that cushioned the rock. "Well, Blabber, what should I do? Should I sell you? We could both make it Out There if I did."

The Blabber's ears perked up. "Talk? Converse? Disgust?" She settled her forty kilo bulk next to him, and nuzzled her head against his chest. The purring from her foretympanum was like some transcendental cat. The sound was pink noise, buzzing through his chest and shaking the rock they sat on. There were few things she enjoyed more than a good talk with a peer. Hamid stroked her black and white pelt. "I said, should I sell you?"

The purring stopped, and for a moment the Blab seemed to give the matter thoughtful consideration. Her head turned this way and that, bobbing—a good imitation of a certain prof at the University. She rolled her big dark eyes at him, "Don't rush me! I'm thinking. I'm thinking." She licked daintily at the sleek fur at the base of her throat. And for all Hamid knew, she really was thinking about what to say. Sometimes she really seemed to try to understand . . . and sometimes she almost made sense. Finally she shut her mouth and began talking.

"Should I sell you? Should I sell you?" The intonation was still Hamid's but she wasn't imitating his voice. When they talked like this, she typically sounded like an adult human female (and a very attractive one, Hamid thought). It hadn't always been that way. When she had been a pup and he a little boy, she'd sounded to him like another little boy. The strategy was clear: she understood the type of voice he most likely wanted to hear. Animal cunning? "Well," she continued, "*I* know what I think. Buy, don't sell. And always get the best price you can."

She often came across like that: oracular. But he had known the Blab all his life. The longer her comment, the less she understood it. In this case . . . Ham remembered his finance class. That was before he got his present apartment, and the Blab had hidden under his desk part of the semester. (It had been an exciting semester for all concerned.) "Buy, don't sell." That was a quote, wasn't it, from some nineteenth century tycoon?

She blabbered on, each sentence having less correlation with the question. After a moment, Hamid grabbed the beast around the neck, laughing and crying at the same time. They wrestled briefly across the rocky slope, Hamid fighting at less than full strength, and the Blab carefully keeping her talons retracted. Abruptly he was on his back and the Blab was standing on his chest. She held his nose between the tips of her long jaws. "Say Uncle! Say Uncle!" she shouted.

The Blabber's teeth stopped a couple of centimeters short of the end of her snout, but the grip was powerful; Hamid surrendered immediately. The Blab jumped off him, chuckling triumph, then grabbed his sleeve to help him up. He stood up, rubbing his nose gingerly. "Okay, monster, let's get going." He waved downhill, toward Ann Arbor Town.

"Ha, ha! For sure. Let's get going!" The Blab danced down the rocks faster than he could hope to go. Yet every few seconds the creature paused an instant, checking that he was still following. Hamid shook his head, and started down. Damned if he was going to break a leg just to keep up with her. Whatever her homeworld, he guessed that winter around Marquette was the time of year most homelike for the Blab. Take her coloring: stark black and white, mixed in wide curves and swirls. He'd seen that pattern in pictures of ice pack seals. When there was snow on the ground, she was practically invisible.

She was fifty meters ahead of him now. From this distance, the Blab could almost pass for a dog, some kind of greyhound maybe. But the paws were too large, and the neck too long. The head looked more like a seal's than a dog's. Of course, she could bark like a dog. But then, she could also sound like a thunderstorm, and make something like human conversation—all at the same time. There was only one of her kind in all Middle America. This last week, he'd come to learn that her kind were almost as rare Out There. A Tourist wanted to buy her . . . and Tourists could pay with coin what Hamid Thompson had sought for more than half his twenty years.

Hamid desperately needed some good advice. It had been five years since he'd asked his father for help; he'd be damned if he did so now. That left the University, and Lazy Larry. . . .

By Middle American standards, Ann Arbor Town was *ancient*. There were older places: out by the landing zone, parts of Old Marquette still stood. School field trips to those ruins were brief—the prefab quonsets were mildly radioactive. And of course there was individual buildings in the present day capital that went back almost to the beginning. But much of the University in Ann Arbor dated from just after those first permanent structures: the University had been a going concern for 190 years.

Something was up today, and it had nothing to do with Hamid's problems. As they walked into town, a couple of police helicopters swept in from Marquette, began circling the school. On the ground, some of Ham's favorite back ways were blocked off by University safety patrols. No doubt it was Tourist business. He might have to come in through the Main Gate, past the Math Building. *Yuck*. Even after ten years he loathed that place: his years as a supposed prodigy; his parents forcing him into math classes he just wasn't bright enough to handle; the tears and anger at home, till he finally convinced them that he was not the boy they thought.

They walked around the Quad, Hamid oblivious to the graceful buttresses, the ivy that meshed stone walls into the flute trees along the street. That was all familiar . . . what was new was all the Federal cop cars. Clusters of students stood watching the cops, but there was no riot in the air. They just seemed curious. Besides, the Feds had never interfered on campus before.

"Keep quiet, okay?" Hamid muttered.

"Sure, sure." The Blab scrunched her neck back, went into her doggie act. At one time they had been notorious on campus, but he had dropped out that summer, and people had other things on their minds today. They walked through the main gate without comment from students or cops.

The biggest surprise came when they reached Larry's slummy digs at Morale Hall. Morale wasn't old enough to be historic; it was old enough to be in decay. It had been an abortive experiment in brick construction. The clay had cracked and rotted, leaving gaps for vines and pests. By now it was more a reddish mound of rubble than a habitable structure. This was where the University Administration stuck tenured faculty in greatest disfavor: the Quad's Forgotten Quarter . . . but not today. Today the cop cars were piled two deep in the parking areas, and there were shotgun-toting guards at the entrance!

Hamid walked up the steps. He had a sick feeling that Lazy Larry might be the hardest prof in the world to see today. On the other hand, working with the Tourists meant Hamid saw some of these security people every day.

"Your business, sir?" Unfortunately, the guard was no one he recognized.

"I need to see my advisor . . . Professor Fujiyama." Larry had never been his advisor, but Hamid was looking for advice.

"Um." The cop flicked on his throat mike. Hamid couldn't hear much, but there was something about "that black and white off-planet creature." Over the last twenty years, you'd have to have been living in a cave never to see anything about the Blabber.

A minute passed, and an older officer stepped through the doorway. "Sorry, son, Mr. Fujiyama isn't seeing any students this week. Federal business."

Somewhere a funeral dirge began playing. Hamid tapped the Blab's forepaw with his foot; the music stopped abruptly. "Ma'am, it's not school business." Inspiration struck: why not tell something like the truth? "It's about the Tourists and my Blabber."

The senior cop sighed. "That's what I was afraid you'd say. Okay, come along." As they entered the dark hallway, the Blabber was chuckling triumph. Someday the Blab would play her games with the wrong people and get the crap beat out of her, but apparently today was not that day.

They walked down two flights of stairs. The lighting got even worse, half-dead fluorescents built into the acoustic tiling. In places the wooden stairs sagged elastically under their feet. There were no queues of students squatting before any of the doors, but the cops hadn't cleared out the faculty: Hamid heard loud snoring from one of the offices. The Forgotten Quarter—Morale Hall in particular—was a strange place. The one thing the faculty here had in common was that they had been an unbearable pain in the neck to someone. That meant that both the most incompetent and the most brilliant were jammed into these tiny offices.

Larry's office was in the sub-basement, at the end of a long hall. Two more cops flanked the doorway, but otherwise it was as Hamid remembered it. There was a brass nameplate: "Professor L. Lawrence Fujiyama, Department of Transhuman Studies." Next to the nameplate, a sign boasted implausible office hours. In the center of the door was the picture of a piglet and the legend: "If a student appears to need help, then appear to give him some."

The police officer stood aside as they reached the door; Hamid was going to have to get in under his own power. Ham gave the door a couple of quick knocks. There was the sound of footsteps, and the door opened a crack. "What's the secret password?" came Larry's voice.

"Professor Fujiyama, I need to talk to—"

"That's not it!" The door was slammed loudly in Hamid's face.

The senior cop put her hand on Hamid's shoulder. "Sorry, son. He's done that to bigger guns than you."

He shrugged off her hand. Sirens sounded from the black and white creature at his feet. Ham shouted over the racket, "Wait! It's me, Hamid Thompson! From your Transhume 201."

The door came open again. Larry stepped out, glanced at the cops, then looked down at the Blabber. "Well, why didn't you say so? Come on in." As Hamid and the Blab scuttled past him, Larry smiled innocently at the Federal officer. "Don't worry, Susie, this is official business."

Fujiyama's office was long and narrow, scarcely an aisle between deep equipment racks. Larry's students (those who dared these depths) doubted the man could have survived on Old Earth before electronic datastorage. There must be tonnes of junk squirreled away on those shelves. The gadgets stuck out this way and that into the aisle. The place was a museum—perhaps literally; one of Larry's specialties was archeology. Most of the machines were dead, but here and there something clicked, something glowed. Some of the gadgets were Rube Goldberg jokes, some were early colonial prototypes . . . and a few were from Out There. Steam and water pipes covered much of the ceiling. The place reminded Hamid of the inside of a submarine.

At the back was Larry's desk. The junk on the table was balanced precariously high: a display flat, a beautiful piece of night black statuary. In Transhume 201, Larry had described his theory of artifact management: Last-In-First-Out, and every year buy a clean bed sheet, date it, and lay it over the previous layer of junk on your desk. Another of Lazy Larry's jokes, most had thought. But there really *was* a bed sheet peeking out from under the mess.

Shadows climbed sharp and deep from the lamp on Larry's desk. The cabinets around him seemed to lean inwards. The open space between them was covered with posters. Those posters were one small reason Larry was down here: ideas to offend every sensible faction of society. A pile of . . . something . . . lay on the visitor's chair. Larry slopped it onto the floor and motioned Hamid to sit.

"Sure, I remember you from Transhume. But why mention that? You own the Blabber. You're Huss Thompson's kid." He settled back in his chair.

I'm not Huss Thompson's kid! Aloud, "Sorry, that was all I could think to say. This is about my Blabber, though. I need some advice."

"Ah!" Fujiyama gave his famous polliwog smile, somehow innocent and predatory at the same time. "You came to the right place. I'm full of it. But I heard you had quit school, gone to work at the Tourist Bureau."

Hamid shrugged, tried not to seem defensive. "Yeah. But I was already a senior, and I know more American Thought and Lit than most graduates . . . and the Tourist caravan will only be here another half year. After that, how long till the next? We're showing them everything I could imagine they'd want to see. In fact, we're showing them more than there really *is* to see. It could be a hundred years before anyone comes down here again."

"Possibly, possibly."

"Anyway, I've learned a lot. I've met almost half the Tourists. But . . ." There were ten million people living on Middle America. At least a million had a romantic yearning to get Out There. At least ten thousand would give everything they owned to leave the Slow Zone, to live in a civilization that spanned thousands of worlds. For the last ten years, Middle America had known of the Caravan's coming. Hamid had spent most of those years—half his life, all the time since he got out of math—preparing himself with the skills that could buy him a ticket Out.

Thousands of others had worked just as hard. During the last decade, every department of American Thought and Literature on the planet had been jammed to the bursting point. And more had been going on behind the scenes. The government and some large corporations had had secret programs that weren't revealed till just before the Caravan arrived. Dozens of people had bet on the long shots, things that no one else thought the Outsiders might want. Some of those were fools: the world class athletes, the chess masters. They could never be more than eighth rate in the vast populations of the Beyond. No, to get a ride you needed something that was odd . . . Out There. Besides the Old Earth angle, there weren't many possibilities—though that could be approached in surprising ways: there was Gilli Weinberg, a bright but not brilliant ATL student. When the Caravan reached orbit, she bypassed the Bureau, announced herself to the Tourists as a genuine American cheerleader and premier courtesan. It was a ploy pursued less frankly and less successfully by others of both sexes. In Gilli's case, it had won her a ticket Out. The big laugh was that her sponsor was one of the few non-humans in the Caravan, a Lothlrimarre slug who couldn't survive a second in an oxygen atmosphere.

"I'd say I'm on good terms with three of the Outsiders. But there are at least five Tour Guides that can put on a better show. And you know the Tourists managed to revive four more corpsicles from the original Middle America crew. Those guys are sure to get tickets Out, if they want 'em." Men and women who had been adults on Old Earth, two thousand light years away and twenty thousand years ago. It was likely that Middle America had no more valuable export this time around. "If they'd just come a few years later, after I graduated . . . maybe made a name for myself."

Larry broke into the self-pitying silence. "You never thought of using the Blabber as your ticket Out?"

"Off and on." Hamid glanced down at the dark bulk that curled around his feet. The Blab was *awfully* quiet.

Larry noticed the look. "Don't worry. She's fooling with some ultrasound imagers I have back there." He gestured at the racks behind Hamid, where a violet glow played hopscotch between unseen gadgets. The boy smiled, "We may have trouble getting her out of here." He had several ultrasonic squawkers around the apartment, but the Blab rarely got to play with high resolution equipment. "Yeah, right at the beginning, I tried to interest them in the Blab. Said I was her trainer. They lost interest as soon as they saw she couldn't be native to Old Earth. . . . These guys are *freaks*, Professor! You could rain transhuman treasure on 'em, and they'd call it spit! But give 'em Elvis Presley singing Bruce Springsteen and they build you a spaceport on Selene!"

Larry just smiled, the way he did when some student was heading for academic catastrophe. Hamid quieted, "Yeah, I know. There are good reasons for some of the strangeness." Middle America had nothing that would interest anybody rational from Out There. They were stuck nine light years inside the Slow Zone: commerce was hideously slow and expensive. Middle American technology was obsolete and—considering their location—it could never amount to anything competitive. Hamid's unlucky world had only one thing going for it. It was a direct colony of Old Earth, and one of the first. Their greatship's tragic flight had lasted twenty thousand years, long enough for the Earth to become a legend for much of humankind.

In the Beyond, there were millions of solar systems known to bear human-equivalent intelligences. Most of these could be in more or less instantaneous communication with one another. In that vastness humanity was a speck—perhaps four thousand worlds. Even on those, interest in a first generation colony within the Slow Zone was near zero. But with four thousand worlds, that was enough: here and there was a rich eccentric, an historical foundation, a religious movement—all strange enough to undertake a twenty year mission into the Slowness. So Middle America should be glad for these rare mixed nuts. Over the last hundred years there had been occasional traders and a couple of Tourists caravans. That commerce had raised the Middle American standard of living substantially. More important to many—including Hamid—it was almost their only peephole on the universe beyond the Zone. In the last century, two hundred Middle Americans had escaped to the Beyond. The early ones had been government workers, commissioned scientists. The Feds' investment had not paid off: of all those who left, only five had returned. Larry Fujiyama and Hussein Thompson were two of those five.

"Yeah, I guess I knew they'd be fanatics. But most of them aren't even much interested in accuracy. We make a big thing of representing twenty-first century America. But we both know what that was like: heavy industry moving up to Earth orbit, five hundred million people still crammed into North America. At best what we have here is like mid-twentieth century America—or even earlier. I've worked very hard to get our past straight. But except for a few guys I really respect, anachronism doesn't seem to bother them. It's like just being here with us is the big thing."

Larry opened his mouth, seemed on the verge of providing some insight. Instead he smiled, shrugged. (One of his many mottos was, "If you didn't figure it out yourself, you don't understand it.")

"So after all these months, where did you dig up the interest in the Blabber?"

"It was the slug, the guy running the Tour. He just mailed me that he had a party who wanted to buy. Normally, this guy haggles. He—wait, you know him pretty well, don't you? Well, he just made a flat offer. A payoff to the Feds, transport for me to Lothlrimarre," that was the nearest civilized system in the Beyond, "and some ftl privileges beyond that."

"And you kiss your pet goodbye?"

"Yeah. I made a case for them needing a handler: me. That's not just bluff, by the way. We've grown up together. I can't imagine the Blab accepting anyone without lots of help from me. But they're not interested. Now, the slug claims no harm is intended her, but . . . do you believe him?"

"Ah, the slug's slime is generally clean. I'm sure he doesn't know of any harm planned . . . and he's straight enough to do at least a little checking. Did he say who wanted to buy?"

"Somebody—something named Ravna&Tines." He passed Larry a flimsy showing the offer. Ravna&Tines had a logo: it looked like a stylized claw. "There's no Tourist registered with that name."

Larry nodded, copied the flimsy to his display flat. "I know. Well, let's see. . . ." He puttered around for a moment. The display was a lecture model, with imaging on both sides. Hamid could see the other was searching internal Federal databases. Larry's eyebrows rose. "Hm*hm!* Ravna&Tines arrived just last week. It's not part of the Caravan at all."

"A solitary trader . . ."

"Not only that. It's been hanging out past the Jovians—at the slug's request. The Federal space net got some pictures." There was a fuzzy image of something long and wasp-waisted, typical of the Outsiders' ramscoop technology. But there were strange fins—almost like the wings on a sailplane. Larry played some algorithmic game with the display and the image sharpened. "Yeah. Look at the aspect ratio on those fins. This guy is carrying high performance ftl gear. No good down here of course, but hot stuff across an enormous range of environment . . ." he whistled a few bars of Nightmare Waltz. "I think we're looking at a High Trader."

Someone from the Transhuman Spaces.

Almost every university on Middle America had a Department of Transhuman Studies. Since the return of the five, it had been a popular thing to do. Yet most people considered it a joke. Transhume was generally the bastard child of Religious Studies and an Astro or Computer Science department, the dumping ground for quacks and incompetents. Lazy Larry had founded the department at Ann Arbor—and spent much class time eloquently proclaiming its fraudulence. Imagine, trying to study what lay *beyond* the Beyond! Even the Tourists avoided the topic. Transhuman Space existed—perhaps it included most of the universe—but it was a tricky, risky, ambiguous thing. Larry said that its reality drove most of the economics of the Beyond . . . but that all the theories about it were rumors at tenuous second hand. One of his proudest claims was that he raised Transhuman Studies to the level of palm reading.

Yet now . . . apparently a trader had arrived that regularly penetrated the Transhuman Reaches. If the government hadn't sat on the news, it would have eclipsed the Caravan itself. And *this* was what wanted the Blab. Almost involuntarily, he reached down to pet the creature. "Y-you don't think there could really be anybody transhuman on that ship?" An hour ago he had been agonizing about parting with the Blab; that might be nothing compared to what they really faced.

For a moment he thought Larry was going to shrug the question off. But the older man sighed. "If there's anything we've got right it's that no transhuman can think at these depths. Even in the Beyond, they'd die or fragment or maybe cyst. I think this Ravna&Tines must be a human-equivalent intellect, but it could be a lot more dangerous than the average Outsider . . . the tricks it would know, the gadgets it would have." His voice drifted off; he stared at the forty-centimeter statue perched on his desk. It was lustrous green, apparently cut from a flawless block of jade. *Green? Wasn't it black a minute ago?*

Larry's gaze snapped up to Hamid. "Congratulations. Your problem is a lot more interesting than you thought. Why would any Outsider want the Blab, much less a High Trader?"

". . . Well, her kind must be rare. I haven't talked to any Tourist who recognized the race."

Lazy Larry just nodded. Space is deep. The Blab might be from somewhere else in the Slow Zone.

"When she was a pup, lots of people studied her. You saw the articles. She has a brain as big as a chimp, but most of it's tied up in driving her tympana and processing what she hears. One guy said she's the ultimate in verbal orientation—all mouth and no mind."

"Ah! A student!"

Hamid ignored the Larryism. "Watch this." He patted the Blab's shoulder.

She was slow in responding; that ultrasound equipment must be fascinating. Finally she raised her head. "What's up?" The intonation was natural, the voice a young woman's.

"Some people think she's just a parrot. She can play things back better than a high fidelity recorder. But she also picks up favorite phrases, and uses them in different voices—and almost appropriately. . . . Hey, Blab. What's that?" Hamid pointed at the electric heater that Larry had propped by his feet. The Blab stuck her head around the corner of the desk, saw the cherry glowing coils. This was not the sort of heater Hamid had in his apartment.

"What's that . . . that . . ." The Blab extended her head curiously toward the glow. She was a bit too eager; her nose bumped the heater's safety grid. "*Hot!*" She jumped back, her nose tucked into her neck fur, a foreleg extended toward the heater. "Hot! Hot!" She rolled onto her haunches, and licked tentatively at her nose. "Jeeze!" She gave Hamid a look that was both calculating and reproachful.

"Honest, Blab, I didn't think you would touch it. . . . She's going to get me for this. Her sense of humor extends only as far as ambushes, but it can be pretty intense."

"Yeah. I remember the Zoo Society's documentary on her." Fujiyama was grinning broadly. Hamid had always thought that Larry and the Blab had kindred humors. It even seemed that the animal's cackling became like the old man's after she attended a couple of his lectures.

Larry pulled the heater back and walked around the desk. He hunched down to the Blab's eye level. He was all solicitude now, and a good thing: he was looking into a mouth full of sharp teeth, and somebody was playing the Timebomb Song. After a moment, the music stopped and she shut her mouth. "I can't believe there isn't human equivalence hiding here somewhere. Really. I've had freshmen who did worse at the start of the semester. How could you get this much verbalization without intelligence to benefit from it?" He reached out to rub her shoulders. "You got sore shoulders, Baby? Maybe little hands ready to burst out?"

The Blab cocked her head. "I like to soar."

Hamid had thought long about the Heinlein scenario; the science fiction of Old Earth was a solid part of the ATL curriculum. "If she is still a child, she'll be dead before she grows up. Her bone calcium and muscle strength have deteriorated about as much as you'd expect for a thirty year old human."

"Hm. Yeah. And we know she's about your age." Twenty. "I suppose she could be an ego frag. But most of those are brain-damaged transhumans, or obvious constructs." He went back behind his desk, began whistling tunelessly. Hamid twisted uneasily in his chair.

He had come for advice. What he got was news that they were in totally over their heads. He shouldn't be surprised; Larry was like that. "What we need is a whole lot more information."

"Well, I suppose I could flat out demand the slug tell me more. But I don't know how I can force any of the Tourists to help me."

Larry waved breezily. "That's not what I meant. Sure, I'll ask the Lothlrimarre about it. But basically the Tourists are at the end of a nine light-year trip to nowhere. Whatever libraries they have are like what you would take on a South Seas vacation—and out of date, to boot. . . . And of course the federal government of Middle America doesn't know what's coming off to begin with. Heh, heh. Why else do they come to me when they're really desperate? . . . No, what we need is direct access to library resourses Out There."

He said it casually, as though he were talking about getting an extra telephone, not solving Middle America's greatest problem. He smiled complacently at Hamid, but the boy refused to be drawn in. Finally, "Haven't you wondered why the campus—Morale Hall, in particular—is crawling with cops?"

"Yeah." *Or I would have, if there weren't lots else on my mind.*

"One of the more serious Tourists—Skandr Vrinimisrinithan—brought along a genuine transhuman artifact. He's been holding back on it for months, hoping he could get what he wants other ways. The Feds—I'll give 'em this—didn't budge. Finally he brought out his secret weapon. It's in this room right now."

Ham's eyes were drawn to the stone carving (now bluish green) that sat on Larry's desk. The old man nodded. "It's an ansible."

"Surely they don't call it that!"

"No. But that's what it is."

"You mean, all these years, it's been a lie that ftl won't work in the Zone?" *You mean I've wasted my life trying to suck up to these Tourists?*

"Not really. Take a look at this thing. See the colors

change. I swear its size and mass do, too. This is a real transhuman artifact. Not an intellect, of course, but not some human design manufactured in Transhuman space. Skandr claims—and I believe him—that no other Tourist has one."

A transhuman artifact. Hamid's fascination was tinged with fear. This was something one heard of in the theoretical abstract, in classes run by crackpots.

"Skandr claims this gadget is 'aligned' on the Lothlrimarre commercial outlet. From there we can talk to any registered address in the Beyond."

"Instantaneously." Hamid's voice was very small.

"Near enough. It would take a while to reach the universal event horizon; there are some subtle limitations if you're moving at relativistic speeds."

"And the catch?"

Larry laughed. "Good man. Skandr admits to a few. This thing won't work more than ten light years into the Zone. I'll bet there aren't twenty worlds in the Galaxy that could benefit from it—but we are *definitely* on one. The trick sucks enormous energy. Skandr says that running this baby will dim our sun by half a percent. Not noticeable to the guy in the street, but it could have long term bad effects." There was a short silence; Larry often did that after a cosmic understatement. "And from your standpoint, Hamid, there's one big drawback. The mean bandwidth of this thing is just under a six bits per minute."

"Huh? Ten seconds to send a single bit?"

"Yup. Skandr left three protocols at the Lothlrimarre end: ASCII, a Hamming map to a subset of English, and an AI scheme that guesses what you'd say if you used more bits. The first is Skandr's idea of a joke, and I wouldn't trust the third more than wishful thinking. But with the Hamming map, you could send a short letter—say five hundred English words—in a day. It's full-duplex, so you might get a good part of your answer in that time. Neat, huh? Anyway, it beats waiting twenty years."

Hamid guessed it would be the biggest news since

first contact, one hundred years ago. "So . . . uh, why did they bring it to you, Professor?"

Larry looked around his hole of an office, smiling wider and wider. "Heh, heh. It's true, our illustrious planetary president is one of the five; he's been Out There. But I'm the only one with real friends in the Beyond. You see, the Feds are very leery of this deal. What Skandr wants in return is most of our zygote bank. The Feds banned any private sale of human zygotes. It was a big moral thing: 'no unborn child sold into slavery or worse'. Now they're thinking of doing it themselves. They really *want* this ansible. But what if it's a fake, just linked up to some fancy database on Skandr's ship? Then they've lost some genetic flexibility, and maybe they've sold some kids into hell—and got nothing but a colorful trinket for their grief.

"So. Skandr's loaned them the thing for a week, and the Feds loaned it to me—with close to *carte blanche*. I can call up old friends, exchange filthy jokes, let the sun go dim doing it. After a week, I report on whether the gadget is really talking to the Outside."

Knowing you, "I bet you have your own agenda."

"Sure. Till you showed up the main item was to check out the foundation that sponsors Skandr, see if they're as clean as he says. Now . . . well, your case isn't as important morally, but it's very interesting. There should be time for both. I'll use Skandr's credit to do some netstalking, see if I can find *anyone* who's heard of Blabbers, or this Ravna&Tines."

Hamid didn't have any really close friends. Sometimes he wondered if that was another penalty of his strange upbringing, or if he was just naturally unlikable. He had come to Fujiyama for help all right, but all he'd been expecting was a round of prickly questions that eventually brought *him* to some insight. Now he seemed to be on the receiving end of a favor of world-shaking proportions. It made him suspicious and very grateful all at once. He gabbled some words of abject gratitude.

Larry shrugged. "It's no special problem for me. I'm curious, and this week I've got the *means* to satisfy my curiosity." He patted the ansible. "There's a real favor I can do though: so far, Middle America has been cheated occasionally, but no Outsider has used force against us. That's one good thing about the Caravan system: it's to the Tourists' advantage to keep each other straight. Ravna&Tines may be different. If this is really a High Trader, it might just make a grab for what it wants. If I were you, I'd keep close to the Blabber. . . . And I'll see if the slug will move one of the Tourist barges over the campus. If you stay in this area, not much can happen without them knowing.

"Hey, see what a help I am? I did nothing for your original question, and now you have a whole, ah, ship-load of new things to worry about. . . ."

He leaned back, and his voice turned serious. "But I don't have much to say about your original question, Hamid. If Ravna&Tines turn out to be decent, you'll still have to decide for yourself about giving up the Blab. I bet every critter that thinks it thinks—even the transhumans—worry about how to do right for themselves and the ones they love. I—uh, oh damn! Why don't you ask your pop, why don't you ask Hussein about these things? The guy has been heartbroken since you left."

Ham felt his face go red. Pop had never had much good to say about Fujiyama. Who'd have guessed the two would talk about him? If Hamid had known, he'd never have come here today. He felt like standing up, screaming at this old man to mind his own business. Instead, he shook his head and said softly, "It's kind of personal."

Larry looked at him, as if wondering whether to push the matter. One word, and Ham knew that all the pain would come pouring out. But after a moment, the old man sighed. He looked around the desk to where the Blab lay, eyeing the heater. "Hey, Blabber. You take good care of this kid."

The Blab returned his gaze. "Sure, sure," she said.

Hamid's apartment was on the south side of campus. It was large and cheap, which might seem surprising so near the oldest university around, and just a few kilometers south of the planetary capital. The back door opened on kilometers of forested wilderness. It would be a long time before there was any land development immediately south of here. The original landing zones were just twenty klicks away. In a bad storm there might be a little hot stuff blown north. It might be only fifty percent of natural background radiation, but with a whole world to colonize, why spread towns toward the first landings?

Hamid parked the commons bicycle in the rack out front, and walked quietly around the building. Lights were on upstairs. There were the usual motorbikes of other tenants. *Something* was standing in back, at the far end of the building. Ah. A Halloween scarecrow.

He and the Blab walked back to his end. It was past twilight and neither moon was in the sky. The tips of his fingers were chilled to numbness. He stuck his hands in his pockets, and paused to look up. The starships of the Caravan were in synch orbit at this longitude. They formed a row of bright dots in the southern sky. Something dark, too regular to be a cloud hung almost straight overhead. That must be the protection Larry had promised.

"I'm hungry."

"Just a minute and we'll go in."

"Okay." The Blab leaned companionably against his leg, began humming. She looked fat now, but it was just her fur, all puffed out. These temperatures were probably the most comfortable for her. He stared across the star fields. *God, how many hours have I stood like this, wondering what all those stars mean?* The Big Square was about an hour from setting. The fifth brightest star in that constellation was Lothlrimarre's sun. At Lothlrimarre and beyond, faster than light travel was possible—even for twenty-first century Old Earth types. If Middle America were just ten more light years further out from the galactic center, Hamid would have had all the Beyond as his world.

His gaze swept back across the sky. Most everything he could see there would be in the Slow Zone. It extended four thousand light years inward from here, if the Outsiders were to be believed. Billions of star systems, millions of civilizations—trapped. Most would never know about the outside.

Even the Outsiders had only vague information about the civilizations down here in the Slow Zone. Greatships, ramscoops, they all must be invented here again and again. Colonies spread, knowledge gained, most often lost in the long slow silence. What theories the Slow Zone civilizations must have for why nothing could move faster than light—even in the face of superluminal events seen at cosmic distances. What theories they must have to explain why human-equivalent intelligence was the highest ever found and ever created. Those ones deep inside, they might at times be the happiest of all, their theories assuring them they were at the top of creation. If Middle America were only a hundred light years further down, Hamid would never know the truth. He would love this world, and the spreading of civilization upon it.

Hamid's eye followed the Milky Way to the western horizon. The glow wasn't really brighter there than above, but he knew his constellations. He was looking at the galactic center. He smiled wanly. In twentieth century science fiction, those star clouds were imagined as the homes of "elder races," godlike intellects. . . . But the Tourists call those regions of the galaxy, the Depths. The Unthinking Depths. Not only was ftl impossible there, but so was sentience. So they guessed. They couldn't know for sure. The fastest round-trip probe to the edge of the Depths took about ten thousand years. Such expeditions were rare, though some were well documented.

Hamid shivered, and looked back at the ground. Four cats sat silently just beyond the lawn, watching the Blab. "Not tonight, Blab," he said, and the two of them went indoors.

The place looked undisturbed: the usual mess. He fixed the Blab her dinner and heated some soup for himself.

"Yuck. This stuff tastes like *shit*!" The Blab rocked back on her haunches and made retching sounds. Few people have their own childhood obnoxiousness come back to haunt them so directly as Hamid Thompson did. He could remember using exactly those words at the dinner table. Mom should have stuffed a sock down his throat.

Hamid glanced at the chicken parts. "Best we can afford, Blab." He was running his savings down to zero to cover the year of the Tourists. Being a guide was such a plum that no one thought to pay for it.

"Yuck." But she started nibbling.

As Ham watched her eat, he realized that one of his problems was solved. If Ravna&Tines wouldn't take him as the Blab's "trainer," they could hike back to the Beyond by themselves. Furthermore, he'd want better evidence from the slug—via the ansible he could get assurances directly from Lothlrimarre—that Ravna&Tines could be held to promises. The conversation with Larry had brought home all the nightmare fears, the fears that drove some people to demand total rejection of the Caravan. Who knew what happened to those that left with Outsiders? Almost all Middle American knowledge of the Beyond came from less than thirty starships, less than a thousand strangers. Strange strangers. If it weren't for the five who came back, there would be zero corroboration. Of those five . . . well Hussein Thompson was a mystery even to Hamid: seeming kind, inside a vicious mercenary. Lazy Larry was a mystery, too, a cheerful one who made it clear that you better think twice about what folks tell you. But one thing came clear from all of them: space is deep. There were millions of civilized worlds in the Beyond, thousands of star-spanning empires. In such vastness, there could be no single notion of law and order. Cooperation and enlightened self-interest were common, but . . . nightmares lurked.

So what if Ravna&Tines turned him down, or couldn't produce credible assurances? Hamid went into the bedroom, and punched up the news, let the color and motion wash over him. Middle America was a beautiful world, still mostly empty. With the agrav plates and the room-temperature fusion electrics that the Caravan had brought, life would be more exciting here than ever before. . . . In twenty or thirty years there would likely be another caravan. If he and the Blab were still restless—well, there was plenty of time to prepare. Larry Fujiyama had been forty years old when he went Out.

Hamid sighed, happy with himself for the first time in days.

The phone rang just as he finished with the news. The name of the incoming caller danced in red letters across the news display: *Ravna*. No location or topic. Hamid swallowed hard. He bounced off the bed, turned the phone pickup to look at a chair in an uncluttered corner of the room, and sat down there. Then he accepted the call.

Ravna was human. And female. "Mr. Hamid Thompson, please."

"T-that's me." *Curse the stutter*.

For an instant there was no reaction. Then a quick smile crossed her face. It was not a friendly smile, more like a sneer at his nervousness. "I call to discuss the animal. The Blabber, you call it. You have heard our offer. I am prepared to improve upon it." As she spoke, the Blab walked into the room and across the phone's field of view. Her gaze did not waver. Strange. He could see that the video transmit light was on next to the screen. The Blab began to hum. A moment passed and *then* she reacted, a tiny start of surprise.

"What is your improvement?"

Again, a half-second pause. Ravna&Tines were a lot nearer than the Jovians tonight, though apparently still not at Middle America. "We possess devices that allow faster than light communication to a world in the . . . Beyond. Think on what this access means. With this, if you stay on Middle America, you will be the richest man on the planet. If you choose to accept passage Out, you will have the satisfaction of knowing you have moved your world a good step out of the darkness."

Hamid found himself thinking faster than he ever had outside of a Fujiyama oral exam. There were plenty of clues here. Ravna's English was more fluent than most Tourists', but her pronunciation was awful. Human but awful: her vowel stress was strange to the point of rendering her speech unintelligible, and she didn't voice things properly: "pleess" instead "pleez," "chooss" instead of "chooz."

At the same time, he had to make sense of what she was saying and decide the correct response. Hamid thanked God he already knew about ansibles. "Miss Ravna, I agree. That is an improvement. Nevertheless, my original requirement stands. I must accompany my pet. Only I know her needs." He cocked his head. "You could do worse than have an expert on call."

As he spoke, her expression clouded. Rage? She seemed hostile toward him *personally*. But when he finished, her face was filled with an approximation of a friendly smile. "Of course, we will arrange that also. We had not realized earlier how important this is to you."

Jeeze. Even I can lie better than that! This Ravna was used to getting her own way without face-to-face lies, or else she had real emotional problems. Either way: "And since you and I are scarcely equals, we also need to work something out with the Lothlrimarre that will put a credible bond on the agreement."

Her poorly constructed mask slipped. "That is absurd." She looked at something off camera. "The Lothlrimarre knows nothing of us. . . . I will try to satisfy you. But know this, Hamid Thompson: I am the congenial, uh, *humane* member of my team. Mr. Tines is very impatient. I try to restrain him, but if he becomes enough desperate . . . things could happen that would hurt us all. Do you understand me?"

First a lie, and now chainsaw subtlety. He fought back a smile. *Careful. You might be mistaking raw insanity for bluff and bluster*. "Yes, Miss Ravna, I do understand, and your offer is generous. But . . . I need to think about this. Can you give me a bit more time?" *Enough time to complain to the Tour Director*.

"Yes. One hundred hours should be feasible."

After she rang off, Hamid sat for a long time, staring sightlessly at the dataset. What *was* Ravna? Through twenty thousand years of colonization, on worlds far stranger than Middle America, the human form had drifted far. Cross fertility existed between most of Earth's children, though they differed more from one another than had races on the home planet. Ravna looked more like an Earth human than most of the Tourists. Assuming she was of normal height, she could almost have passed as an American of Middle East descent: sturdy, dark-skinned, black haired. There were differences. Her eyes had epicanthic folds, and the irises were the most intense violet he had ever seen. Still, all that was trivial compared to her manner.

Why hadn't she been receiving Hamid's video? Was she blind? She didn't seem so otherwise; he remembered her looking at things around her. Perhaps she was some sort of personality simulator. That had been a standard item in American science fiction at the end of the twentieth century; the idea passed out of fashion when computer performance seemed to top out in the early twenty-first. But things like that should be possible in the Beyond, and certainly in Transhuman Space. They wouldn't work very well down here, of course. Maybe she was just a graphical front end for whatever Mr. Tines was.

Somehow, Hamid thought she was real. She certainly had a human effect on him. Sure she had a good figure, obvious under soft white shirt and pants. And sure, Hamid had been girl crazy the last five years. He was so horny most of the time, it felt good just to ogle femikins in downtown Marquette stores. But for all-out sexiness, Ravna wasn't *that* spectacular. She had nothing on Gilli Weinberg or Skandr Vrinimisrinithan's wife. Yet, if he had met her at school, he would have tried harder to gain her favor than he had Gilli's . . . and that was saying *a lot*.

Hamid sighed. That probably just showed that *he* was nuts.

"I wanna go out." The Blab rubbed her head against his arm. Hamid realized he was sweating even though the room was chill.

"God, not tonight, Blab." He realized that there was a lot of bluff in Ravna&Tines. At the same time, it was clear they were the kind who might just *grab* if they could get away with it.

"I wanna go out!" Her voice came louder. The Blab spent many nights outside, mainly in the forest. That made it easier to keep her quiet when she was indoors. For the Blab, that was a chance to play with her pets: the cats—and sometimes the dogs—in the neighborhood. There had been a war when he and the Blab first arrived here. Pecking orders had been abruptly revised, and two of the most ferocious dogs had just disappeared. What was left was very strange. The cats were fascinated by the Blab. They hung around the yard just for a glimpse of her. When she was here they didn't even fight among themselves. Nights like tonight were the best. In a couple of hours both Selene and Diana would rise, the silver moon and the gold. On nights like this, when gold and silver lay between deep shadows, Hamid had seen her pacing through the edge of the forest, followed by a dozen faithful retainers.

But, "*Not tonight, Blab!*" There followed a major argument, the Blabber blasting rock music and kiddie shows at high volume. The noise wasn't the loudest she could make. That would have been physically painful to Ham. No, this was more like a cheap music player set way high. Eventually it would bring complaints from all over the apartment building. Fortunately for Hamid, the nearest rooms were unoccupied just now.

After twenty minutes of din, Hamid twisted the fight into a "game of humans." Like many pets, the Blab thought of herself as a human being. But unlike a cat or a dog or even a parrot, she could do a passable job of imitating one. The trouble was, she couldn't always find people with the patience to play along.

They sat across from each other at the dinette table, the Blab's forelegs splayed awkwardly across its surface. Hamid would start with some question—it didn't matter the topic. The Blab would nod wisely, ponder a reply. With most abstractions, anything she had to say was nonsense, meaningful only to tea-leaf readers or wishful thinkers. Never mind that. In the game, Hamid would respond with a comment, or laugh if the Blab seemed to be in a joke-telling behavior. The pacing, the intonation—they were all perfect for real human dialog. If you didn't understand English, the game would have sounded like two friends having a good time.

"How about an imitation, Blab? Joe Ortega. President Ortega. Can you do that?"

"Heh, heh." That was Lazy Larry's cackle. "Don't rush me. I'm thinking. I'm thinking!" There were several types of imitation games. For instance, she could speak back Hamid's words instantly, but with the voice of some other human. Using that trick on a voice-only phone was probably her favorite game of all, since her audience really *believed* she was a person. What he was asking for now was almost as much fun, if the Blab would play up to it.

She rubbed her jaw with a talon, "Ah yes." She sat back pompously, almost slid onto the floor before she caught herself. "We must all work together in these exciting times." That was from a recent Ortega speech, a simple playback. But even when she got going, responding to Hamid's questions, adlibbing things, she was still a perfect match for the President of Middle America. Hamid laughed and laughed. Ortega was one of the five who came back, not a very bright man but self-important and ambitious. It said something that even his small knowledge of the Outside was enough to propel him to the top of the world state. The five were very big fish in a very small pond—that was how Larry Fujiyama put it.

The Blab was an enormous show-off, and was quickly carried away by her own wit. She began waving her forelegs around, lost her balance and fell off the chair. "Oops!" She hopped back on the chair, looked at Hamid—and began laughing herself. The two were in stitches for almost half a minute. This had happened before; Hamid was sure the Blab could not appreciate humor above the level of pratfalls. Her laughter was imitation for the sake of congeniality, for the sake of being a person. "Oh, God!" She flopped onto the table, "choking" with mirth, her forelegs across the back of her neck as if to restrain herself.

The laughter died away to occasional snorts, and then a companionable silence. Hamid reached across to rub the bristly fur that covered the Blab's forehead tympanum. "You're a good kid, Blab."

The dark eyes opened, turned up at him. Something like a sigh escaped her, buzzing the fur under his palm. "Sure, sure," she said.

Hamid left the drapes partly pulled, and a window pane cranked open where the Blab could sit and look out. He lay in the darkened bedroom and watched her silhouette against the silver and gold moonlight. She had her nose pressed up to the screen. Her long neck was arched to give both her head and shoulder tympana a good line on the outside. Every so often her head would jerk a few millimeters, as if something very interesting had just happened outside.

The loudest sound in the night was faint roach racket, out by the forest. The Blab was being very quiet—in the range Hamid could hear—and he was grateful. She really was a good kid.

He sighed and pulled the covers up to his nose. It had been a long day, one where life's problems had come out ahead.

He'd be very careful the next few days; no trips away from Marquette and Ann Arbor, no leaving the Blab unattended. At least the slug's protection looked solid. *I better tell Larry about the second ansible, though*. If Ravna&Tines just went direct to the government with it . . . that might be the most dangerous move of all. For all their pious talk and restrictions on private sales, the Feds would sell their own grandmothers if they thought it would benefit the Planetary Interest. Thank God they already had an ansible—or almost had one.

Funny. After all these years and all the dreams, that it was the Blab the Outsiders were after. . . .

Hamid was an adopted child. His parents had told him that as soon as he could understand the notion.

And somewhere in those early years, he had guessed the truth . . . that his father had brought him in . . . from the Beyond. Somehow Huss Thompson had kept that fact secret from the public. Surely the government knew, and cooperated with him. In those early years—before they forced him into Math—it had been a happy secret for him; he thought he had all his parents' love. Knowing that he was really from Out There had just given substance to what most well-loved kids believe anyway—that somehow they are divinely special. His secret dream had been that he was some Outsider version of an exiled prince. And when he grew up, when the next ships from the Beyond came down . . . he would be called to his destiny.

Starting college at age eight had just seemed part of that destiny. His parents had been so confident of him, even though his tests results were scarcely more than bright normal. . . . That year had been the destruction of innocence. He wasn't a genius, no matter how much his parents insisted. The fights, the tears, their insistence. In the end, Mom had left Hussein Thompson. Not till then did the man relent, let his child return to normal schools. Life at home was never the same. Mom's visits were brief, tense . . . and rare. But it wasn't for another five years that Hamid learned to hate his father. The learning had been an accident, a conversation overheard. Hussein had been *hired* to raise Hamid as he had, to push him into school, to twist and ruin him. The old man had never denied the boy's accusations. His attempts to "explain" had been vague mumbling . . . worse than lies. . . . If Hamid was a prince, he must be a very hated one indeed.

The memories had worn deep grooves, ones he often slid down on his way to sleep. . . . But tonight there was something new, something ironic to the point of magic. All these years . . . it had been the Blab who was the lost princeling. . . !

There was a hissing sound. Hamid struggled toward wakefulness, fear and puzzlement playing through his dreams. He rolled to the edge of the bed and forced his eyes to see. Only stars shone through the window. The Blab. She wasn't sitting at the window screen anymore. She must be having one of her nightmares. They were rare, but spectacular. One winter's night Hamid had been wakened by the sounds of a full-scale thunderstorm. This was not so explosive, but. . . .

He looked across the floor at the pile of blankets that was her nest. Yes. She was there, and facing his way.

"Blab? It's okay, baby."

No reply. Only the hissing, maybe louder now. *It wasn't coming from the Blab*. For an instant his fuzzy mind hung in a kind of mouse-and-snake paralysis. Then he flicked on the lights. No one here. The sound was from the dataset; the picture flat remained dark. *This is crazy*.

"Blab?" He had never seen her like this. Her eyes were open wide, rings of white showing around the irises. Her forelegs reached beyond the blankets. The talons were extended and had slashed deep into the plastic flooring. A string of drool hung from her muzzle.

He got up, started toward her. The hissing formed a voice, and the voice spoke. "I want her. Human, I want her. And I will have her." Her, the Blab.

"How did you get access? You have no business disturbing us." Silly talk, but it broke the nightmare spell of this waking.

"My name is Tines." Hamid suddenly remembered the claw on the Ravna&Tines logo. Tines. Cute. "We have made generous offers. We have been patient. That is past. I will have her. If it means the death of all you m-meat animals, so be it. But I *will* have her."

The hissing was almost gone now, but the voice still sounded like something from a cheap synthesizer. The syntax and accent were similar to Ravna's. They were either the same person, or they had learned English from the same source. Still, Ravna had seemed angry. Tines sounded flat-out nuts. Except for the single stutter over "meat," the tone and pacing were implacable. And that voice gave away more than anything yet about why the Outsider wanted his pet. There was a *hunger* in its voice, a lust to feed or to rape.

Hamid's rage climbed on top of his fear. "Why don't you just go screw yourself, comic monster! We've got *protection*, else you wouldn't come bluffing—"

"Bluffing! *Bluffiiyowru*—" the words turned into choked gobbling sounds. Behind him, Hamid heard the Blab scream. After a moment the noises faded. "I do not bluff. Hussein Thompson has this hour learned what I do with those who cross me. You and all your people will also die unless you deliver her to me. I see a ground car parked by your . . . house. Use it to take her east fifty kilometers. Do this within one hour, or learn what Hussein Thompson learned—that *I do not bluff*." And Mr. Tines was gone.

It has *to be a bluff! If Tines has that power why not wipe the Tourists from the sky and just grab the Blab?* Yet they were so stupid about it. A few smooth lies a week ago, and they might have gotten everything without a murmur. It was as if they couldn't imagine being disobeyed—or were desperate beyond reason.

Hamid turned back to the Blab. As he reached to stroke her neck, she twisted, her needle-toothed jaws clicking shut on his pyjama sleeve. "Blab!"

She released his sleeve, and drew back into the pile of blankets. She was making whistling noises like the time she got hit by a pickup trike. Hamid's father guessed those must be true Blabber sounds, like human sobs or chattering of teeth. He went to his knees and made comforting noises. This time she let him stroke her neck. He saw that she had wet her bed. The Blab had been toilet trained as long as he had. Bluff or not, this had thoroughly terrified her. Tines claimed he could kill everyone. Hamid remembered the ansible, a god-damned telephone that could dim the sun.

Bluff or madness?

He scrambled back to his dataset, and punched up the Tour Director's number. Pray the slug was accepting more than mail tonight. The ring pattern flashed twice, and then he was looking at a panorama of cloud tops and blue sky. It might have been an aerial view of Middle America, except that as you looked downwards the clouds seemed to extend forever, more and more convoluted in the dimness. This was a picture clip from the ten bar level over Lothlrimarre. No doubt the slug chose it to soothe human callers, and still be true to the nature of his home world—a subjovian thirty-thousand kilometers across.

For five seconds they soared through the canyons of cloud. *Wake up, damn you!*

The picture cleared and he was looking at a human—Larry Fujiyama! Lazy Larry did not look surprised to see him. "You got the right number, kid. I'm up here with the slug. There have been developments."

Hamid gaped for an appropriate reply, and the other continued. "Ravna&Tines have been all over the slug since about midnight. Threats and promises, mostly threats since the Tines critter took their comm. . . . I'm sorry about your dad, Hamid. We should've thought to—"

"*What?*"

"Isn't that what you're calling about? . . . Oh. It's been on the news. Here—" The picture disolved into a view from a news chopper flying over Eastern Michigan farmland. It took Hamid a second to recognize the hills. This was near the Thompson spread, two thousand klicks east of Marquette. It would be past sunup there. The camera panned over a familiar creek, the newsman bragging how On-Line News was ahead of the first rescue teams. They crested a range of hills and . . . where were the trees? Thousands of black lines lay below, trunks of blown-over trees, pointing inevitably inward, toward the center of the blast. The newsman babbled on about the meteor strike and how fortunate it was that ground zero was in a lake valley, how only one farm had been affected. Hamid swallowed. That farm . . . was Hussein Thompson's. The place they lived after Mom left. Ground zero itself was obscured by rising steam—all that was left of the lake. The reporter assured his audience that the crater consumed all the land where the farm buildings had been.

The news clip vanished. "It was no Middle American nuke, but it wasn't natural, either," said Larry. "A lighter from Ravna&Tines put down there two hours ago. Just before the blast, I got a real scared call from Huss, something about 'the tines' arriving. I'll show it to you if—"

"No!" Hamid gulped. "No," he said more quietly. How he had hated Hussein Thompson; how he had loved his father in the years before. Now he was gone, and Hamid would never get his feelings sorted out. "Tines just called me. He said he killed my—Hussein." Hamid played back the call. "Anyway, I need to talk to the slug. Can he protect me? Is Middle America really in for it if I refuse the Tines thing?"

For once Larry didn't give his "you figure it" shrug. "It's a mess," he said. "And sluggo's waffling. He's around here somewhere. Just a sec—" More peaceful cloud-soaring. Damn, damn, damn. Something bumped gently into the small of his back. The Blab. The black and white neck came around his side. The dark eyes looked up at him. "What's up?" she said quietly.

Hamid felt like laughing and crying. She was very subdued, but at least she recognized him now. "Are you okay, Baby?" he said. The Blabber curled up around him, her head stretched out on his knee.

On the dataset, the clouds parted and they were looking at both Larry Fujiyama and the slug. Of course, they were not in the same room; that would have been fatal to both. The Lothlrimarre barge was a giant pressure vessel. Inside, pressure and atmosphere were just comfy for the slug—about a thousand bars of ammonia and hydrogen. There was a terrarium for human visitors. The current view showed the slug in the foreground. Part of the wall behind him was transparent, a window into the terrarium. Larry gave a little wave, and Hamid felt himself smiling. No question who was in a zoo.

"Ah, Mr. Thompson. I'm glad you called. We have a very serious problem." The slug's English was perfect, and though the voice was artificial, he sounded like a perfectly normal Middle American male. "Many problems would be solved if you could see your way clear to give—"

"No." Hamid's voice was flat. "N-not while I'm alive, anyway. This is no business deal. You've heard the threats, and you saw what they did to my father." The slug had been his ultimate employer these last six months, someone rarely spoken to, the object of awe. None of that mattered now. "You've always said the first responsibility of the Tour Director is to see that no party is abused by another. I'm asking you to live up to that."

"Um. Technically, I was referring to you Middle Americans and the Tourists in my caravan. I know I have the power to make good on my promises with them. . . . But we're just beginning to learn about Ravna&Tines. I'm not sure it's reasonable to stand up against them." He swiveled his thousand kilo bulk toward the terrarium window. Hamid knew that under Lothlrimarre gravity, the slug would have been squashed into the shape of a flatworm, with his manipulator fringe touching the ground. At one gee, he looked more like an overstuffed silk pillow, fringed with red tassles. "Larry has told me about Skandr's remarkable Slow Zone device. I've heard of such things. They are *very* difficult to obtain. A single one would have more than financed my caravan. . . . And to think that Skandr pleaded his foundation's poverty in begging passage. . . . Anyway, Larry has been using the 'ansible' to ask about what your Blabber really is."

Larry nodded. "Been at it since you left, Hamid. The machine's down in my office, buzzing away. Like Skandr says, it is aligned on the commercial outlet at Lothlrimarre. From there I have access to the Known Net. Heh, heh. Skandr left a *sizable* credit bond at Lothlrimarre. I hope he and Ortega aren't too upset by the phone bill I run up testing this gadget for them. I described the Blab, and put out a depth query. There are a million subnets, all over the Beyond, searching their databases for anything like the Blab. I—" His happy enthusiasm wavered, "Sluggo thinks we've dug up a reference to the Blabber's race. . . ."

"Yes, and it's frightening, Mr. Thompson." It was no surprise that none of the Tourists had heard of a blabber. The only solid lead coming back to Larry had been from halfway around the galactic rim, a nook in the Beyond that had only one occasional link with the rest of the Known Net. That far race had no direct knowledge of the Blabbers. But they heard rumors. From a thousand light years below them, deep within the Slow Zone, there came stories . . . of a race matching the Blab's appearance. The race was highly intelligent, and had quickly developed the relativistic transport that was the fastest thing inside the Zone. They colonized a vast sphere, held an empire of ten thousand worlds—all without ftl. And the tines—the name seemed to fit—had not held their empire through the power of brotherly love. Races had been exterminated, planets busted with relativistic kinetic energy bombs. The tines' technology had been about as advanced and deadly as could exist in the Zone. Most of their volume was a tomb now, their story whispered through centuries of slow flight toward the Outside.

"Wait, wait. Prof Fujiyama told me the ansible's bandwidth is a tenth of a bit per second. You've had less than twelve hours to work this question. How can you possibly know all this?"

Larry looked a little embarrassed—a first as far as Hamid could remember. "We've been using the AI protocol I told you about. There's massive interpolation going on at both ends of our link to Lothlrimarre."

"I'll bet!"

"Remember, Mr. Thompson, the data compression applies only to the first link in the chain. The Known Net lies in the Beyond. Bandwidth and data integrity are very high across most of its links."

The slug sounded very convinced. But Hamid had read a lot about the Known Net; the notion was almost as fascinating as ftl travel itself. There was no way a world could have a direct link with all others—partly because of range limitations, mainly because of the *number* of planets involved. Similarly, there was no way a single "phone company" (or even ten thousand phone companies!) could run the thing. Most likely, the information coming to them from around the galaxy had passed through five or ten intermediate hops. The intermediates—not to mention the race on the far rim—were likely nonhuman. Imagine asking a question in English to someone who also speaks Spanish, and that person asking the question in Spanish to someone who understands Spanish and passes the question on in German. This was a million times worse. Next to some of the creatures Out There, the slug could pass for human!

Hamid said as much. "F-furthermore, even if this *is* what the sender meant, it could still be a lie! Look at what local historians did to Richard the Third, or Mohamet Rose."

Lazy Larry smiled his polliwog smile, and Hamid realized they must have been arguing about this already. Larry put in, "There's also this, sluggo: the nature of the identification. The tines must have something like hands. See any on Hamid's Blabber?"

The slug's scarlet fringe rippled three quick cycles. Agitation? Dismissal? "The text is still coming in. But I have a theory. You know, Larry, I've always been a great student of sex. I may be a 'he' only by courtesy, but I think sex is fascinating. It's what makes the 'world go around' for so many races." Hamid suddenly understood Gilli Weinberg's success. "So. Grant me my expertise. My guess is the tines exhibit *extreme* sexual dimorphism. The males' forepaws probably are hands. No doubt it's the males who are the killers. The females—like the Blab—are by contrast friendly, mindless creatures."

The Blab's eyes rolled back to look at Hamid. "Sure, sure," she murmurred. The accident of timing was wonderful, seeming to say *who is this clown?*

The slug didn't notice. "This may even explain the viciousness of the male. Think back to the conversation Mr. Thompson had. These creatures seem to regard their own females as property to exploit. Rather the ultimate in sexism." Hamid shivered. That *did* ring a bell. He couldn't forget the *hunger* in the tines's voice.

"Is this the long way to tell me you're not going to protect us?"

The slug was silent for almost fifteen seconds. Its scarlet fringe waved up and down the whole time. Finally: "Almost, I'm afraid. My caravan customers haven't heard this analysis, just the threats and the news broadcasts. Nevertheless, they are tourists, not explorers. They demand that I refuse to let you aboard. Some demand that we leave your planet immediately. . . . How secure is this line, Larry?"

Fujiyama said, "Underground fiberoptics, and an encrypted laser link. Take a chance, sluggo."

"Very well. Mr. Thompson, there is what you can expect from me: I can stay over the city, and probably defend against direct kidnapping—that unless I see a planetbuster coming. I doubt very much they have that set up, but if they do—well, I don't think even you would want to keep your dignity at the price of a relativistic asteroid strike.

"I can *not* come down to pick you up. That would be visible to all, a direct violation of my customers' wishes. On the other hand," there was another pause, and his scarlet fringe whipped about even faster than before, "if you should appear, uh, up here, I would take you aboard my barge. Even if this were noticed, it would be a *fait accompli*. I could hold off my customers, and likely our worst fate would be a premature and unprofitable departure from Middle America."

"T-that's very generous." *Unbelievably so*. The slug was thought to be an honest fellow—but a very hard trader. Even Hamid had to admit that the claim on the slug's honor was tenuous here, yet he was risking a twenty-year mission for it.

"Of course, *if* we reach that extreme, I'll want a few years of your time once we reach the Outside. My bet is that hard knowledge about your Blabber might make up for the loss of everything else."

A day ago, Hamid would have quibbled about contracts and assurances. Today, well, the alternative was Ravna&Tines. . . . With Larry as witness, they settled on two years indenture and a pay scale.

Now all he and the Blab had to do was figure how to

climb five thousand meters straight up. There was one obvious way.

It was Dave Larson's car, but Davey owed him. Hamid woke his neighbor, explained that the Blab was sick and had to go into Marquette. Fifteen minutes later, Hamid and the Blab were driving through Ann Arbor Town. It was a Saturday, and barely into morning twilight; he had the road to himself. He'd half expected the place to be swarming with cops and military. If Ravna&Tines ever guessed how easy it was to intimidate Joe Ortega. . . . If the Feds knew exactly what was going on, they'd turn the Blab over to Tines in an instant. But apparently the government was simply confused, lying low, hoping it wouldn't be noticed till the big boys upstairs settled their arguments. The farm bombing wasn't in the headline list anymore. The Feds were keeping things quiet, thereby confining the mindless panic to the highest circles of government.

The Blab rattled around the passenger side of the car, alternately leaning on the dash and sniffing in the bag of tricks that Hamid had brought. She was still subdued, but riding in a private auto was a novelty. Electronics gear was cheap, but consumer mechanicals were still at a premium. And without a large highway system, cars would never be the rage they had been on Old Earth; most freight transport was by rail. A lot of this would change because of the Caravan. They brought one hundred thousand agrav plates—enough to revolutionize transport. Middle America would enter the Age of the Aircar—and for the first time surpass the homeworld. So saith Joe Ortega.

Past the University, there was a patch of open country. Beyond the headlights, Hamid caught glimpses of open fields, a glint of frost. Hamid looked up nervously every few seconds. Selene and Diana hung pale in the west. Scattered clouds floated among the Tourist barges, vague grayness in the first light of morning. No intruders, but three of the barges were gone, presumably moved to orbit. The Lothlrimarre vessel floated just

East of Marquette, over the warehouse quarter. It looked like the slug was keeping his part of the deal.

Hamid drove into downtown Marquette. Sky signs floated brightly amid the two hundred storey towers, advertising dozens of products—some of which actually existed. Light from discos and shopping malls flooded the eight lane streets. Of course the place was deserted; it was Saturday morning. Much of the business section was like this—a reconstruction of the original Marquette as it had been on Earth in the middle of the twenty-first century. That Marquette had sat on the edge of an enormous lake, called Superior. Through that century, as Superior became the splash down point for heavy freight from space, Marquette had become one of the great port cities of Earth, the gateway to the solar system. The Tourists said it was legend, ur-mother to a thousand worlds.

Hamid turned off the broadway, down an underground ramp. The Marquette of today was for show, perhaps one percent the area of the original, with less than one percent the population. But from the air it looked good, the lights and bustle credible. For special events, the streets could be packed with a million people—everyone on the continent that could be spared from essential work. And the place wasn't really a fraud; the Tourists knew this was a reconstruction. The point was, it was an *authentic* reconstruction, as could only be done by a people one step from the original source—that was the official line. And in fact, the people of Middle America had made enormous sacrifices over almost twenty years to have this ready in time for the Caravan.

The car rental was down a fifteen storey spiral, just above the train terminal. *That* was for real, though the next arrival was a half hour away. Hamid got out, smelling the cool mustiness of the stone cavern, hearing only the echoes of his own steps. Millions of tonnes of ceramic and stone stood between them and the sky. Even an Outsider couldn't see through that . . . he hoped. One sleepy-eyed attendant watched him fill out the forms. Hamid stared at the display, sweating even in the cool; would the guy in back notice? He almost laughed at the thought. His first sally into crime was the least of his worries. If Ravna&Tines were plugged into the credit net, then in a sense they really *could* see down here—and the bogus number Larry had supplied was all that kept him invisible.

They left in a Millennium Commander, the sort of car a Tourist might use to bum around in olden times. Hamid drove north through the underground, then east, and when finally they saw open sky again, they were driving south. Ahead was the warehouse district . . . and hanging above it, the slug's barge, its spheres and cupolas green against the brightening sky. So huge. It looked near, but Hamid knew it was a good five thousand meters up.

A helicopter might be able to drop someone on its topside, or maybe land on one of the verandas—though it would be a tight fit under the overhang. But Hamid couldn't fly a chopper, and wasn't even sure how to rent one at this time of day. No, he and the Blab were going to try something a lot more straightforward, something he had done every couple of weeks since the Tourists arrived.

They were getting near the incoming lot, where Feds and Tourists held payments-to-date in escrow. Up ahead there would be cameras spotted on the roofs. He tinted all but the driver side window, and pushed down on the Blab's shoulders with his free hand. "Play hide for a few minutes."

"Okay."

Three hundred meters more and they were at the outer gate. He saw the usual three cops out front, and a fourth in an armored box to the side. If Ortega was feeling the heat, it could all end right here.

They looked *real* nervous, but they spent most of their time scanning the sky. They knew something was up, but they thought it was out of their hands. They took a quick glance at the Millennium Commander and waved him through. The inner fence was almost as easy, though here he had to enter his Guide ID. . . . If

Ravna&Tines were watching the nets, Hamid and the Blab were running on borrowed time now.

He pulled into the empty parking lot at the main warehouse, choosing a slot with just the right position relative to the guard box. "Keep quiet a little while, Blab," he said. He hopped out and walked across the gravel yard. Maybe he should move faster, as if panicked? But no, the guard had already seen him. *Okay, play it cool.* He waved, kept walking. The glow of morning was already dimming the security lamps that covered the lot. No stars shared the sky with the clouds and the barges.

It was kind of a joke that merchandise from the Beyond was socked away here. The warehouse was big, maybe two hundred meters on a side, but an old place, sheet plastic and aging wood timbers.

The armored door buzzed even before Hamid touched it. He pushed his way through. "Hi, Phil."

Luck! The other guards must be on rounds. Phil Lucas was a friendly sort, but not too bright, and not very familiar with the Blab. Lucas sat in the middle of the guard cubby, and the armored partition that separated him from the visitor trap was raised. To the left was a second door that opened into the warehouse itself. "Hi, Ham." The guard looked back at him nervously. "Awful early to see you."

"Yeah. Got a little problem. There's a Tourist out in the Commander." He waved through the armored window. "He's drunk out of his mind. I need to get him Upstairs and quietly."

Phil licked his lips. "Christ. Everything happens at once. Look, I'm sorry, Ham. We've got orders from the top at Federal Security: nothing comes down, nothing goes up. There's some kind of a ruckus going on amongst the Outsiders. If they start shooting, we want it to be at each other, not us."

"That's the point. We think this fellow is part of the problem. If we can get him back, things should cool off. You should have a note on him. It's Antris ban Reempt."

"Oh. *Him.*" Ban Reempt was the most obnoxious

Tourist of all. If he'd been an ordinary Middle American, he would have racked up a century of jail time in the last six months. Fortunately, he'd never killed anyone, so his antics were just barely ignorable. Lucas pecked at his dataset. "No, we'd don't have anything."

"Nuts. Everything stays jammed unless we can get this guy Upstairs," Hamid paused judiciously, as if giving the matter serious thought. "Look, I'm going back to the car, see if I can call somebody to confirm this."

Lucas was dubious. "Okay, but it's gotta be from the top, Ham."

"Right."

The door buzzed open, and Hamid was jogging back across the parking lot. Things really seemed on track. Thank God he'd always been friendly with the cops running security here. The security people regarded most of the Guides as college trained snots—and with some reason. But Hamid had had coffee with these guys more than once. He knew the system . . . he knew the incoming phone number for security confirmations.

Halfway across the lot, Hamid suddenly realized that he didn't have the shakes anymore. The scheme, the adlibbing, it almost seemed normal—a skill he'd never guessed he had. Maybe that's what desperation does to a fellow. . . . Somehow this was almost fun.

He pulled open the car door. "Back! Not yet," he pushed the eager Blab onto the passenger seat. "Big game, Blab." He rummaged through his satchel, retrieved the two comm sets. One was an ordinary head and throat model, the other had been modified for the Blab. He fastened the mike under the collar of his windbreaker. The earphone shouldn't be needed, but it was small; he put it on, turned the volume down. Then he strapped the other commset around the Blab's neck, turned off *its* mike, and clipped the receiver to her ear. "The game, Blab: Imitation. Imitation." He patted the commset on her shoulder. The Blab was fairly bouncing around the Commander's cab. "For sure. Sure, sure! Who, who?"

"Joe Ortega. Try it: 'We must all pull together . . .' "

The words came back from the Blab as fast as he spoke them, but changed into the voice of the Middle American President. He rolled down the driver side window; this worked best if there was eye contact. Besides, he might need her out of the car. "Okay. Stay here. I'll go get us the sucker." She rattled his instructions back in pompous tones.

One last thing: He punched a number into the car phone, and set its timer and no video option. Then he was out of the car, jogging back to the guard box. This sort of trick had worked often enough at school. Pray that it would work now. Pray that she wouldn't ad lib.

He turned off the throat mike as Lucas buzzed him back into the visitor trap. "I got to the top. Someone—maybe even the Chief of Federal Security—will call back on the Red Line."

Phil's eyebrows went up. "That would do it." Hamid's prestige had just taken a giant step up.

Hamid made a show of impatient pacing about the visitor trap. He stopped at the outer door with his back to the guard. Now he really *was* impatient. Then the phone rang, and he heard Phil pick it up.

"Escrow One, Agent Lucas speaking, Sir!"

From where he was standing, Hamid could see the Blab. She was in the driver's seat, looking curiously at the dash phone. Hamid turned on the throat mike and murmured, "Lucas, this is Joseph Stanley Ortega."

Almost simultaneously, "Lucas, this is Joseph Stanley Ortega," came from the phone behind him. The words were weighted with all the importance Hamid could wish, and something else: a furtiveness not in the public speeches. That was probably because of Hamid's original delivery, but it didn't sound too bad.

In any case, Phil Lucas was impressed. "Sir!"

"Agent Lucas, we have a problem." Hamid concentrated on his words, and tried to ignore the Ortega echo. For him, that was the hardest part of the trick, especially when he had to speak more than a brief sentence. "There could be nuclear fire, unless the Tourists cool off. I'm with the National Command Authorities in deep shelter: it's that serious." Maybe that would explain why there was no video.

Phil's voice quavered. "Yes, sir." *He* wasn't in deep shelter.

"Have you verified—" *clicket* "—my ID?" The click was in Hamid's earphone; he didn't hear it on the guard's set. A loose connection in the headpiece?

"Yes, sir. I mean . . . just one moment." Sounds of hurried keyboard tapping. There should be no problem with a voiceprint match, and Hamid needed things nailed tight to bring this off. "Yes sir, you're fine. I mean—"

"Good. Now listen carefully: The guide, Thompson, has a Tourist with him. We need that Outsider returned, *quickly and quietly*. Get the lift ready, and keep everybody clear of these two. If Thompson fails, millions may die. Give him whatever he asks for." Out in the car, the Blab was having a high old time. Her front talons were hooked awkwardly over the steering wheel. She twisted it back and forth, "driving" and "talking" at the same time: the apotheosis of life—to be taken for a person by real people!

"Yes, sir!"

"Very well. Let's—" *clicket-click* "—get moving on this." And on that last click, the Ortega voice was gone. *God damned cheapjack commset!*

Lucas was silent a moment, respectfully waiting for his President to continue. Then, "Yes, sir. What must we do?"

Out in the Millennium Commander, the Blab was the picture of consternation. She turned toward him, eyes wide. *What do I say now?* Hamid repeated this line, as loud as he dared. No Ortega. *She can't hear anything I'm saying!* He shut off his mike.

"Sir? Are you still there?"

"Line must be dead," Hamid said casually, and gave the Blab a little wave to come running.

"Phone light says I still have a connection, Ham. . . . Mr. President, can you hear me? You were saying what we must do. Mr. President?"

The Blab didn't recognize his wave. Too small. He

tried again. She tapped a talon against her muzzle. *Blab! Don't ad lib!* "Well, uh," came Ortega's voice, "don't rush me. I'm thinking. I'm thinking! . . . We must all pull together or else millions may die. Don't you think? I mean, it makes sense—" which it did not, and less so by the second. Lucas was making "uh-huh" sounds, trying to fit reason on the Blabber. His tone was steadily more puzzled, even suspicious.

No help for it. Hamid slammed his fist against the transp armor, and waved wildly to the Blab. *Come here!* Ortega's voice died in midsyllable. He turned to see Lucas staring at him, surprise and uneasiness on his face. "Something's going on here, and I don't like it—" Somewhere in his mind, Phil had figured out he was being taken, yet the rest of him was carried forward by the inertia of the everyday. He leaned over the counter, to get Hamid's line of view on the lot.

The original plan was completely screwed, yet strangely he felt no panic, no doubt; there were still options: Hamid smiled—and jumped across the counter, driving the smaller man into the corner of wall and counter. Phil's hand reached wildly for the tab that would bring the partition down. Hamid just pushed him harder against the wall . . . and grabbed the guard's pistol from its holster. He jammed the barrel into the other's middle. "Quiet down, Phil."

"*Son of a bitch!*" But the other stopped struggling. Hamid heard the Blab slam into the outer door.

"Okay. Kick the outside release." The door buzzed. A moment later, the Blab was in the visitor trap, bouncing around his legs.

"Heh heh heh! That was good. That was really good!" The cackle was Lazy Larry's but the voice was still Ortega's.

"Now buzz the inner door." The other gave his head a tight shake. Hamid punched Lucas's gut with the point of the pistol. "*Now!*" For an instant, Phil seemed frozen. Then he kneed the control tab, and the inner door buzzed. Hamid pushed it ajar with his foot, then heaved Lucas away from the counter. The other bounced to his feet, his eyes staring at the muzzle of the pistol, his face very pale. *Dead men don't raise alarums*. The thought was clear on his face.

Hamid hesitated, almost as shocked by his success as Lucas was. "Don't worry, Phil." He shifted his aim and fired a burst over Lucas's shoulder . . . into the warehouse security processor. Fire and debris flashed back into the room—and now alarms sounded everywhere.

He pushed through the door, the Blab close behind. The armor clicked shut behind them; odds were it would stay locked now that the security processor was down. Nobody in sight, but he heard shouting. Hamid ran down the aisle of upgoing goods. They kept the agrav lift at the back of the building, under the main ceiling hatch. Things were definitely not going to plan, but if the lift was there, he could still—

"There he is!"

Hamid dived down an aisle, jigged this way and that between pallets . . . and then began walking very quietly. He was in the downcoming section now, surrounded by the goods that had been delivered thus far by the Caravan. These were the items that would lift Middle America beyond Old Earth's twenty-first century. Towering ten meters above his head were stacks of room-temperature fusion electrics. With them—and the means to produce more—Middle America could trash its methanol economy and fixed fusion plants. Two aisles over were the raw agrav units. These looked more like piles of fabric than anything high-tech. Yet the warehouse lifter was built around one, and with them Middle America would soon make aircars as easily as automobiles.

Hamid knew there were cameras in the ceiling above the lights. Hopefully they were as dead as the security processor. Footsteps one aisle over. Hamid eased into the dark between two pallets. Quiet, quiet. The Blab didn't feel like being quiet. She raced down the aisle ahead of him, raking the spaces between the pallets with a painfully loud imitation of his pistol. They'd see her in a second. He ran the other direction a few meters, and fired a burst into the air.

"Jesus! How many did asshole Lucas let in?" Someone very close replied, "That's still low power stuff." Much quieter: "We'll show these guys some firepower." Hamid suddenly guessed there were only two of them. And with the guard box jammed, they might be trapped in here till the alarm brought guards from outside.

He backed away from the voices, continued toward the rear of the warehouse.

"Boo!" The Blab was on the pallets above him, talking to someone on the ground. Explosive shells smashed into the fusion electrics around her. The sounds bounced back and forth through the warehouse. Whatever it was, it was a cannon compared to his pistol. No doubt it was totally unauthorized for indoors, but that did Hamid little good. He raced forward, heedless of the destruction. "Get down!" he screamed at the pallets. A bundle of shadow and light materialized in front of him and streaked down the aisle.

A second roar of cannon fire, tearing through the space where he had just been. But something else was happening now. Blue light shone from somewhere in the racks of fusion electrics, sending brightness and crisp shadows across the walls ahead. It felt like someone had opened a furnace door behind him. He looked back. The blue was spreading, an arc-welder light that promised burns yet unfelt. He looked quickly away, afterimages dancing on his eyes, afterimages of the pallet shelves *sagging* in the heat.

The autosprinklers kicked on, an instant rainstorm. But this was a fire that water would not quench—and might even fuel. The water exploded into steam, knocking Hamid to his knees. He bounced up sprinting, falling, sprinting again. The agrav lift should be around the next row of pallets. In the back of his mind, something was analyzing the disaster. That explosive cannon fire had started things, a runaway melt in the fusion electrics. They were supposedly safer than meth engines—but they could melt down. This sort of destruction in a Middle American nuclear plant would have meant rad poisoning over a continent. But the Tourists claimed their machines melted clean—shedding low energy photons and an enormous flood of particles that normal matter scarcely responded to. Hamid felt an urge to hysterical laughter; Slow Zone astronomers lightyears away might notice this someday, a wiggle on their neutrino scopes, one more datum for their flawed cosmologies.

There was lightning in the rainstorm now, flashes between the pallets and across the aisle—into the raw agrav units. The clothlike material jerked and rippled, individual units floating upwards. Magic carpets released by a genie.

Then giant hands clapped him, sound that was pain, and the rain was gone, replaced by a hot wet wind that swept around and up. Morning light shown through the steamy mist. The explosion had blasted open the roof. A rainbow arced across the ruins. Hamid was crawling now. Sticky wet ran down his face, dripped redly on the floor. The pallets bearing the fusion electrics had collapsed. Fifteen meters away, molten plastic slurried atop flowing metal.

He could see the agrav lift now, what was left of it. The lift sagged like an old candle in the flow of molten metal. So. No way up. He pulled himself back from the glare, and leaned against the stacked agravs. They slid and vibrated behind him. The cloth was soft, yet it blocked the heat, and some of the noise. The pinkish blue of a dawn sky shown through the last scraps of mist. The Lothlrimarre barge hung there, four spherical pressure vessels embedded in intricate ramps and crenellations.

Jeeze. Most of the warehouse roof was just . . . gone. A huge tear showed through the far wall. *There!* The two guards. They were facing away from him, one half leaning on the other. Chasing him was very far from their minds at the moment. They were picking their way through the jumble, trying to get out of the warehouse. Unfortunately, a rivulet of silver metal crossed their path. One false step and they'd be ankle deep in the stuff. But they were lucky, and in fifteen seconds passed from sight around the outside of the building.

No doubt he could get out that way, too. . . . But that wasn't why he was here. Hamid struggled to his feet, and began shouting for the Blab. The hissing, popping sounds were loud, but not like before. If she were conscious, she'd hear him. He wiped blood from his lips and limped along the row of agrav piles. *Don't die, Blab. Don't die.*

There was motion everywhere. The piles of agravs had come alive. The top ones simply lifted off, tumbled upwards, rolling and unrolling. The lower layers strained and jerked. Normal matter might not notice the flood of never-never particles from the melt-down; the agravs were clearly not normal. Auras flickered around the ones trapped at the bottom. But this was not the eye-sizzling burn of the fusion electrics. This was a soft thing, an awakening rather than an explosion. Hamid's eyes were caught on the rising. Hundreds of them just floating off, gray and russet banners in the morning light. He leaned back. Straight up, the farthest ones were tiny specks against the blue. *Maybe—*

Something banged into his legs, almost dumping him back on the floor. "Wow. So loud." The Blab had found *him*! Hamid knelt and grabbed her around the neck. She looked fine! A whole lot better than he did anyway. Like most smaller animals, she could take a lot of bouncing around. He ran his hands down her shoulders. There were some nicks, a spattering of blood. And she looked subdued, not quite the hellion of before. "Loud. Loud," she kept saying.

"I know, Blab. But that's the worst." He looked back into the sky. At the rising agravs . . . at the Lothlrimarre barge. *It would be crazy to try* . . . but he heard sirens outside.

He patted the Blab, then stood and clambered up the nearest pile of agravs. The material, hundreds of separate units piled like blankets, gave beneath his boots like so much foam rubber. He slid back a ways after each step. He grabbed at the edges of the units above him, and pulled himself near the top. He wanted to test one that was free to rise. Hamid grabbed the top layer, already rippling in an unsensed wind. He pulled out his pocket knife, and slashed at the material. It parted smoothly, with the resistence of heavy felt. He ripped off a strip of the material, stuffed it in his pocket, then grabbed again at the top layer. The unit fluttered in his hands, a four-meter square straining for the sky. It slowly tipped him backwards. His feet left the pile. It was rising as fast as the unloaded ones!

"Wait for me! Wait!" The Blab jumped desperately at his boots. Two meters up, three meters. Hamid gulped, and let go. He crashed to the concrete, lay stunned for a moment, imagining what would have happened if he'd dithered an instant longer. . . . Still. He took the scrap of agrav from his pocket, stared at it as it tugged on his fingers. There was a pattern in the reddish-gray fabric, intricate and recursive. The Tourists said it was in a different class from the fusion electrics. The electrics involved advanced technology, but were constructable within the Slow Zone. Agrav, on the other hand . . . the effect could be explained in theory, but its practical use depended on instant-by-instant restabilization at atomic levels. The Tourists claimed there were billions of protein-sized processors in the fabric. This was an import—not just from the Beyond—but from Transhuman Space. Till now, Hamid had been a skeptic. Flying was such a prosaic thing. But . . . these things had no simple logic. They were more like living creatures, or complex control systems. They seemed a lot like the "smart matter" Larry claimed was common in Transhuman technology.

Hamid cut the strip into two different-sized pieces. The cut edges were smooth, quite unlike cuts in cloth or leather. He let the fragments go. . . . They drifted slowly upwards, like leaves on a breeze. But after a few seconds, the large one took the lead, falling higher and higher above the smaller. *I could come down just by trimming the fabric!* And he remembered how the carpet had drifted sideways, in the direction of his grasp.

The sirens were louder. He looked at the pile of agravs. Funny. A week ago he had been worried about flying commercial air to Westland. "You want games, Blab? This is the biggest yet."

He climbed back up the pile. The top layer was just beginning to twitch. They had maybe thirty seconds, if it was like the others. He pulled the fabric around him, tying it under his arms. "Blab! Get your ass up here!"

She came, but not quite with the usual glee. Things had been rough this morning—or maybe she was just brighter than he was. He grabbed her, and tied the other end of the agrav under her shoulders. As the agrav twitched toward flight, the cloth seemed to shrink. He could still cut the fabric, but the knots were tight. He grabbed the Blab under her hind quarters, and drew her up to his chest—just like Pop used to do when the Blab was a pup. Only now, she was big. Her forelegs stuck long over his shoulders.

The fabric came taut around his armpits. Now he was standing. Now—his feet left the pile. He looked *down* at the melted pallets, the silver metal rivers that dug deep through the warehouse floor. The Blab was making the sounds of a small boy crying.

They were through the roof. Hamid shuddered as the morning chill turned his soaked clothing icy. The sun was at the horizon, its brilliance no help against the cold. Shadows grew long and crisp from the buildings. The guts of the warehouse lay open below them; from here it looked dark, but lightning still flickered. More reddish-gray squares floated up from the ruins. In the gravel lot fronting the warehouse, there were fire trucks and armored vehicles. Men ran back and forth from the guard box. A squad was moving around the side of the building. Two guys by the armored cars pointed at him, and others just stopped to stare. A boy and his not-dog, swinging beneath a wrong way parachute. He'd seen enough Feds 'n' Crooks to know they could shoot him down easily, any number of ways. One of the figures climbed into the armored car. If they were half as trigger happy as the guards inside the warehouse . . .

Half a minute passed. The scene below could fit between his feet now. The Blab wasn't crying anymore, and he guessed the chill was no problem for her. The Blab's neck and head extended over his shoulder. He could feel her looking back and forth. "Wow," she said softly. "Wow."

Rockabye baby. They swung back and forth beneath the agrav. Back and forth. The swings were getting wider each time! In a sickening whirl, the sky and ground traded places. He was buried head first in agrav fabric. He struggled out of the mess. They weren't hanging below the agrav now, they were *lying* on top of it. This was crazy. How could it be stable with them on top? In a second it would dump them back under. He held tight to the Blab . . . but no more swinging. It was as if the hanging down position had been the unstable one. More evidence that the agrav was smart matter, its processors using underlying nature to produce seemingly unnatural results.

The damn thing really was a flying carpet! Of course, with all the knots, the four-meter square of fabric was twisted and crumpled. It looked more like the Blab's nest of blankets back home than the flying carpets of fantasy.

The warehouse district was out of sight beneath the carpet. In the spaces around and above them, dozens of agravs paced him—some just a few meters away, some bare specks in the sky. Westwards, they were coming even with the tops of the Marquette towers: brown and ivory walls, vast mirrors of windows reflecting back the landscape of morning. Southwards, Ann Arbor was a tiny crisscross of streets, almost lost in the bristle of leafless trees. The quad was clearly visible, the interior walks, the tiny speck of red that was Morale Hall. He'd had roughly this view every time they flew back from the farm, but now . . . there was nothing around him. It was just Hamid and the Blab . . . and the air stretching away forever beneath them. Hamid gulped, and didn't look down for a while.

They were still rising. The breeze came straight down upon them—and it seemed to be getting stronger. Hamid shivered uncontrollably, teeth chattering. How high up were they? Three thousand meters? Four? He was going numb, and when he moved he could hear ice crackling in his jacket. He felt dizzy and nauseous—five thousand meters was about the highest you'd want to go without oxygen on Middle America. He *thought* he could stop the rise; if not, they were headed for space, along with the rest of the agravs.

But he had to do more than slow the rise, or descend. He looked up at the Lothlrimarre's barge. It was much nearer—and two hundred meters to the east. If he couldn't move this thing sideways, he'd need the slug's active cooperation.

It was something he had thought about—for maybe all of five seconds—back in the warehouse. If the agrav had been an ordinary lighter-than-air craft, there'd be no hope. Without props or jets, a balloon goes where the wind says; the only control comes from finding the *altitude* where the wind and you want the same thing. But when he grabbed that first carpet, it really had slid horizontally toward the side he was holding. . . .

He crept toward the edge. The agrav yielded beneath his knees, but didn't tilt more than a small boat would. Next to him, the Blab looked over the edge, straight down. Her head jerked this way and that as she scanned the landscape. "Wow," she kept saying. Could she really understand what she was seeing?

The wind shifted a little. It came a bit from the side now, not straight from above. He really did have control! Hamid smiled around chattering teeth.

The carpet rose faster and faster. The downward wind was an arctic blast. They must be going up at fifteen or twenty klicks per hour. The Lothlrimarre barge loomed huge above them . . . now almost beside them.

God, they were *above* it now! Hamid pulled out his knife, picked desperately at the blade opener with numbed fingers. It came open abruptly—and almost popped out of his shaking hand. He trimmed small pieces from the edge of the carpet. The wind from heaven stayed just as strong. Bigger pieces! He tore wildly at the cloth. One large strip, two. And the wind eased . . . stopped. Hamid bent over the edge of the carpet, and stuffed his vertigo back down his throat. *Perfect*. They were directly over the barge, and closing.

The nearest of the four pressure spheres was so close it blocked his view of the others. Hamid could see the human habitat, the conference area. They would touch down on a broad flat area next to the sphere. The aiming couldn't have been better. Hamid guessed the slug must be maneuvering too, moving the barge precisely under his visitor.

There was a flash of heat, and an invisible fist slammed into the carpet. Hamid and the Blab tumbled—now beneath the agrav, now above. He had a glimpse of the barge. A jet of yellow-white spewed from the sphere, ammonia and hydrogen at one thousand atmospheres. The top pressure sphere had been breached. The spear of superpressured gas was surrounded by pale flame where the hydrogen and atmospheric oxygen burned.

The barge fell out of view, leaving thunder and burning mists. Hamid held onto the Blab and as much of the carpet as he could wrap around them. The tumbling stopped; they were upside down in the heavy swaddling. Hamid looked out:

"Overhead" was the brown and gray of farmland in late autumn. Marquette was to his left. He bent around, peeked into the sky. There! The barge was several klicks away. The top pressure vessel was spreading fire and mist, but the lower ones looked okay. Pale violet flickered from between the spheres. Moments later, thunder echoed across the sky. The slug was fighting back!

He twisted in the jumble of cloth, trying to see the high sky. To the north . . . a single blue-glowing trail lanced southwards . . . split into five separate, jigging paths that cooled through orange to red. It was beautiful . . . but somehow like a jagged claw sketched against the sky. The claw tips dimmed to nothing, but whatever caused them still raced forward. The attackers' answering fire slagged the north-facing detail of the barge. It crumpled like trash plastic in a fire. The bottom pressure vessels still looked okay, but if the visitors' deck got zapped like that, Larry would be a dead man.

Multiple sonic booms rocked the carpet. Things swept past, too small and fast to clearly see. The barge's guns still flickered violet, but the craft was rising now—faster than he had ever seen it move.

After a moment, the carpet drifted through one more tumble, and they sat heads up. The morning had been transformed. Strange clouds were banked around and above him, some burning, some glowing, all netted with the brownish-reds of nitrogen oxides. The stench of ammonia burned his eyes and mouth. The Blab was making noises through her mouth, true coughing and choking sounds.

The Tourists were long gone. The Lothlrimarre was a dot at the top of the sky. All the other agravs had passed by. He and the Blab were alone in the burning clouds. *Probably not for long*. Hamid began sawing at the agrav fabric—tearing off a slice, testing for an upwelling breeze, then tearing off another. They drifted through the cloud deck into a light drizzle, a strange rain that burned the skin as it wet them. He slid the carpet sideways into the sunlight, and they could breathe again. Things looked almost normal, except where the clouds cast a great bloody shadow across the farmland.

Where best to land? Hamid looked over the edge of the carpet . . . and saw the enemy waiting. It was a cylinder, tapered, with a pair of small fins at one end. It drifted through the carpet's shadow, and he realized the enemy craft was *close*. It couldn't be more than ten meters long, less than two meters across at the widest. It hung silent, pacing the carpet's slow descent. Hamid looked up, and saw the others—four more dark shapes. They circled in, like killer fish nosing at a possible lunch. One slid right over them, so slow and near he could have run his palm down its length. There were no ports, no breaks in the dull finish. But the fins—red glowed dim from within them, and Hamid felt a wave of heat as they passed.

The silent parade went on for a minute, each killer getting its look. The Blab's head followed the craft around and around. Her eyes were wide, and she was making the terrified whistling noises of the night before. The air was still, but for the faint updraft of the carpet's descent. Or was it? . . . The sound grew, a hissing sound like Tines had made during his phone call. Only now it came from all the killers, and there were overtones lurking at the edge of sensibility, tones that never could have come from an ordinary telephone.

"Blab." He reached to stroke her neck. She slashed at his hand, her needle-teeth slicing deep. Hamid gasped in pain, and rolled back from her. The Blab's pelt was puffed out as far as he had ever seen it. She looked twice normal size, a very large carnivore with death glittering in her eyes. Her long neck snapped this way and that, trying to track all the killers at once. Fore and rear talons dragged long rips through the carpet. She climbed onto the thickest folds of the carpet, and *shrieked* at the killers . . . and collapsed.

For a moment, Hamid couldn't move. His hand, the scream: razors across his hand, icepicks jammed in his ears. He struggled to his knees and crawled to the Blabber. "Blab?" No answer, no motion. He touched her flank: limp as something fresh dead.

In twenty years, Hamid Thompson had never had close friends, but he had never been alone, either. Until now. He looked up from the Blabber's body, at the circling shapes.

Alone at four thousand meters. He didn't have much choice when one of the killer fish came directly at him, when something wide and dark opened from its belly. The darkness swept around them, swallowing all.

Hamid had never been in space before. Under other circumstances, he would have reveled in the experience. The glimpse he'd had of Middle America from low orbit was like a beautiful dream. But now, all he could see through the floor of his cage was a bluish dot, nearly lost in the sun's glare. He pushed hard against the clear softness, and rolled onto his back. It was harder than a one-handed pushup to do that. He guessed the mothership was doing four or five gees . . . and had been for hours.

When they had pulled him off the attack craft, Hamid had been semiconscious. He had no idea what acceleration that shark boat reached, but it was more than he could take. He remembered that glimpse of Middle America, blue and serene. Then . . . they'd taken the Blab—or her body—away. *Who?* There had been a human, the Ravna woman. She had done something to his hand; it wasn't bleeding anymore. And . . . and there had been the Blabber, up and walking around. No, the pelt pattern had been all wrong. *That must have been Tines*. There had been the hissing voice, and some kind of argument with Ravna.

Hamid stared up at the sunlight on the ceiling and walls. His own shadow lay spread-eagled on the ceiling. In the first hazy hours, he had thought it was another prisoner. The walls were gray, seamless, but with scrape marks and stains, as though heavy equipment was used here. He thought there was a door in the ceiling, but he couldn't remember for sure. There was no sign of one now. The room was an empty cubical, featureless, its floor showing clear to the stars: surely not an ordinary brig. There were no toilet facilities—and at five gees they wouldn't have helped. The air was thick with the stench of himself. . . . Hamid guessed the room was an airlock. The transparent floor might be nothing more than a figment of some field generator's imagination. A flick of a switch and Hamid would be swept away forever.

The Blabber gone, Pop gone, maybe Larry and the slug gone. . . . Hamid raised his good hand a few centimeters and clenched his fist. Lying here was the first time he'd ever thought about killing anyone. He thought about it a lot now. . . . It kept the fear tied down.

"Mr. Thompson." Ravna's voice. Hamid suppressed a twitch of surprise: after hours of rage, to hear the enemy. "Mr. Thompson, we are going to free fall in fifteen seconds. Do not be alarmed."

So, airline courtesy of a sudden.

The force that had squished him flat these hours, that had made it an exercise even to breathe, slowly lessened. From beyond the walls and ceiling he heard small popping noises. For a panicky instant, it seemed as though the floor had disappeared and he was falling through. He twisted. His hand hit the barrier . . . and he floated slowly across the room, toward the wall that had been the ceiling. A door had opened. He drifted through, into a hall that would have looked normal except for the intricate pattern of grooves and ledges that covered the walls.

"Thirty meters down the hall is a latrine," came Ravna's voice. "There are clean clothes that should fit you. When you are done . . . when you are done, we will talk."

Damn right. Hamid squared his shoulders and pulled himself down the hall.

She didn't look like a killer. There was anger—tension?—on her face, the face of someone who has been awake a long time and has fought hard—and doesn't expect to win.

Hamid drifted slowly into the—conference room? bridge?—trying to size everything up at once. It was a large room, with a low ceiling. Moving across it was easy in zero gee, slow bounces from floor to ceiling and back. The wall curved around, transparent along most of its circumference. There were stars and night dark beyond.

Ravna had been standing in a splash of light. Now she moved back a meter, into the general dimness. Somehow she slipped her foot into the floor, anchoring herself. She waved him to the other side of a table. They stood in the half crouch of zero gee, less than two meters apart. Even so, she looked taller than he had guessed from the phone call. Her mass might be close to his. The rest of her was as he remembered, though she looked very tired. Her gaze flickered across him, and away. "Hello, Mr. Thompson. The floor will hold your foot, if you tap it gently."

Hamid didn't take the advice; he held onto the table edge and jammed his feet against the floor. He would have something to brace against if the time came to move quickly. "Where is my Blabber?" His voice came out hoarse, more desperate than demanding.

"Your pet is dead."

There was a tiny hesitation before the last word. She was as bad a liar as ever. Hamid pushed back the rage: if the Blab was alive, there was something still possible beyond revenge. "Oh." He kept his face blank.

"However, we intend to return you safely to home." She gestured at the star fields around them. "The six gee boost was to avoid unnecessary fighting with the Lothlrimarre being. We will coast outwards some further, perhaps even go into ram drive. But Mr. Tines will take you back to Middle America in one of our attack boats. There will be no problem to land you without attracting notice . . . perhaps on the western continent, somewhere out of the way." Her tone was distant. He noticed that she never looked directly at him for more than an instant. Now she was staring just to one side of his face. He remembered the phone call, how she seemed to ignore his video. Up close, she was just as attractive as before—more. Just once he would like to see her smile. *And somewhere there was unease that he could be so attracted by a murderous stranger.*

If only, "If only I could understand *why*. Why did you kill the Blab? Why did you kill my father?"

Ravna's eyes narrowed. "That cheating piece of filth? He is too tricky to kill. He was gone when we visited his farm. I'm not sure I have killed anyone on this operation. The Lothlrimarre is still functioning, I know that." She sighed. "We were all very lucky. You have no idea what Tines has been like these last days. . . . He called you last night."

Hamid nodded numbly.

"Well, he was mellow then. He tried to kill me when

I took over the ship. Another day like this and he would have been dead—and most likely your planet would have been so too."

Hamid remembered the Lothlrimarre's theory about the tines's need. And now that the creature had the Blab. . . . "So now Tines is satisfied?"

Ravna nodded vaguely, missing the quaver in his voice. "He's harmless now and very confused, poor guy. Assimilation is hard. It will be a few weeks . . . but he'll stabilize, probably turn out better than he ever was."

Whatever that means.

She pushed back from the table, stopped herself with a hand on the low ceiling. Apparently their meeting was over. "Don't worry. He should be well enough to take you home quite soon. Now I will show you your—"

"Don't rush him, Rav. Why should he want to go back to Middle America?" The voice was a pleasant tenor, human sounding but a little slurred.

Ravna bounced off the ceiling. "I thought you were going to stay out of this! Of course the boy is going back to Middle America. That's his home; that's where he fits."

"I wonder." The unseen speaker laughed. He sounded cheerfully—*joyfully*—drunk. "Your name is shit down there, Hamid, did you know that?"

"Huh?"

"Yup. You slagged the Caravan's entire shipment of fusion electrics. 'Course you had a little help from the Federal Police, but that fact is being ignored. Much worse, you destroyed most of the agrav units. *Whee.* Up, up and away. And there's no way those can be replaced short of a trip back to the Outsi—"

"Shut up!" Ravna's anger rode over the good cheer. "The agrav units were a cheap trick. Nothing that subtle can work in the Zone for long. Five years from now they would all have faded."

"Sure, sure. I know that, and you know that. But both Middle America and the Tourists figure you've trashed this Caravan, Hamid. You'd be a fool to go back."

Ravna shouted something in a language Hamid had never heard.

"English, Rav, English. I want him to understand what is happening."

"*He is going back!*" Ravna's voice was furious, almost desperate. "We *agreed!*"

"I know, Rav." A little of the rampant joy left the voice. It sounded truly sympathetic. "And I'm sorry. But I was different then, and I understand things better now. . . . Hey, I'll be down in a minute, okay?"

She closed her eyes. It's hard to slump in free fall, but Ravna came close, her shoulders and arms relaxing, her body drifting slowly up from the floor. "Oh, Lord," she said softly.

Out in the hall, someone was whistling a tune that had been popular in Marquette six months ago. A shadow floated down the walls, followed by . . . *the Blab?* Hamid lurched off the table, flailed wildly for a handhold. He steadied himself, got a closer look.

No. Not the Blab. It was of the same race certainly, but this one had an entirely different pattern of black and white. The great patch of black around one eye and white around the other would have been laughable . . . if you didn't know what you were looking at: at last to see Mr. Tines.

Man and alien regarded each other for a long moment. It was a little smaller than the Blab. It wore a checkered orange scarf about its neck. Its paws looked no more flexible than his Blab's . . . but he didn't doubt the intelligence that looked back from its eyes. The tines drifted to the ceiling, and anchored itself with a deft swipe of paw and talons. There were faint sounds in the air now, squeaks and twitters almost beyond hearing. If he listened close enough, Hamid guessed he would hear the hissing, too.

The tines looked at him, and laughed pleasantly—the tenor voice of a minute before. "Don't rush me! I'm not all here yet."

Hamid looked at the doorway. There were two more there, one with a jeweled collar—the leader? They glided through the air and tied down next to the first. Hamid saw more shadows floating down the hall.

"How many?" he asked.

"I'm six now." He thought it was a different tines that answered, but the voice was the same.

The last three floated in the doorway. One wore no scarf or jewelry . . . and looked very familiar.

"Blab!" Hamid pushed off the table. He went into a spin that missed the door by several meters. The Blabber—it must be her—twisted skillfully around and fled the room.

"Stay away!" For an instant the tines's voice changed, held the same edge as the night before. Hamid stood on the wall next to the doorway and looked down the hall. The Blab was there, sitting on the closed door at the far end. Hamid's orientation flipped . . . the hall could just as well be a deep, bright-lit well, with the Blab trapped at the bottom of it.

"Blab?" He said softly, aware of the tines behind him.

She looked up at him. "I can't play the old games anymore, Hamid," she said in her softest femvoice. He stared for a moment, uncomprehending. Over the years, the Blab said plenty of things that—by accident or in the listeners' imagination—might seem humanly intelligent. Here, for the first time, he knew that he was hearing sense. . . . And he guessed what Ravna meant when she said the Blab was dead.

Hamid backed away from the edge of the pit. He looked at the other tines, remembered that their speech came as easily from one as the other. "You're like a hive of roaches, aren't you?"

"A little," the tenor voice came from somewhere among them.

"But telepathic," Hamid said.

The one who had been his friend answered, but in the tenor voice: "Yes, between myselves. But it's no sixth sense. You've known about it all your life. I like to talk a lot. Blabber." The squeaking and the hissing: just the edge of all they were saying to each other across their two hundred kiloherz bandwidth. "I'm sorry I flinched. Myselves are still confused. I don't know quite who I am."

The Blab pushed off and drifted back into the bridge. She grabbed a piece of ceiling as she came even with Hamid. She extended her head toward him, tentatively, as though he were a stranger. *I feel the same way about you*, thought Hamid. But he reached out to brush her neck with his fingers. She twitched back, glided across the room to nestle among the other tines.

Hamid stared at them staring back. He had a sudden image: a pack of long necked rats beadily analyzing their prey. "So. Who is the real Mr. Tines? The monster who'd smash a world, or the nice guy I'm hearing now?"

Ravna answered, her voice tired, distant. "The monster tines is gone . . . or going. Don't you see? The pack was unbalanced. It was dying."

"There were five in my pack, Hamid. Not a bad number: some of the brightest packs are that small. But I was down from seven—two of myselves had been killed. The ones remaining were mismatched, and only one of them was female." Tines paused. "I know humans can go for years without contact with the opposite sex, and suffer only mild discomfort—"

Tell me about it.

"—but tines are very different. If a pack's sex ratio gets too lopsided, especially if there is a mismatch of skills, then the mind disintegrates. . . . Things can get very nasty in the process." Hamid noticed that all the time it talked, the two tines next to the one with the orange scarf had been nibbling at the scarf's knots. They moved quickly, perfectly coordinated, untying and retying the knots. *Tines doesn't need hands*. Or put another way, he already had six. Hamid was seeing the equivalent of a human playing nervously with his tie.

"Ravna lied when she said the Blab is dead. I forgive her: she wants you off our ship, with no more questions, no more hassle. But the Blabber isn't dead. She was *rescued* . . . from being an animal the rest of her life. And her rescue saved the pack. I feel so . . .

happy. Better even than when I was seven. I can understand things that have been puzzles for years. Your Blab is far more language oriented than any of my other selves. I could never talk like this without her."

Ravna had drifted toward the pack. Now she had her feet planted on the floor beneath them. Her head brushed the shoulder of one, was even with the eyes of another. "Imagine the Blabber as the verbal hemisphere of a human brain," she said to Hamid.

"Not quite," Tines said. "A human hemisphere can almost carry on by itself. The Blab by itself could never be a person."

Hamid remembered how the Blab's greatest desire had often seemed just to *be* a real person. And listening to this creature, he heard echoes of the Blab. It would be easy to accept what they were saying. . . . Yet if you turned the words just a little, you had enslavement and rape—the slug's theory with frosting.

Hamid turned away from all the eyes and looked across the star clouds. *How much should I believe? How much should I seem to believe?* "One of the Tourists wanted to sell us a gadget, an 'ftl radio.' Did you know that we used it to ask about the tines? Do you know what we found?" He told them about the horrors Larry had found around the galactic rim.

Ravna exchanged a glance with the tines by her head. For a moment the only sound was the twittering and hissing. Then Tines spoke. "Imagine the most ghastly villains of Earth's history. Whatever they are, whatever holocausts they set, I assure you much worse has happened elsewhere. . . . Now imagine that this regime was so vast, so effectively *evil* that no honest historians survived. What stories do you suppose would be spread about the races they exterminated?"

"Okay. So—"

"Tines are not monsters. On average, we are no more bloodthirsty than you humans. But we are descended from packs of wolf-like creatures. We are deadly warriors. Given reasonable equipment and numbers, we can outfight most anything in the Slow Zone." Hamid remembered the shark pack of attack boats. With one animal in each, and radio communication . . . no team of human pilots could match their coordination. "We were once a great power in our part of the Slow Zone. We had enemies, even when there was no war. Would you trust creatures who live indefinitely, but whose personalities may drift from friendly to indifferent—even to inimical—as their components die and are replaced?"

"And you're such a peach of a guy because you've got the Blab?"

"*Yes!* Though you liked . . . I know you would have liked me when I was seven. But the Blab has a lovely outlook; she makes it fun to be alive."

Hamid looked at Ravna and the pack who surrounded her. So the tines had been great fighters. That he believed. So they were now virtually extinct, having run into something even deadlier. That he could believe, too. Beyond that . . . he'd be a fool to believe anything. He could imagine Tines as a friend, he wanted Ravna as one. But all the talk, all the seeming argument—it could just as well be manipulation. One thing was sure: if he returned to Middle America, he would never know the truth. He might live the rest of his life safe and cozy, but he wouldn't have the Blab, and he would never know what had really happened to her.

He gave Ravna a lopsided smile. "Back to square one then. I want passage to the Beyond with you."

"Out of the question. I-I made that clear from the beginning."

Hamid pushed nearer, stopped a meter in front of her. "Why won't you look at me?" he said softly. "Why do you hate me so much?"

For a full second, her eyes looked straight into his. "I *don't* hate you!" Her face clouded, as if she were about to weep. "It's just that you're such a God *damned* disappointment!" She pushed back abruptly, knocking the tines out of her way.

He followed her slowly back to the conference table.

She "stood" there, talking to herself in some unknown language. "She's swearing to her ancestors," murmurred a tines that drifted close by Hamid's head. "Her kind is big on that sort of thing."

Hamid anchored himself across from her. He looked at her face. Young, no older than twenty it looked. But Outsiders had some control over aging. Besides, Ravna had spent at least the last ten years in relativistic flight. "You hired my—you hired Hussein Thompson to adopt me, didn't you?"

She nodded.

"Why?"

She looked back at him for a moment, this time not flinching away. Finally she sighed. "Okay, I will try but . . . there are many things you from the Slow Zone do not understand. Middle America is close to the Beyond, but you see out through a tiny hole. You can have even less concept of what lies beyond the Beyond, in the Transhuman reaches." She was beginning to sound like Lazy Larry.

"I'm willing to start with the version for five-year-olds."

"Okay." The faintest of smiles crossed her face. It was everything he'd guessed it would be. He wondered how he could make her do it again. " 'Once upon a time,' "—the smile again, a little wider!—"there was a very wise and good man, as wise and good as any mere human or human equivalent can ever be: a mathematical genius, a great general, an even greater peacemaker. He lived five hundred years subjective, and half that time he was fighting a very great evil."

The Tines put in, "Just a part of that evil chewed up my race for breakfast."

Ravna nodded. "Eventually it chewed our hero, too. He's been dead almost a century objective. The enemy has been very alert to keep him dead. Tines and I may be the last people trying to bring him back. . . . How much do you know about cloning, Mr. Thompson?"

Hamid couldn't answer for a moment; it was too clear where all this was going. "The Tourists claim they can build a viable zygote from almost any body cell. They say it's easy, but that what you get is no more than an identical twin of the original."

"That is about right. In fact, the clone is often *much* less than an identical twin. The uterine environment determines much of an individual's adult characteristics. Consider mathematical ability. There is a genetic component—but part of mathematical genius comes from the fetus getting just the right testosterone overdose. A little too much and you have a *dummy*.

"Tines and I have been running for a long time. Fifty years ago we reached Lothlrimarre—the back end of nowhere if there ever was one. We had a clonable cell from the great man. We did our best with the humaniform medical equipment that was available. The newborn *looked* healthy enough. . . ."

Rustle, hiss.

"But why not just raise the—child—yourself?" Hamid said. "Why hire someone to take him into the Slow Zone?"

Ravna bit her lip and looked away. It was Tines who replied: "Two reasons. The enemy wants you permanently dead. Raising you in the Slow Zone was the best way to keep you out of sight. The other reason is more subtle. We don't have records of your original memories; we can't make a perfect copy. But if we could give you an upbringing that mimicked the original's . . . then we'd have someone with the same outlook."

"Like having the original back, with a bad case of amnesia."

Tines chuckled. "Right. And things went very well at first. It was great good luck to run into Hussein Thompson at Lothlrimarre. He seemed a bright fellow, willing to work for his money. He brought the newborn in suspended animation back to Middle America, and married a woman equally bright, to be your mother.

"We had everything figured, the original's background imitated better than we had ever hoped. I even gave up one of my selves, a newborn, to be with you."

"I guess I know most of the rest," said Hamid. "Everything went fine for the first eight years," the happy years of a loving family, "till it became clear that I wasn't a math genius. Then your hired hand didn't know what to do, and your plan fell apart."

"It didn't have to!" Ravna slapped the table. The motion pulled her body up, almost free of the foot anchors. "The math ability was a big part, but there was still a chance—if Thompson hadn't welshed on us." She glared at Hamid, and then at the pack. "The original's parents died when he was ten years old. Hussein and his woman were supposed to disappear when the clone was ten, in a faked air crash. *That was the agreement!* Instead—" she swallowed. "We talked to him. He wouldn't meet in person. He was full of excuses, the clever bastard. 'I didn't see what good it would do to hurt the boy any more,' he said. 'He's no superman, just a good kid. I wanted him to be happy!' " She choked on her own indignation. "*Happy!* If he knew what we have been through, what the stakes are—"

Hamid's face felt numb, frozen. He wondered what it would be like to throw up in zero gee. "What—what about my mother?" he said in a very small voice.

Ravna gave her head a quick shake. "She tried to persuade Thompson. When that didn't work, she left you. By then it was too late; besides, that sort of abandonment is not the trauma the original experienced. But she did her part of the bargain; we paid her most of what we promised. . . . We came to Middle America expecting to find someone very wonderful, living again. Instead, we found—"

"—a piece of trash?" He couldn't get any anger into the question.

She gave a shaky sigh. ". . . no, I don't really think that. Hussein Thompson probably did raise a good person, and that's more than most can claim. But if you were the one we had hoped, you would be known all over Middle America by now, the greatest inventor, the greatest mover since the colony began. And that would be just the beginning." She seemed to be looking through him . . . remembering?

Tines made a diffident throat-clearing sound. "Not a

piece of trash at all. And not just a 'good kid', either. A part of me lived with Hamid for twenty years; the Blabber's memories are about as clear as a tines fragment's can be. Hamid is not just a failed dream to me, Rav. He's different, but I like to be around him almost as much as with . . . the other one. And when the crunch came—well, I saw him fight back. Given his background, even the original couldn't have done better. Hitching a ride on a raw agrav was the sort of daring that—"

"Okay, Tiny, the boy is daring and quick. But there's a difference between suicidal foolishness and calculated risk-taking. This late in life, there's no way he'll become more than a 'good man.' " Sarcasm lilted in the words.

"We could do worse, Rav."

"We *must* do far better, and you know it! See here. It's two years subjective to get out of the Zone, and our suspension gear is failed. I will *not* accept seeing his face every day for two years. He goes back to Middle America." She kicked off, drifted toward the tines that hung over Hamid.

"I think not," said Tines. "If he doesn't want to go, I won't fly him back."

Anger and—strangely—panic played on Ravna's face. "This isn't how you were talking last week."

"Heh heh heh." Lazy Larry's cackle. "I've changed. Haven't you noticed?"

She grabbed a piece of ceiling and looked down at Hamid, calculating. "Boy. I don't think you understand. We're in a hurry; we won't be stopping any place like Lothlrimarre. There is one last way we might bring the original back to life—perhaps even with his own memories. You'll end up in Transhuman space if you come with us. The chances are that none of us will surv—" She stopped, and a slow smile spread across her face. Not a friendly smile. "Have you not thought what use your body might still be to us? You know nothing of what we plan. We may find ways of using you like a—like a blank data cartridge."

Hamid looked back at her, hoping no doubts showed

on his face. "Maybe. But I'll have two years to prepare, won't I?"

They glared at each other for a long moment, the greatest eye contact yet. "So be it," she said at last. She drifted a little closer. "Some advice. We'll be two years cooped up here. It's a big ship. Stay out of my way." She drew back and pulled herself across the ceiling, faster and faster. She arrowed into the hallway beyond, and out of sight.

Hamid Thompson had his ticket to the Outside. Some tickets cost more than others. What much would he pay for his?

Eight hours later, the ship was under ram drive, outward bound. Hamid sat in the bridge, alone. The "windows" on one side of the room showed the view aft. Middle America's sun cast daylight across the room.

Invisible ahead of them, the interplanetary medium was being scooped in, fuel for the ram. The acceleration was barely perceptible, perhaps a fiftieth of a gee. The ram drive was for the long haul. That acceleration would continue indefinitely, eventually rising to almost half a gravity—and bringing them near light speed.

Middle America was a fleck of blue, trailing a white dot and a yellow one. It would be many hours before his world and its moons were lost from sight—and many days before they were lost to telescopic view.

Hamid had been here an hour—two?—since shortly after Tines showed him his quarters.

The inside of his head felt like an abandoned battlefield. A monster had become his good buddy. The man he hated turned out to be the father he had wanted . . . and his mother now seemed an uncaring manipulator. *And now I can never go back and ask you truly what you were, truly if you loved me.*

He felt something wet on his face. One good thing about gravity, even a fiftieth of a gee: it cleared the tears from your eyes.

He must be very careful these next two years. There was much to learn, and even more to guess at. What was lie and what was truth? There were things about the story that . . . how could one human being be as important as Ravna and Tines claimed? Next to the Transhumans, nó human equivalent could count for much.

It might well be that these two believed the story they told him—*and that could be the most frightening possibility of all*. They talked about the Great Man as though he were some sort of messiah. Hamid had read of similar things in Earth history: twentieth century Nazis longing for Hitler, the fanatics of the Afghan Jihad scheming to bring back their Imam. The story Larry got from the ansible could be true, and the Great Man might have been accomplice to the murder of a thousand worlds.

Hamid found himself laughing. *Where does that put me?* Could the clone of a monster rise above the original?

"What's funny, Hamid?" Tines had entered the bridge quietly. Now he settled himself on the table and posts around Hamid. The one that had been the Blab sat just a meter away.

"Nothing. Just thinking."

They sat for several minutes in silence, watching the sky. There was a wavering there—like hot air over a stove—the tiniest evidence of the fields that formed the ram around them. He glanced at the tines. Four of them were looking out the windows. The other two looked back at him, their eyes as dark and soft as the Blab's had ever been.

"Please don't think badly of Ravna," Tines said. "She had a real thing going with the almost-you of before. . . . They loved each other very much."

"I guessed."

The two heads turned back to the sky. These next two years he must watch this creature, try to decide. . . . But suspicions aside, the more he saw of Tines, the more he liked him. Hamid could almost imagine that he had not lost the Blab, but gained five of her siblings. And the bigmouth had finally become a real person.

The companionable silence stretched on. After a moment, the one that had been the Blab edged across the table and bumped her head against his shoulder. Hamid hesitated, then stroked her neck. They watched the sun and the fleck of blue a moment more. "You know," said Tines, but in the femvoice that was the Blab's favorite, "I will miss that place. And most of all . . . I will miss the cats and the dogs."

Introduction

"Anyone who cannot cope with mathematics is not fully human. At best he is a tolerable subhuman who has learned to wear shoes, bathe, and not make messes in the house."

—Lazarus Long,
from his notebooks

If you, like me, never got much further than quadratic equations, this particular note has probably left you a tad uncomfortable. I hereby take it upon myself to say that this was Lazarus talking, and not Robert. If the phrase were changed from "cannot cope with mathematics" to "unwilling to attempt quantitative analysis" I would not be so certain.

The reason I can be so certain on this matter is that once, years ago, Robert happened to call while I was running a high fever. In my weakness I confessed my deficiency in the arts mathematical and he assured me categorically that it was "all right."

Counting Up

Charles Sheffield

1. THE THINGS THAT COUNT

The ancient Greeks gave a good deal of thought to the definition of Man (Woman, back in the fourth century B.C., was not considered a suitable subject for philosophy). The Greeks wanted to know what it is that makes humans different from all the animals. Early attempted definitions, e.g. the Platonist one: "Man is a featherless animal with two feet," were not well received. Kangaroos were unknown in ancient Greece, but Diogenes offered a plucked chicken and asked if it were human (he was not serious, and this must be the original chicken joke). Even when amended to "a featherless animal with two feet without claws," the Platonist definition did not exactly sparkle. The Greeks never did come up with a good answer.

By the nineteenth century, definitions were more oriented to function than to appearance. "Man is a tool-using animal," declared Thomas Carlyle, in *Sartor Resartus*, following an idea of Ben Franklin, but neither man knew, as we know now, that some chimpanzees make tools out of sticks and rocks.

"Mankind is the only animal with language," say the linguists, but not as loudly as they once did. The extent to which Washoe, the famous chimpanzee with a symbol vocabulary of 180 words, and her primate friends are capable of working with a real language remains a matter of hot debate; and the complex sounds produced by the humpback whale may not be messages at all; but in any case, the claim to uniqueness by humans is in question.

—*"Man is the only animal that laughs."*

—*"Man is the only animal that cries."*

—*"Man is the only animal that blushes—or needs to."*

—*"Man is a thinking reed."*

—*"Man is Nature's sole mistake."*

All interesting, and all suspect, especially as more and more of the things that we once thought uniquely human, including murder and rape, are found to be shared with our animal relatives.

"Man is the fire-using animal" still sounds good, but my own favorite definition is this one: "Mankind is a counting animal." If I substitute "entity" for "animal" in this sentence it becomes far less persuasive, since if computers do one thing well, they count—but only with human direction. Also, certain birds are supposed to be able to count the eggs in their nests, or at least to know when one is missing. However, it is certainly true that we know of no animal able to count to more than ten. Humans can, or at least, most humans can. (It was George Gamow, in his delightful book, *One Two Three . . . Infinity*, who told the story of two Hungarian aristocrats who challenged each other to think of the bigger number. "Well," said one of them, "you name your number first."

"Three," said the second one, after a little hard thought.

"Right," said the other. "You win.")

Humans are "the things that count." Counting is something most of us learn early and learn well, to the point where there is something unnatural about the sequence 1, 2, 3, 5, 6, 7 . . . Counting is the subject of this article, but we will be concerned ultimately with counting as it applies to physics and the natural sciences, rather than to the role of counting and numbers in mathematics. I hope to start with things familiar to everyone, and end with novelties.

2. NUMBERS

The most familiar numbers are the integers, the whole numbers that we use whenever we start counting, 1, 2, 3. They are basic to everything else, to the point where the nineteenth-century German mathematician Leopold Kronecker proclaimed: "God made the integers; all the rest is the work of man." Personally, I think Kronecker had it backwards. Humans were quite capable of creating the integers, from the need to enumerate everything from cabbages to kings. It is the other sorts of number, the ones we need to describe lengths and times and weights, that may need divine intervention to explain them. We will get to them in a moment.

First, let us ask an odd question. Can we define the biggest number that we normally need for counting? The conventional answer is, no, there is no such biggest number. We start counting at 1, but we never reach a "last number." No matter how far we go, there will always be a number bigger than the one we have just reached. However, there is another way to look at this, because when we get numbers larger than about a hundred, we don't think of them as made up of a whole lot of ones. We think of them in groups. A thousand is ten hundreds, a hundred is ten tens. We need that structure, to allow us to work with anything more than we can count conveniently on our fingers and toes.

The largest number of objects that I ever have to deal with in my everyday life, where I am not able to group them into subsets in a useful way, are the bits of a jigsaw puzzle. Even here, with a 1000-piece puzzle, I try to impose some sort of system that will help me to put the pieces into their structured form of the actual picture. I pick out all the edge pieces and do those first, and I organize pieces according to their colors. And even with this help, I take many hours to assemble a hard puzzle of more than 500 pieces. Given a puzzle of ten thousand pieces, I'm not sure I'd ever put it together; and yet ten thousand is not a particularly big number. We work with much larger ones all the time, merely by organizing them into sets of smaller ones. Ten thousand dollars is not a massive stack of singles, it's a hundred one-hundred dollar bills.

The same principle works when we have to deal with something that's too small to be handled conveniently by straight counting. For example, the heights of people, or the size of a room, are not usually an exact number of feet or meters. So we say that a foot is a group of smaller objects, inches; and if we have to, we say that each inch is also a group of still smaller objects, tenths of inches. Since we can define as many levels of subgroups as we like, we can describe anyone's height, or the size of any room, as closely as we like, just by counting.

The Greeks had reached this conclusion by about five hundred B.C. They believed that they had a system that would allow them to define any given number. It was a horrible intellectual shock for them to discover that there were certain numbers that cannot be described in this way. The result seemed to fly in the face of common sense—to be irrational. And the name "irrational numbers" is used to this day, to describe numbers that can't be written exactly as whole numbers, and subsets of whole numbers. Numbers that *can* be so written are called rational numbers.

The original example of an irrational number, discovered to be so by Pythagoras, is the square root of two. It's easy to write this number approximately, as something a little bigger than 1.4 and less than 1.5. We can even specify very easily a value that is as good as we are ever likely to need for practical calculation, 1.41421 35623 7309. In terms of our whole numbers and subsets of whole numbers, this is just 1, plus 4 one-tenths, plus

1 one-hundredth, plus 4 one-thousandths, and so on. (I should add that the Greeks themselves did not have a decimal notation. That came much later, introduced in Europe in 1586, and useful as it is, it is not popular with everyone. Jerome K. Jerome wrote of visiting the city of Bruges, where he "had the pleasure of throwing a stone at the statue of Simon Stevin, the man who invented decimals.")

The problem comes when we ask when the sequence of numbers occurring in the square root of 2, namely, 1 + 4/10 + 1/100 + 4/1000 + 2/10000 . . . , stops.

It doesn't. The first thought might be that this is a problem created because we are using the decimal system. After all, ⅓ is described very nicely by dividing a unit into threes, but when we write it as a decimal, 0.3333 . . . it goes on forever.

The Greeks were able to show that this was not the cause of the problem, using a very simple and elegant proof, as follows:

Suppose that the square root of 2 can be written as a fraction in the form p/q, where p and q are whole numbers with no common divisors, i.e. there are no whole numbers other than 1 that divide both p and q. For example, 1.414 would be written as 1,414/1000 = 707/500.

Then $(p/q)^2 = 2$, so $p^2 = 2q^2$.

Now if p is an odd number, then so is p^2. But p^2 is even, so p must be even, and can be written as 2r, where r is also a whole number. Then since $4r^2 = (2r)^2 = 2q^2$, we must have $2r^2 = q^2$, and so q must be even. But before we began, we agreed that p and q would have no common divisors, and now we have decided they are both divisible by two. Thus our assumption that the square root of 2 can be written as a ratio of whole numbers must be wrong.

(This is such an easy proof that the reader may feel anyone could find it, and that mathematics must therefore be simple stuff. If so, here's another problem to try your teeth on. It can also be proved by very simple arguments:

Let m and n be whole numbers with n having no divisors other than 1. Then when m^n is divided by n, it will leave the same remainder as when m itself is divided by n. For example, if m is 15 and n is 7, then 15^7 = 170,859,375. Divide by 7, and we get the remainder 1—the same remainder as when we divide 15 by 7.

If you can prove this, without assistance or looking up the proof in a book on number theory, I would like to hear from you.)

The implications of the fact that not all numbers can be written as fractions were disturbing to the Greeks, and they ought to be equally disturbing to us. I mentioned Kronecker's idea of divine influence in connection with the whole numbers, but many people struggling over the years with irrational numbers would give credit for them to the devil.

Let's look at one of the other peculiar facts about irrationals. If we imagine a long ruler, marked off in inches, then in any inch there will be an infinite number of points that can be marked on the ruler as rational numbers, of the form p/q; but we have found that not all points within the inch can be marked that way. There are points corresponding to irrational numbers, sandwiched in among the rationals. Thus, if you want to label *all* the points on the line, you must include the irrational numbers. Worse than that, and most surprising, it can be shown that there are *many more* irrational numbers than there are rational ones. The rational numbers, in mathematical terminology, constitute a set of measure zero on the line—which means they account for zero percent of the line's length. Almost every number is irrational.

3. INFINITY

That last paragraph may sound odd, even crazy. We have already agreed that there is an infinite number of whole numbers, so there is certainly an infinite number of rational numbers, since the rational numbers include the whole numbers as a subset. Now we are saying that there are even more irrational numbers than rational ones—more than infinity. How can anything be more than infinity?

Until a hundred years ago, the answer to that question would have been simple: it can't. Then another German mathematician, Georg Cantor, suggested a different way of looking at things relating to infinity (Cantor died in a lunatic asylum, and that may be more than coincidence).

Cantor said that you don't need to enumerate things to agree that there are the same number of them. You can line them up, and if to each member of one set there corresponds exactly one member of the other, then there must be the same number in each set. Just as in musical chairs, you don't need to count the players or the chairs to see if the game will work; all you need to do is give a chair to every player, then take one chair away and start the music.

This idea of exact matching, or one-to-one correspondence as it is usually called, allows us to compare sets having an infinite number of members, but it quickly leads to curious consequences. As Galileo pointed out in the seventeenth century, the whole numbers can be matched one-for-one with the squares of the whole numbers, thus:

1, 2, 3, 4, 5, 6, 7, 8, 9, 10, 11, 12 . . .
1, 4, 9, 16, 25, 36, 49, 64, 81, 100, 121, 144 . . .

According to Cantor, we must say there are as many squares as there are numbers, because they can be put into one-to-one correspondence. On the other hand, there seem to be a lot more whole numbers that are not squares than numbers that are. The squares omit 2,3, 5,6,7,8, 10,11,12,13,14,15, and so on. Most numbers are not squares.

In spite of this, Cantor insisted that it makes sense to say that there are the same number of whole numbers as there are of squares; an infinite number of both,

true, but the same *sort* of infinity. There are similarly as many even numbers as there are whole numbers. (They can be put into one-to-one correspondence, thus:
1, 2, 3, 4, 5, 6, 7 . . .
2, 4, 6, 8, 10, 12, 14 . . . .)

Using the same idea, we find that there are as many squares as whole numbers, as many cubes, even as many rational numbers. But there are more irrational numbers, a different order of infinity. The irrational numbers cannot be placed in one-to-one correspondence with the whole numbers, and Cantor was able to prove that fact using an elementary argument.

Cantor was able to go farther. There are higher orders of infinite numbers than the points on the line, in fact, there is an infinite set of orders of infinity. The whole numbers define the "least infinite" infinite set. The question of whether the number of points on a line constitutes the *second* smallest infinite set, i.e. there is no third infinite set which includes the set of whole numbers and is included by the set of points on a line, was a famous unsolved problem of mathematics. In 1967 Paul Cohen showed that it is impossible to prove this conjecture (called the continuum hypothesis) using the standard axioms of set theory. This negative proof diminished mathematical interest in the question.

Infinite sets are seductive stuff, and it is tempting to pursue them further. However, that route will not take us towards the physics we want. That road is found by looking at numbers that are finite, but very large by everyday standards.

4. BIG NUMBERS

> *". . . Man, proud Man! Dressed in a little brief authority, most ignorant of what he's most assured . . ."*

Pure mathematics, as its name suggests, should be mathematics uncontaminated by anything so crude as an application. As G.H. Hardy, an English mathematician of the first half of this century, said in a famous toast: "Here's to pure mathematics. No damned use to anyone, and let's hope it never will be."

Bertrand Russell went even farther in stressing the lack of utility of mathematics: "Mathematics may be defined as the subject in which we never know what we are talking about, nor whether what we are saying is true."

In spite of these lofty sentiments, mathematics that began its life as the purest form of abstract thought has an odd tendency to be just what scientists need to describe the physical world. For example, the theory of conic sections, developed by the Greeks before the birth of Christ, was the tool that Kepler needed to formulate his laws of planetary motion. The theory of matrices was ready and waiting when it was needed in quantum mechanics (and today in hundreds of other places in applied mathematics); and Einstein found the absolute differential calculus of Ricci and Levi-Civita just the thing to describe curved space-times in general relativity.

(It doesn't always work out so conveniently. When Newton was setting up the laws of motion and of universal gravitation, he needed calculus. It didn't exist. That would have been the end of the story for almost everyone. Newton, being perhaps the greatest intellect who ever lived, went ahead and invented calculus, then applied it to his astronomical calculations.)

Conversely, the needs of the applied scientist often stimulate the development of mathematics. And by the seventeenth century, the main attention of physicists and astronomers was not with counting finite sets of objects; it was with describing things that varied continuously, like moving planets, or spinning tops, or heat flow. For such studies, counting things seemed to have little relevance.

That state of affairs continued until the third quarter of the nineteenth century. By that time continuous-variable mathematics had done a wonderful job in the development of astronomy, hydrodynamics, mechanics, and thermodynamics. The main tool was the calculus, which had been developed into a dozen different forms, such as the theory of functions of a complex variable and the calculus of variations.

Now, back before 400 B.C. the Greek Democritus had already suggested on philosophical grounds that matter must be composed of separate indivisible particles, called atoms (*atomos* in Greek means "uncut"). However, people had rather lost sight of that idea until 1805, when John Dalton re-introduced an atomic theory. But this time, there was experimental evidence to support the notion that matter was made up of individual atoms. Thus the behavior of such atoms, regarded as separate, countable objects, must somehow be able to explain the apparently continuous properties of the matter that we observe in everyday life. Unfortunately, the numbers involved are so huge—nearly a trillion trillion atoms in a gram of hydrogen gas—that it was difficult to visualize the properties of so large an assembly of objects.

If we have direct counting experience of numbers only up to a few dozen, any number as big as a billion is beyond intuition. It is possible that some crazy human has actually counted up to a million, but it is certain that no human has ever counted up to a billion. At one number a second (try saying 386,423,569 in *less* than a second), ten hours a day, every day of the year, a billion would take 76 years to finish.

It is worrying to me when I hear politicians throw around so glibly "this many millions" and "that many billions." I wonder if they actually know the difference between the two. It's an old theory that the expenditure of $100 on a new bicycle rack will engender more debate than $500,000,000 for a new weapons system. People have a feel for a hundred dollars, they know what it's like. A billion dollars is just an abstract number.

When we look at the counting needed to enumerate the atoms of a bar of soap or a breath of air, we are well beyond the billion mark. We are talking a trillion trillion atoms; and when we reach numbers so large, we are all like Gamow's Hungarian aristocrats. We simply have no experience base, no intuitive feel for the properties of a system with so many pieces.

To take a simple example, suppose that we toss an unbiased coin in the air. We all believe we understand coil-tossing pretty well. Half the time it will come down heads, the other half it will come down tails. Now suppose that we toss two coins. What's the chance of getting two heads? Of two tails? Of one head and one tail?

Any gambler can give you the answer. You have a one in four chance of two heads, a one in four chance of two tails, and a one in two chance of a head and a tail. The same gambler can probably tell you the odds if you toss three or four coins, and ask him for the probability of getting some given number of heads.

Now throw a million coins in the air. We know that if they are all unbiased coins, the most likely situation will be that half of the coins will land heads, and half tails. But we have no feel for the chance of getting a particular number, say, 400,000 heads, and 600,000 tails. How does it compare with the chance of getting 500,000 heads and 500,000 tails?

The probabilities obey what is known as a binomial distribution, and can be calculated exactly. Table 1 shows how many times we will get a given number of heads, divided by the number of times we will get exactly equal numbers of heads and tails. As we expected, this ratio is always less than one, because equal heads and tails is the most likely situation.

TABLE 1. Coin-tossing probabilities (following page)

R is the probability of throwing N heads, divided by the probability of throwing an equal number of heads and tails. Small numbers are written in exponent form, so for example, 3.1 E–05 = 3.1×10^{-5} = 0.000031. Probabilities less than one in a million are not printed.

TABLE 1 Coin-tossing probabilities

NUMBER OF COINS = 6

N	R
0	0.05
1	0.3
2	0.75
3	1

NUMBER OF COINS = 10

N	R
0	0.004
1	0.040
2	0.179
3	0.476
4	0.833
5	1

NUMBER OF COINS = 100

N	R
25	2.40 E–06
30	2.91 E–04
35	0.0108
40	0.136
45	0.609
50	1

NUMBER OF COINS = 1,000

N	R
420	2.65 E–06
430	5.42 E–05
440	7.39 E–04
450	6.72 E–03
460	0.041
470	0.165
480	0.450
490	0.819
500	1

NUMBER OF COINS = 10,000

N	R
4750	3.71 E–06
4800	3.35 E–04
4850	0.011
4900	0.135
4950	0.607
5000	1

NUMBER OF COINS = 100,000

N	R
49,200	2.76 E–06
49,400	7.47 E–04
49,600	0.041
49,800	0.449
50,000	1

NUMBER OF COINS = 1,000,000

N	R
497,500	3.73 E–06
498,000	3.35 E–04
498,500	0.011
499,000	0.135
499,500	0.607
500,000	1

NUMBER OF COINS = 10,000,000

N	R
4,992,000	2.76 E–06
4,994,000	7.47 E–04
4,996,000	0.041
4,998,000	0.449
5,000,000	1

As the number of coins thrown increases, the chance of a large inequality between heads and tails rapidly decreases.

However, the general behavior of the table as the number of coins increases is not at all intuitive. For small numbers of coins, there is a good chance of getting any number of heads we like to choose. For a million coins, however, the chance of getting anything far from equal numbers of heads and tails is totally negligible. And as the number of coins keeps on increasing, the shape of the curve keeps squeezing narrower and narrower. By the time we reach a trillion trillion coins, the curve has become a single spike. The chance of getting a quarter heads and three quarters tails, or 51% heads and 49% tails, or even 50.00001% heads and 49.99999% tails is vanishingly small.

This result may seem to have no relevance to anything in the real world. But such probabilities are now central to our understanding of everything from refrigerators to lasers.

5. COUNTING AND PHYSICS

"Man is slightly nearer to the atom than the star."

—A.S. Eddington

A small room contains about 1 E27 molecules of air. (As usual, I am using an exponent notation for big numbers. Thus 5 E05 is the same as 5×10^5, i.e. 500,000). The molecules are in ceaseless random motion, and the air pressure on the walls of the room is generated by their impact. Suppose that the walls of the room face north, south, east, and west, and that the room is perfectly sealed, so that no molecule can arrive or escape. Then at any moment, some fraction of the molecules inside the room have a component of their motion taking them generally towards the north wall, and the rest are heading generally towards the south wall (the number who happen to be heading due east or due west is negligible).

All the molecules bounce off the walls, and occasionally off each other. If the motions are, as we said, truly random, then we would be most surprised if the same number were heading for the north wall at all times.

Thus the air pressure on any area of the wall ought to keep changing, fluctuating from one second to the next depending on the number of molecules striking there. If we measured the pressure, we ought to get constantly changing values.

We don't. Unless the temperature in the room changes, we always measure the same pressure on the walls.

To see how this can be so, imagine that the molecules had originally been introduced into the room one at a time. They are to have random motions, so to decide on the motion of these molecules, let's suppose a coin had been tossed. If it lands heads, the molecule will move north; tails, it moves south. Since coin-tossing is random, so are the movements of the molecules.

When we have tossed 1 E27 coins, the room will be filled with air. Now recall our earlier result on tossing a very large number of coins. The chance that *exactly* as many coins land heads as tails is extremely small, so the chance that *exactly* equal numbers of molecules are heading north and south is effectively zero. However, as we saw from Table 1, even with as "few" as ten million coins, the chance that we will get substantially more heads than tails is also negligible. This result applies even more strongly when we have trillions of trillions of coins. The ratio of heads to tails will be so close to one that we will never measure anything other than an even split. Since air pressure is generated by the impact of randomly-moving molecules on the room's walls, and since there is a negligible probability that we have substantially more than half the molecules heading for any given wall, we measure the same pressure on each wall. We will also find no change in the pressure over time.

A similar argument can be used to analyze the position of the molecules. Imagine a partition drawn across the middle of the room. Since molecules move at random, at any moment any number of the molecules may be to the right of the partition. What is to prevent a situation arising where all the molecules happen to be down at one end of the room, with a perfect vacuum at the other?

The distribution of molecules within the room can again be simulated by the tossing of a coin. Let us spin the coin, and each time it lands as heads, we will place a molecule to the right of the partition; when it lands as tails, we place the molecule to the left of the partition. After 1 E27 coin tosses, the room is full of air. However, we know from our coin-tossing probabilities that there is negligible chance of, say, 60% of the molecules being to the right, and 40% to the left, or even of 50.00001% being on the right and 49.99999% on the left. The danger of finding one end of the room suddenly airless is small enough to be totally ignored. It will never happen, not in a time span billions of times longer than the age of the universe.

These examples may seem rather trivial, since we know from our own experience that the air in one end of the room doesn't suddenly vanish, and we don't feel continuous popping in our ears from fluctuating air pressure. However, the same technique, expressed in suitable mathematical form, is much more than it may seem. In the hands of the Scotsman, James Clerk Maxwell, the German, Ludwig Boltzmann, and the American, J. Willard Gibbs, this statistical approach had by the end of the nineteenth century become a powerful tool that allowed global properties of continuous systems (such as temperature) to be understood from the statistical properties governing the movement of their individual pieces—the atoms and molecules.

The science that governs the motion of individual particles is *mechanics;* the science that describes the global pressure and temperatures of continuous systems is *thermodynamics*. *Statistical mechanics*—the statistical analysis of very large assemblies of particles, each governed by the laws of mechanics—provides the bridge between individual particle behavior and whole system behavior. The central mathematical technique is one of counting, enumerating the number of possible arrangements of very large numbers of particles.

What do we lose in adopting such an approach? In the words of Maxwell, "I wish to point out that, in adopting this statistical method of considering the average number of groups of molecules selected according to their velocities, we have abandoned the strict kinetic method of tracing the exact circumstances of each individual molecule in all its encounters. It is therefore possible that we may arrive at results which, though they fairly represent the facts as long as we are supposed to deal with a gas in mass, would cease to be applicable if our faculties and instruments were so sharpened that we could detect and lay hold of each molecule and trace it, through all its course."

Atoms and molecules are tiny objects, only billionths of an inch in diameter and visible only with the aid of the most powerful electron microscopes. Can the effects of their encounters as individual particles ever be seen, as Maxwell suggests? They can, under the right circumstances, with the aid of no more than a low-power microscope. In 1828 an English botanist, Robert Brown, was observing tiny grains of pollen suspended in water. He noticed that instead of remaining in one place, or slowly rising or sinking, the pollen grains were in constant, jerky, and unpredictable motion. They were moving to the buffeting of water molecules. Pollen is at the size threshold where the probability of different numbers of molecules hitting each side is big enough to show a visible effect. A detailed analysis of "Brownian motion," as it is now called, was the subject of one of three ground-breaking papers published in 1905 by Albert Einstein. (The other two set forth the theory of relativity and explained the photoelectric effect.)

6. COUNTING AND BIOLOGY

"Man is judge of all things, a feeble earthworm, the depository of truth, a sink of uncertainty and error, the glory and shame of the universe."

—Blaise Pascal

Simple counting can be the basis of a field of science, as is the case with statistical mechanics; or it can provide the logical destruction of one, as is the case of homeopathic medicine.

In 1795, the doctrine of "like cures like" was proposed by Samuel Hahnemann as the basis for a new practice of medicine, basing his theory upon earlier ideas by Paracelsus. The central notion is that if a strong dose of a particular drug produces in a healthy person symptoms like those of a certain disease, then a minute dose of the same drug will cure the disease. To assure that small dose, the procedure is as follows:

The original drug forms the "mother tincture." A fixed quantity of this, say one gram, is added to a kilogram of pure water, and thoroughly mixed. From this "first dilution," one gram is taken, and added to a kilogram of pure water to form the "second dilution." The procedure is repeated, each time taking one gram and mixing with one kilogram of water, to form third dilutions, fourth dilutions, and so on. This is often done as many as ten or twenty times, arguing that the greater the dilution, the more potent the healing effect of the final mixture.

The logic behind the process is obscure, but never mind that. Let's look at the molecular counts, something that was not possible in the first days of homeopathy.

One gram of a drug will contain no more than 6 E23 molecules. If that gram is diluted with one kilogram of water, the number of molecules of the drug in one gram of the result is reduced by a factor of one thousand, so one gram of the first dilution will contain at most 6 E20 drug molecules. The second dilution will be reduced to 6 E17 molecules, the third dilution to 6 E14, and so on. The tenth dilution has on average 6 E–7 molecules of drug—in other words, there is less than one chance in a million that the tenth dilution contains a single molecule of the drug we started with! The tenth or twentieth dilution is pure water. There is not a trace of the original drug in it.

Even if the like-cures-like idea were correct, how can

pure water with no drug cure the disease? The simple answer is, it can't.

Presented with the counting argument for number of molecules, the practitioners of homeopathic medicine mutter vaguely about residual influences and healing fields. But no one can explain what they are, or how they fit with any other scientific ideas.

So homeopathic medicine can't work.

Or can it?

At this point, skeptical as I am, I have to point out another example of large-number counting drawn from the biological sciences, one that shows how careful we must be when we say that something is impossible.

On the evening of May 6th, 1875, the French naturalist Jean Henri Fabre performed an interesting experiment. He took a young female of Europe's largest moth, the Great Peacock, and placed her in a wire cage. Then he watched in amazement as male moths of the species—and only of that species—began to appear from all over, some of them flying considerable distances to get to the female.

They could sense her presence. But how?

After more experiments, sight and sound were ruled out. Smell was all that remained. The male moths could smell some substance emitted by the female, and they could detect it in unbelievably small quantities. (The female silk moth, *Bombyx mori*, secretes a substance called *bombykol* with scent glands on her abdomen; the male silk moth will recognize and respond to a single molecule of bombykol. Moths hold the record in the *Guinness Book of World Records* for the organism with the most acute sense of smell.)

The moth attractant is one of a class of substances known as *pheromones*, a coined word meaning "hormone-bearing." Pheromones are chemicals secreted and given off by animals, to convey information to or elicit particular responses from other members of the same species. One class of pheromones conveys sexual information, telling the males that a female of the species is ready, willing, and able to mate.

Before we get too excited by this, let me mention that pheromones are employed as a sexual lure mainly by insects. The same thing does occur in humans, but our noses have become so civilized and insensitive that we have trouble picking up the signal. We have to resort to other methods, more uniquely human. ("Man is the 'How'd you like to come back to my place?'-saying animal.")

Female moths, ready to mate, attract their male counterparts over incredible distances—several miles, if the male is downwind.

Now let's do some counting. A female moth emits a microgram or so of pheromones, possibly as much as ten micrograms under unusual circumstances. That's a lot of molecules, about 1 E15 of them (airborne pheromone molecules are large and heavy, 100 to 300 times as massive as a hydrogen atom, and you don't get all that many to a gram). But by the time those molecules have diffused through the atmosphere and dispersed themselves over a large airspace, they will be spread very thin.

So thin that the chance of a male moth, three miles away, receiving even a single molecule from the source female seems to be almost vanishingly small. For example, suppose that the aerial plume of pheromones stays within 20 feet of the ground, and spreads in three miles to a width of 1,000 feet—which is a tight, narrow-angle plume. Then we are looking at pheromone concentrations of about one part in a hundred billion. Even the incredibly sensitive odor detection apparatus of the moth needs at least one molecule to work with, and chances are high that it will not get it.

The natural conclusion might be that, *Guinness Book of World Records* notwithstanding, the story of a single female moth attracting a male miles away must be no more than a story. And yet the experiments have been done many times. The males, unaware of the statistics, appear from the distance to cluster around the fertile females.

Now, in England a few months ago I was given a very

intriguing explanation of how this might be possible. If other female moths who receive pheromones from a fertile female themselves produce more pheromones, then these intermediate moths can play a crucial role by serving as *amplifiers* for the pheromonal message. Each moth that receives a molecule or two of the female pheromone emits more than that of the same substance. Like tiny repeater stations for an electronic signal, the moths pass the word on, increasing the intensity of the message in the process. The distant male moth receives the pheromonal signal, and heads upwind toward the fertile female.

This is such an attractive idea that it would be hard to forget it once you have heard it mentioned. I was sure I had never encountered it before. So before I said it was a fact in this article, I wanted to check references. And that is where the trouble started.

I began with the obvious sources: reference texts. There are a number on pheromones, and all of them stress the incredible sensitivity of moths to these chemical messengers. However, not one of them mentioned the idea of pheromonal amplifiers. (One of the most interesting books on the subject is *Sexual Strategy*, by Tim Halliday. On its cover is a bright red frog on top of a black frog. I found the contents, all about the tricks used by animals in locating their mates, fascinating. It was only when I saw the expression on the desk clerk's face as I checked the book out of a university library that I realized the title and front illustration might cause questions.)

With no help from books, or from a search of the *General Science Index*, I cast my net wider. I called David Brin, who had been present when the pheromonal amplifier idea was mentioned. He didn't have a reference, either—but he had the telephone number in Worcestershire of Jack Cohen, who had told us both about it.

I called England, and reached Jack after a couple of efforts. He was not sure quite where or when he had read about the idea, but he could offer me two key words:

Lymantria, the genus of moth used in the experiments; and *Rothschild*, the name of the person who had done the work.

At that point, it seemed to be a snap. I had names. I expected to have full references in no time. All I needed was a good entomologist, and I set out to track one down by placing telephone calls.

Roger Allen led me to Craig Philips, a wonderful naturalist who is worth an article in his own right. He keeps tropical cockroaches and tarantulas in his apartment, and apparently enjoys their company.

("I've only been bitten once by a tarantula," he said, "and that was my own fault. I was wearing shorts in my apartment, and the tarantula was sitting on my bare leg. Suddenly the mynah bird" —not previously mentioned at all in our conversation— "swooped down to have a go at the tarantula. I covered it with my hand to protect it. And naturally it bit me."

A perfectly ordinary day in the life of a dedicated naturalist. "It didn't hurt," he added, "the way that a bee sting would. But after a while a kind of ulcer developed that took weeks and weeks to heal.")

Well, we had a very enjoyable conversation, but he had not heard of pheromonal amplifiers, either. Nor had another friend of mine, an amateur entomologist in Oklahoma City (my phone bills were mounting) but he had a vague recollection of hearing something odd like this about a different moth. *Cecropia*, he thought.

I checked that one in the reference texts, too. *Cecropia*, yes. Pheromone amplifiers, no. No writer had heard of it.

Nor had any of the many entomologists that I spoke to over the next few days. Moths may not pass on pheromonal messages, but entomologists sure pass on interesting questions. I heard from Sheila Mutchler, who ran the Insect Zoo at the National Museum of Natural History; Gates Clarke, an entomologist at the same organization; Mark Jacobson, who works on moths and pheromones at the U.S. Department of Agriculture; and Jerome Klun, who works in the Agricultural

Research Service and who told me more intriguing things about moth mating habits than I had dreamed existed.

All very helpful, all hugely knowledgeable, all fascinating to talk to. But no pheromonal amplifiers. Everyone agreed what an interesting concept it was—the sort of thing that *ought* to be true, in an interesting world. But no one could give me a single reference, or recall anything that had ever been written about the idea.

So where do I stand now?

Undecided. But it has become a minor mania with me. I can't stop looking. And I've become reluctant to use the word "impossible" when something seems to be ruled out on counting arguments alone.

7. THE FUTURE OF COUNTING

"Man is the measure of all things."

—Protagoras

Counting has been important to humans since the beginning of recorded history, but I can make a case for the idea that the real Age of Counting began only in 1946. That's when the world's first electronic computer, the ENIAC, went into operation.

Computers count wonderfully well. Although no human has ever counted to a billion, today's fastest computers can do it in less than one second. And that is going to have profound effects on the way that science is performed, and on everything else in our future.

To take one minor example, consider the values in Table 1. I did not copy them from some standard reference work, but computed the necessary ratios of binomial coefficients from scratch, on a lap-top computer that is small and slow by today's standards. The number of arithmetic operations involved was no more than a few million. The program took less than half an hour to write, and maybe the same to run—I went off to have lunch, so I didn't bother to time it.

Compare that with the situation only forty years ago. I would have been forced to use quite different computational methods, or spend months on calculating that single table. For small values of N, say, less than 30, I would have computed the coefficients directly on a mechanical or an electric calculating machine. That would have been several hours of work, with a non-negligible chance of error. If the results were important, I would have had a second person repeat the whole computation as an independent check. For larger values of N, direct calculation would have taken far too long. Instead, I would have made use of an approximation known as Stirling's formula, calling for the use of logarithm tables and involving me in several more hours of tedious calculations. Again, there would be a strong possibility of human error.

This example illustrates the general principle: what could have been done a hundred years ago only by ingenious analysis and approximation will be done in the future more and more by direct calculation—i.e. by counting.

The trend can be seen again and again, in dozens of different problem areas. The motion of the planets used to be calculated by a clever set of analytic approximations known as general perturbation theory. Many of history's greatest scientists, from Kepler to Newton to Laplace, spent years toiling over hand-calculations. Today, planetary motion (and spacecraft motion) are computed by direct numerical integration of the differential equations of motion. Instead of being treated as a continuous variable, time is chopped up into many small intervals, and the motion of the body is calculated by a computer from one time interval to the next.

This method of "finite differences" and numerical integration is used in everything from weather prediction to aircraft design to stellar evolution. The time and space variables of the continuous problem are chopped up into sufficiently large numbers of finite pieces, and the calculation consists of coupling neighboring times and places so as to calculate global behavior.

Statisticians have rather different needs. Instead of using finite difference methods to solve their problems, they often rely on repeated trials of a statistical process. A random element is introduced in each trial to mimic the variations seen in nature. Many thousands of trials are usually needed before a valid statistical inference can be drawn. Often the number of trials is not known in advance, since it is the behavior of the computed solution itself that tells you whether you can safely stop, or must keep on going to more trials. These appropriately-named "Monte Carlo" methods are quite impractical without a fast computer.

That's the situation in 42 A.C.—and the Age of Computers has just begun. Whole new sciences are emerging, relying on a symbiosis of computer experiment and human analysis: nonlinear stability theory, irreversible thermodynamics, chaos theory, fractals. Even pure mathematics is being changed. The proof a few years ago of the four-color theorem ("Any plane map can be colored, with neighboring regions having different colors, using no more than four colors") was done using a computer to enumerate the thousands of possible cases.

The diversity of available computing equipment is increasing, as well as its speed. I'm writing these words on a small portable computer with only 192K of memory, and one programing language (BASIC). On the other hand, it weighs less than four pounds and I can easily carry it with me for use on planes and trains. For heavy-duty work I wouldn't dream of using it. I have access to a Connection Machine, a large parallel-logic computer with 16,384 separate processors, able to perform about three and a half billion floating-point multiplications a second (3.5 *gigaflops*, a word I like very much). That's where the real number-crunching takes place. Thirty years from now, I expect to have available a machine the size and weight of the portable, but with the computing power of the Connection Machine.

Implausible? Not if we look at the past. Today's small portables have the computer power of a large mainframe of 1958 vintage, and they are infinitely easier to use. The rate of increase of computer speed shows no signs of slowing, and arithmetic calculations are only the beginning. Computer hardware is as dumb as ever, but software gets smarter all the time. We are entering the age of expert systems, where human experience is captured in complex programs and used as a starting point for efficient computer algorithms.

The list of applications grows all the time, everything from messy algebraic manipulations to realtime flight simulators to crop forecasting to department store management. In addition to counting, today's computers can do algebra and complex logic far faster and more accurately than humans. A few years ago, a computer was used to make an algebraic check of the Delaunay theory of the motion of the moon, a vast mass of complicated formulae that took the French astronomer C. E. Delaunay over twenty years to develop. Most people find it amazing that his 1,800 pages of working, contained in two huge volumes published in 1860 and 1867, are correct except for a couple of insignificant errors. But should we be more amazed by this, or by the fact that today's computers can perform a complete check of the algebra in a few hours? Or that ten years from now, the same calculations will take minutes or maybe seconds?

Time to stop.

We have come a long way from the simple 1, 2, 3 . . . counting that we learn before we can read. How far can computers go, in performing functions that only a few decades ago were considered solely the prerogative of humans?

A long way. I don't want to get into the old argument about whether or not a computer can ever think, particularly when there is so much evidence that people can't. But let me summarize my own opinions, by suggesting that a thousand years from now there will (finally) be a new and wholly satisfactory definition of humankind:

"Man is the ideal computer I/O unit."

Introduction

In Days of Yore when Marxism was in flower, it was often said that "The end justifies the means"—if the end in view was The Dictatorship of the Proletariat. Shortly this became vulgarized to "The end justifies the means if a Marxist is doing it." Nowadays, many gulags and killing fields later (not to mention food and ration lines that would stretch from here to Arcturus) we don't believe that anymore.

Still, desperate situations can call for desperate remedies . . .

MEGAPHONE

Rick Cook

The key, Senator Steven Cherney told himself, *is to talk a language they'll understand.*

The Virginia dawn was glorious, the late spring air alive with birdsong and the woods were green and lovely. But Cherney's mind was on politics, as usual.

He scuffed the dead leaves thoughtfully with his foot and considered his options carefully. The votes were there to bring the dams and waterways bill out of committee, but there was going to be a messy floor fight unless he could head it off.

Too expensive, they complained. Full of pork, they said. Well, maybe there was something there for a lot of people, but that didn't make it less important to his state's farmers—and those farmers were damned important to him. They'd pulled him through a tough election and now it was his turn.

He had come here, to a friend's farm, as he so often did to get away from the bustle and pressures of the capital. "My own private Camp David," he sometimes called it when he was feeling presidential. He would tramp the woods at dawn and sleep in the upstairs bedroom of a farmhouse which had been old when Union and Confederate armies clashed in its sight. On

Monday he would return to the city refreshed, restored and with his plans laid.

As *for the expense, we'll just have to find the money,* he thought. We'll slice someplace to make up for it, something that doesn't have a real constituency. Research? NASA? The bill would go easier if he had a victim lined up beforehand.

Cherney was so absorbed he barely heard the leaves rustle behind him. He remembered the odor of musk and violets and struggling for breath and consciousness. Then nothing.

He awoke on a bench, lying under a sheet. He sat up suddenly and clutched the edge of the bench as the world reeled. He closed his eyes and breathed deeply several times to steady himself and when he opened them he saw he was not alone.

He was, however, the only person in the room.

The creature behind the desk was small, a little over five feet he guessed, humanoid, and frail. Not frail, the senator corrected himself, delicate. Like fine porcelain. What skin he could see was golden brown and hairless. The head was much wider at the top than the bottom so it seemed to balance precariously on the thin neck. But it was the eyes that grabbed his attention. They were huge, dark, and so luminous a man could lose himself forever in them.

My God! he thought. *Oh my God!* His heart hammered and he closed his eyes once more against a new wave of dizziness. When he opened them the creature was still there, unmoving, unblinking. He licked his lips and tasted metal, a taste he hadn't known since Vietnam.

Say something dammit! This is a historic event. "Ahhh . . . umm." Not exactly famous words or even his usual standard of eloquence, but Senator Steven Cherney was happy to find his mouth worked at all.

The creature raised a thin, inhumanly long arm and Cherney saw that it ended in a knot of worm-like tentacles. The tentacles moved over the surface of a small gray box on the desk and the box spoke.

"Why have you decided not to explore space?" The creature asked, softly, gently and with all the sadness in the world.

"Huh? I mean, I beg your pardon?" Cherney had expected almost anything but that.

"Why have you turned away from space?"

"Forgive us," the box said as the creature stroked it. "But we have to know. There are so very few intelligent races which jump the gap." The tendrils hesitated on the surface and then the voice went on. "And we are lonely, you see."

"But we have an active space program," Cherney protested. "We've been to the Moon, we've sent probes to the outer planets. We've even built a Space Shuttle."

"You use the form of speech for past events." The tone did not change. The voice was as soft and gentle and—regretful?—as ever. "You have done these things and now you do them no more. We wish to understand why." The creature added apologetically, "It is important to us."

"There's the space station . . ." Cherney began and then stopped. He knew all too well what had happened to the space station. How it had been turned from a jumping-off point for planetary exploration into a research base and then whittled down and stretched out repeatedly. He had done some of the whittling himself.

The creature said nothing, only looked at him.

Hell, thought Cherney. *How in God's name do you answer a question like that? How do you explain to something from beyond the sky about budget deficits and social needs and priorities in a time of limited resources?* Never mind the really deciding things like deals and quiet understandings. For the first time in a long time, Senator Steven Cherney felt small and inadequate.

"Other things are more important right now," he said finally. "We have problems we must meet first."

"Yet those problems grow constantly worse," the voice

said gently, inexorably. "Each year it gets harder for you to devote the resources to exploration. Soon it becomes impossible." The creature gestured. "We have seen it before."

Fermi paradox, Cherney thought dully. That's what they call it. Why don't we find signs of intelligent life in the universe? Is that the answer? They all just quit? He had a vision of an alien Budget Committee solemnly holding hearings on its space program. He could even picture old Senator Cronkite with scaly green skin and tentacles waving dramatically as he thundered against the waste of it all.

"Well look," Cherney said. "If it's that important to you why don't you help us? You could show us how to do it."

"That has been tried," the creature said. "It has turned out—badly."

Remembering the plight of his state's Indians Cherney was silent again.

"You said there were other races," he said at last. "How many?"

"Intelligent races? Many. Those that have made the leap to space? Just ourselves." The tentacles paused and then caressed the box again. "Just ourselves."

"What about the others?"

"Most of them do not survive," the voice said sadly.

Cherney's breath caught in his throat. "What happens to them?"

The creature made an odd "palm"–up gesture. "Many things," the box said. "A planet's resources are finite. Eventually a species finds limits to its growth. Some of them battle to extinction, some lay down and die quietly. A very few survive by regression and stagnation."

Cherney went cold. Two years before he had toured refugee camps in Ethiopia on a fact-finding mission on world hunger. The walking skeletons and the children with pipestem legs, enormous dark eyes and swollen bellies would be with him always. Sometimes he had nightmares about those emaciated, dying children and their parents walking the streets of his city.

He licked his lips. "No other choice?" he asked.

The alien inclined its head and stroked the box. "We have found none. In all our searching."

"Oh my God," he breathed.

"As you will," the alien stroked the box again. "Only tell us—why?"

"Because we're fools," Senator Steven Cherney snapped. "We're blind, stupid fools who will dig our own graves if we're given half a chance." The alien reached for its box and he held up a hand to interrupt it.

"But we're something else too," he said, lapsing into the style he'd learned as a kid sergeant leading a squad in the Delta. "We're fighters and we don't quit. Stopped? No, we've just paused. And I'll tell you another thing. We're about through pausing. We would have gone on anyway because it's always been our way to push over the next hill. But that pause will end one holy hell of a lot quicker when I get back to Washington.

"No, whoever you are. You're not going to be alone much longer. We're coming out to you and we're coming fast. By God, we will not lay down and die!"

Senator Steven Cherney realized his cheeks were wet and that he really didn't give a damn. It felt good to go beyond all the shitty compromises and arcane manueverings that had brought him where he was; to have a clear simple goal and to know it was worth fighting for with every ounce of breath in his body. Besides everything else, it felt good.

The alien inclined its head. "It is not an easy thing to do."

He grinned mirthlessly. "We've got a saying. The difficult we do immediately. The impossible takes a little longer. Keep looking up, fella, because you're going to have something to see damn quick."

The alien fingers caressed the box. "That is your answer?"

Steven Cherney, once a sergeant in Company K, 1st Battalion First Air Cavalry and now the junior senator from his state squared his shoulders and stared deep into the dark eyes before him. "Damn straight."

"Then you have told us what we wish to know," the box said, less regretfully. "Thank you." The creature lifted its hand from the box and gestured. Cherney smelled musk and violets and dizziness washed over him again.

The alien's final words seemed to come from the bottom of a deep, distant well. "And good luck."

He awoke under a tree on the hill overlooking the farmhouse. The sky had turned slate gray and thunder muttered through it. He raised his head, felt the familiar dizziness and then settled back to rest, thinking.

His aides wouldn't appreciate being rousted for an evening staff meeting, but he had to get rolling. It was already late in the session to schedule new hearings, not to mention the deals that would have to be cut to make things happen. As he lay there his politician's brain went into high gear, weighing alternative approaches, considering potential allies and maneuvers.

One thing he was not going to do was tell anyone what had happened. The last thing he needed was to be front-page news in every supermarket tabloid in the country. No, he'd come up with some reasonable, plausible explanation for his new policy—and then he would push like hell to get the space program rolling.

"We're going to do it," he said to the leaden sky. "By God, we'll make that jump. Just see if we don't." It began to sprinkle lightly as Senator Steven Cherney got slowly to his feet and started on the path back.

"It's all in the presentation," said the golden-skinned alien, tugging roughly at her antennae. They came away, and with them large chunks of latex makeup. A few more tugs and the woman underneath was revealed. She was tiny with dark hair and eyes almost as dark as the costume's—even if they weren't as luminous.

"I still say this is a crazy idea," said the tall, slender man who was carefully cleaning latex "skin" and makeup off the tentacled "hands" before packing the delicate mechanisms in their storage case.

"Then why did you turn down a job with Spielberg to fly clear across the country to help us with it?"

He grinned. "Hell Sis, you know I could never resist a challenge. And you've got to admit, that's some makeup job."

"I'll say," the woman agreed. "I think my skin ages ten years every time I put it on."

"Well, there's just one more to go," said the second man, as he repacked the oxygen mask. "I'll be glad when this is over. Aside from details like legality, that knockout gas is dangerous."

"What is that stuff anyway?" the other man asked.

The man with the oxygen mask grinned. "Ethyl chloride with some scent added. It's fast, but it's tricky as hell and I'd hate to OD someone on it."

"It's in a good cause," the small woman said as she began to pull the fake skin off her arms. "One more senator and our list will be complete."

"I'm still surprised no one has said anything," said the anesthesiologist.

The other man smiled. "That was the one thing we were sure wouldn't happen. These men are realists. That means that to them unreal things like their reputations are the most important things in the world. They won't talk."

"Do you really think this will do any good?" the doctor asked.

The woman frowned. "You mean can we change the course of history? No. But we can attract attention. So far we've pulled this gag on five key people: Two congressmen, a NASA offical, a White House staffer and now a senator. The ones who have been major stumbling blocks. With them either convinced or neutralized, maybe we can get some momentum into space again."

"Lobbying would be a whole lot more legal," her brother said neutrally.

The woman's eyes sparkled. "Yeah, but lobbying's not nearly as much fun."

"Besides which it doesn't work," the doctor said practically. "We've tried. It isn't that people like Cherney disagree with us, they're just more concerned with other things. We can't speak loudly enough to be heard in their scheme of things. So we present them with someone or something they will listen to."

"And we're telling them the truth," the woman said, ripping off another chunk of her face in an angry gesture and wincing as the latex pulled her skin raw. "You've seen the computer simulations. You know where they lead."

"Still, it seems immoral to me," her brother said.

She smiled sweetly, luminously. "So was the bill of goods Columbus sold Isabella." Then she reached for the jar of cold cream. "Now come on, let's get ready for the next one."

MORE FROM THE NOTEBOOKS OF LAZARUS LONG

Robert A. Heinlein

Always tell her she is beautiful, especially if she is not.

*

If you are part of a society that votes, then do so. There may be no candidates and no measures you want to vote *for* . . . but there are certain to be ones you want to vote *against*. In case of doubt, vote *against*. By this rule you will rarely go wrong.

If this is too blind for your taste, consult some well-meaning fool (there is always one around) and ask his advice. Then vote the other way. This enables you to be a good citizen (if such is your wish) without spending the enormous amount of time on it that truly intelligent exercise of franchise requires.

*

Sovereign ingredient for a happy marriage: Pay cash or do without. Interest charges not only eat up a household budget; awareness of debt eats up domestic felicity.

*

Those who refuse to support and defend a state have no claim to protection by that state. Killing an anarchist or a pacifist should not be defined as "murder" in a legalistic sense. The offense against the state, if any, should be "Using deadly weapons inside city limits," or "Creating a traffic hazard," or "Endangering bystanders," or other misdemeanor.

However, the state may reasonably place a closed season on these exotic asocial animals whenever they are in danger of becoming extinct. An authentic buck pacifist has rarely been seen off Earth, and it is doubtful that any have survived the trouble there . . . regrettable, as they had the biggest mouths and the smallest brains of any of the primates.

The small-mouthed variety of anarchist has spread through the Galaxy at the very wave front of the Diaspora; there is no need to protect them. But they often shoot back.

*

Another ingredient for a happy marriage: Budget the luxuries *first!*

*

And still another— See to it that she has her own desk—then keep your hands off it!

*

And another— In a family argument, if it turns out you are right—apologize at once!

*

"God split himself into a myriad parts that he might have friends." This may not be true, but it sounds good—and is no sillier than any other theology.

*

To stay young requires unceasing cultivation of the ability to unlearn old falsehoods.

*

Does history record *any* case in which the majority was right?

*

When the fox gnaws—*smile!*

*

A "critic" is a man who creates nothing and thereby feels qualified to judge the work of creative men. There is logic in this; he is unbiased—he hates all creative people equally.

*

Money is truthful. If a man speaks of his honor, make him pay cash.

*

Never frighten a little man. He'll kill you.

*

Only a sadistic scoundrel—or a fool—tells the bald truth on social occasions.

*

This sad little lizard told me that he was a brontosaurus on his mother's side. I did not laugh; people who boast of ancestry often have little else to sustain them. Humoring them costs nothing and adds to happiness in a world in which happiness is always in short supply.

*

In handling a stinging insect, move very slowly.

*

To be "matter of fact" about the world is to blunder into fantasy—and dull fantasy at that, as the real world is strange and wonderful.

*

The difference between science and the fuzzy subjects is that science requires reasoning, while those other subjects merely require scholarship.

*

Copulation is spiritual in essence—or it is merely friendly exercise. On second thought, strike out "merely." Copulation is not "merely"—even when it is just a happy pastime for two strangers. But copulation at its spiritual best is so much more than physical coupling that it is different in kind as well as in degree.

The saddest feature of homosexuality is not that it is "wrong" or "sinful" or even that it can't lead to progeny—but that it is more difficult to reach through it this spiritual union. Not impossible—but the cards are stacked against it.

But—most sorrowfully—many people never achieve spiritual sharing even with the help of male-female advantage; they are condemned to wander through life alone.

*

Touch is the most fundamental sense. A baby experiences it, all over, before he is born and long before he learns to use sight, hearing, or taste, and no human ever ceases to need it. Keep your children short on pocket money—but long on hugs.

*

Secrecy is the beginning of tyranny.

*

The greatest productive force is human selfishness.

*

Be wary of strong drink. It can make you shoot at tax collectors—and miss.

*

The profession of shaman has many advantages. It offers high status with a safe livelihood free of work in the dreary, sweaty sense. In most societies it offers legal privileges and immunities not granted to other men. But it is hard to see how a man who has been given a mandate from on High to spread tidings of joy to all mankind can be seriously interested in taking up a collection to pay his salary; it causes one to suspect that the shaman is on the moral level of any other con man.

But it's lovely work if you can stomach it.

*

A whore should be judged by the same criteria as other professionals offering services for pay—such as dentists, lawyers, hairdressers, physicians, plumbers, etc. Is she professionally competent? Does she give good measure? Is she honest with her clients?

It is possible that the percentage of honest and competent whores is higher than that of plumbers and much higher than that of lawyers. And *enormously* higher than that of professors.

*

Minimize your therbligs until it becomes automatic; this doubles your effective lifetime—and thereby gives time to enjoy butterflies and kittens and rainbows.

*

Have you noticed how much they look like orchids? Lovely!

*

Expertise in one field does not carry over into other fields. But experts often think so. The narrower their field of knowledge the more likely they are to think so.

*

Never try to outstubborn a cat.

*

Tilting at windmills hurts you more than the windmills.

*

Yield to temptation; it may not pass your way again.

*

Waking a person unnecessarily should not be considered a capital crime. For a first offense, that is.

*

"Go to hell!" or other insult direct is all the answer a snoopy question rates.

*

The correct way to punctuate a sentence that starts: "Of course it is none of my business but—" is to place a period after the word "but." Don't use excessive force in supplying such moron with a period. Cutting his throat is only a momentary pleasure and is bound to get you talked about.

*

A man does not insist on physical beauty in a woman who builds up his morale. After a while he realizes that she *is* beautiful—he just hadn't noticed it at first.

*

A skunk is better company than a person who prides himself on being "frank."

*

"All's fair in love and war"—what a contemptible lie!

*

Beware of the "Black Swan" fallacy. Deductive logic is tautological; there is no way to get a new truth out of it, and it manipulates false statements as readily as true ones. If you fail to remember this, it can trip you—with perfect logic. The designers of the earliest computers called this the "Gigo Law," i.e., "Garbage in, garbage out."

Inductive logic is *much* more difficult—but can produce new truths.

*

A "practical joker" deserves applause for his wit according to its quality. Bastinado is about right. For exception wit one might grant keelhauling. But staking him out on an anthill should be reserved for the very wittiest.

*

Natural laws have no pity.

*

On the planet Tranquille around KM849 (G-O) lives a little animal known as a "knafn." It is herbivorous and has no natural enemies and is easily approached and may be petted—sort of a six-legged puppy with scales. Stroking it is very pleasant; it wiggles its pleasure and broadcasts euphoria in some band that humans can detect. It's worth the trip.

Someday some bright boy will figure out how to record this broadcast, then some smart boy will see commercial angles—and not long after that it will be regulated and taxed.

In the meantime I have faked that name and catalog number; it is several thousand light-years off in another direction. Selfish of me—

*

Freedom begins when you tell Mrs. Grundy to go fly a kite.

*

Take care of the cojones and the frijoles will take care of themselves. Try to have getaway money—but don't be fanatic about it.

*

If "everybody knows" such-and-such, then it ain't so, by at least ten thousand to one.

*

Political tags—such as royalist, communist, democrat, populist, fascist, liberal, conservative, and so forth—are never basic criteria. The human race divides politically into those who want people to be controlled and those who have no such desire. The former are idealists acting from highest motives for the greatest good of the greatest number. The latter are surly curmudgeons, suspicious and lacking in altruism. But they are more comfortable neighbors than the other sort.

*

All cats are *not* gray after midnight. Endless variety—

*

Sin lies only in hurting other people unnecessarily. All other "sins" are invented nonsense. (Hurting yourself is not sinful—just stupid.)

*

Being generous is inborn; being altruistic is a learned perversity. No resemblance—

*

It is impossible for a man to love his wife wholeheartedly without loving all women somewhat. I suppose that the converse must be true of women.

*

You can go wrong by being too skeptical as readily as by being too trusting.

*

Formal courtesy between husband and wife is even more important than it is between strangers.

*

Anything free is worth what you pay for it.

*

Don't store garlic near other victuals.

*

Climate is what we expect, weather is what we get.

*

Pessimist by policy, optimist by temperament—it is possible to be both. How? By never taking an unnecessary chance and by minimizing risks you can't avoid. This permits you to play out the game happily, untroubled by the certainty of the outcome.

Do not confuse "duty" with what other people expect of you; they are utterly different. Duty is a debt you owe to yourself to fulfill obligations you have assumed voluntarily. Paying that debt can entail anything from years of patient work to instant willingness to die. Difficult it may be, but the reward is self-respect.

But there is no reward at all for doing what other people expect of you, and to do so is not merely difficult, but impossible. It is easier to deal with a footpad than it is with the leech who wants "just a few minutes of your time, please—this won't take long." Time is your total capital, and the minutes of your life are painfully few. If you allow yourself to fall into the vice of agreeing to such requests, they quickly snowball to the point where these parasites will use up 100 percent of your time—and squawk for more!

So learn to say No—and to be rude about it when necessary.

Otherwise you will not have time to carry out your duty, or to do your own work, and certainly no time for love and happiness. The termites will nibble away your life and leave none of it for you.

(This rule does not mean that you must not do a favor for a friend, or even a stranger. But let the choice be *yours*. Don't do it because it is "expected" of you.)

*

"I came, I saw, she conquered." (The original Latin seems to have been garbled.)

*

A committee is a life form with six or more legs and no brain.

*

Animals can be driven crazy by placing too many in too small a pen. Homo sapiens is the only animal that voluntarily does this to himself.

*

Don't try to have the last word. You might get it.

Introduction

"Ars longa, vita brevis." —Robert A. Heinlein, *Glory Road**

There is a feeling of terrible waste and deprivation when a great artist dies. What more might he have given us had he only been able to cheat death? Writer's of the Future finalist John Moore tells of such an artist's duel with death—and an establishment attempting to pervert his art, his eternal vision.

—TW

**That's where I first read it!*

Freeze Frame

John Moore

The vision came and he held it. It came in the thirty-third year of his sleep and for seventy-nine years he held it, examined it, twisted it, expanded the dream until it left his brain and traveled right down to his fingertips. Outside the cryocoffin the seasons passed, the world turned and the moon eclipsed, fortunes were made and squandered, babies and stars were born and died or, worse, forgotten. Inside the heavy silvered tube one human hibernated with an endless dream circulating through an endless sleep. But if he ever got out of this damned icebox then he, Vincent Vernio, greatest artist that ever lived, then he would paint that dream and make it his last masterpiece.

Vincent's readaption counselor was a bland smiling young man, his personality worn dull by years of paper pushing. Vincent could never remember his name. He unhurriedly examined Vincent's file. "You seem to be adapting quite nicely, Mr. Vernio."

Vincent said yes.

"I guess things really haven't changed that much in the last hundred twelve years."

Vincent said no.

"And those memory proteins are a big help too. Before those came out, why, you would have had to spend twice as long on the hypno-tapes just to get the language."

Vincent tried to look impressed.

"Anyway, the doctors say you'll be able to start work in a week."

Good.

"You realize that everyone must have a job these days. Otherwise you go into the army."

Yes.

"Your file is somewhat incomplete. Normally when a person is revived his sponsor, that is, the person making the revival application, must agree to accept responsibility for making that person a useful and productive member of society. But I can't seem to find the sponsor in your case. Usually it's a relative, unless the sponsor is rather wealthy."

"I left no children."

"Yes. Your case is somewhat out of the ordinary. However, you seem to appreciate your responsibility towards society so we'll just go right ahead. Do you have any skills or crafts that you think may be marketable today?"

Vincent resisted the temptation to say he was the greatest artist of his time. "I was a painter."

"A painter. Excellent. We just had a call for painters from the aircraft factory. Can you work an airbrush?"

Vincent stood in line for two hours. Everyone else seemed used to it. He supposed that someone somewhere had calculated the most cost-effective length for a line. He waited another ten minutes at the counter while the girl examined his applications. She looked a lot like his adaption counselor.

"Hello, my name is Linda and I'm here to help you." She sounded like him too. "I see you would like a new apartment."

"A different apartment. One with a north window."

"Your present apartment has two windows."

"They face south."

"Most people prefer south windows because they get more sun."

Vincent hated to explain. "I'm painting a picture. North light is better to paint by. It's more consistent."

"We can have indirect lighting installed. The wait is only three months. We can get you the same kind they use at the gallery."

"I never paint by artificial light."

"Well, the gallery is where people go to look at paintings, so isn't that the kind of light you need? I mean, that's the whole point of painting a picture, for people to look at."

Vincent said nothing.

"I have a room with a skylight."

"A skylight would be perfect."

Vincent went to the art gallery. He was not surprised to see his own work prominently displayed; he had never doubted that his name would live. Scanning the sparse crowd, he mused that things hadn't changed too much in a hundred years; it seemed to consist mostly of young men trying to pick up girls. He wandered the quiet hallways in deep reverie, his mind filled with swirls of bright colors and clean crisp lines. His masterpiece, yes. His vision. For a hundred years he had dreamed it.

"What?" He looked about. A young woman was beside him. Pretty face.

"I hope I didn't break your train of thought. You seemed so absorbed in this painting. Do you know why the sunflowers are such a sickening color?"

Vincent checked out the painting. It was a familiar van Gogh. He smiled. "Oh. Well, when van Gogh painted those flowers he used a bright new yellow with a chrome base. Cadmium yellow hadn't been invented then. It looked just fine when he painted it but chrome yellow slowly decomposes and in, let's see, another hundred years it will be almost black."

The girl made a face. "It's pretty far gone already."

"Are you an artist?" So far he hadn't met any.

She blushed. "I'm . . . sort of aspiring. Why? Do I have paint under my fingernails? I thought I got it all out."

"I caught the scent of turpentine."

Now she looked upset. "I think that's my perfume. I can't understand it. It smelled so nice in the store. I don't use turps. I use mineral spirits."

"My name is Vincent."

"I'm Derra."

They made their way to the single Vernio work exhibited. Vincent was pleased with the brilliance and clarity his work still held. Derra was awed. "Every person in that mural reminds me of someone I know."

"Me too."

"Vernio was the greatest artist who ever lived."

"Yes, I've heard that."

"Almost the entire Vernio collection is owned by Nolan Marcus. He only releases one in a terrible long while. That one sold for twelve million credits. Vernio would have traded it for a sandwich."

"Oh?"

"All great artists are never appreciated until they are dead."

"Vernio managed to amass some fame during his lifetime."

"Still, I think it's terrible that somebody is making fortunes off his work while Vernio starved to death. He did, you know, starve to death in his garret in Rome. That's kind of romantic."

"It is not bad that art collectors profit." Vincent strove to keep his voice neutral. "The problems arise when the patron trys to order the artist to paint what is profitable. Anyway, I thought Vernio died of cancer in Newark, New Jersey."

"What a strange idea."

Vincent bent down and scooped a paintbrush off the carpet. He had leaned the paintbrush against the door-jamb when he left. Now it was on the floor. Someone had been in his room. He frowned. They were keeping closer tabs on him than he had expected. Still, they wouldn't dare try anything while the painting was still unfinished. He uncovered it and scanned it carefully. No, no damage. Coming along nicely. It had taken weeks of saving to obtain the proper canvasboard. The right paints, on the other hand, had been quite reasonable. And the electronic easel had been wonderful for doing the preliminary outlines and sketches. Unscrewing three tubes, he squeezed globs of pigment onto a palette and mixed them in small bright circles with a plastic spoon. The paint hardened rapidly and he worked with quick, short strokes, his brush dancing across the canvas in skips and jumps, tiny beads of color flicking to his face and hands. He hummed a little as he worked.

The aircraft factory no longer built aircraft. It built large space station components. Vincent put down his airbrush and tugged on his dust mask. The shift supervisor came over, a big man that everyone called Rock. "Safety glasses, Vince."

"Okay."

"I mean it. We got a bunch of executives coming through. Nolan Marcus and some of the other bigwigs. So look sharp."

"Seems like I've heard that name before."

"Sure. He owns this company and just about half the world. One of the power elite."

When the clique of executives came through Vincent had resumed spraying sheets of violet mylar with a selenium compound. "We are manufacturing solar panels in this division," Rock told them. "Most of these will go to the Capricorn station. They are made of a lightweight plastic coated with a photoelectric chemical."

An executive said, "Why is the plastic purple?"

"I don't know."

Vincent removed his dust mask. "The violet end of the visible spectrum contains the higher-energy photons. With a violet coating there is more tendency for these photons to be reflected onto the energy-generating surfaces."

Nolan Marcus leaned forward. "Very interesting, Mr. . . . ah?"

"Vincent."

"Mr. Vincent. Do you have a knowledge of optics?"

"No," Vincent said. "I know something about color."

Derra's one-room apartment was wall-to-wall with pictures: her own work, and a lot of prints. An art catalog lay open on the couch; he leaned over for a closer look. Ah, yes. Brittly. Vincent had been present at his first show, a wispy, sallow kid who had yet to sell his first watercolor. He would ask Derra about Brittly and some of his contemporaries. He continued to flip through the book, stopping in sudden recognition. Hurriedly he scanned the caption. ". . . several unsuccessful lawsuits against his corporate patrons resulted in his being prohibited from selling his own paintings. These sketches (plates 36–39), which have never been released to the public, indicate that he was planning a major work at the time of his death."

Derra came back in holding a bag of ice cubes. "Let there be ice. Want a drink?"

Vincent closed the book. "Sure. I see you're using natural fiber brushes now."

"Yes, cat hair. And they're costing me a fortune. I don't know why I let you talk me into using them. I keep thinking of poor little cats with their tails cut off."

"Have you started mixing your own black?"

"That too. At least I can see the difference there."

"The brushes will make a difference too. But your technique must improve first to where that kind of subtlety will reflect in paint."

"I think I have a while to go." Derra uncovered her latest landscape in progress and sighed. "Years to go."

"Uh oh," said Vincent. "Bad scene."

Derra turned instantly defensive. "What's wrong with it?"

"It's fine, it's a good strong composition." In fact, he

thought Derra showed excellent talent. "But you're using cadmium yellow."

"Well, so what? Cadmium yellow holds its color."

"Except you're mixing it with flake white, which contains lead. And cadmium yellow contains sulfur. Eventually they will darken and distort the picture."

Derra pouted. "But I'm not painting for posterity. Unless you're another van Gogh, what difference does it make?"

Vincent was silent.

"I guess I'll switch to zinc white anyway." She handed Vincent his drink. "Does it ever bother you?"

"What?"

'Well, working on an assembly line and living in a one-room, and the people who ignored you in your . . . uh . . . first life got rich off your paintings."

Vincent raised an arm to his forehead dramatically. "Ah, to be an artist one truly has to suffer."

"Now you're making fun of me."

"Derra. I wish you would rid yourself of these starving-artist cliches. I had no small reputation then. I sold paintings, I taught, I lectured. My work was critically acclaimed."

"But that was nothing compared to now. You may have been respected as an artist, but no one considered you one of the great masters."

Vincent was quiet a long while. Finally he said in a voice almost too low for Derra to hear, "*I* did."

The taxi let Vincent off on the roof of his apartment, then dropped two hundred stories into the darkness. He punched the code into the lock and let himself in. A few stars shone through the skylight. They had been in his room again, he could tell. He went to the electronic easel and ran off one copy of each of his sketches, carefully signing and dating each one as it came out of the printer, knowing how important these would be to art historians.

They would know the painting was almost finished. Then what. Would they make their move, or wait?

Vincent took the best of the sketches, rolled it into a mailing tube, and addressed it to Derra. He didn't think they would wait long.

"Slow down, Vince. You're building up a sweat." Rock crossed over the factory floor. "And it's almost break time."

"Sure. I'll just finish this one off."

Rock watched him move the airbrush in tight arcs. "That's the eighth panel you've sprayed today, Vince. The last guy only got six the whole day. And that was on a good day."

"I like to get into a rhythm."

"It cost the company almost nothing to make these panels and they sell them for thousands. You get the same few bucks of that whether you produce six panels or nine. So why sweat to make Nolan Marcus richer?"

"Have you ever considered satisfaction in a job well done?"

"I'd get just as much satisfaction if I made a few bucks more and the company a few less out of it."

Vincent stood back from his painting. He moved from side to side and examined it from every angle, then stepped forward, his eyes only an inch from the canvasboard, and scrutinized the brush work. Finally he stood back, satisfied. The painting was finished. When one has dreamed a painting for a hundred years, there can be no doubt.

"Truly your finest creation. Indeed, your old sketches were but a taste of what was to come."

Vincent turned slowly, neither feeling nor showing surprise at the sudden voice. He recognized the figure in the doorway, although he had seen Nolan Marcus only once before. "I thought I'd hear from you sooner or later, but I didn't think you would come in person. I suppose I should feel honored. You must have been keeping pretty close tabs on me, to time it this well."

Nolan Marcus spoke as though he hadn't heard. "I hope you don't mind my letting myself in." He crossed in front of Vincent and contemplated the painting. "Wonderful. I can't tell you what a privilege it has been watching this grow. Exquisite combinations of form and color. Fraught with subtle meaning. And of course, the famous signature. Vincent. No last name. Like Twiggy or Makila. Rather egotistical, don't you think, to assume people will know who you are?"

Vincent shrugged. "No one ever paid twelve million for anything you painted."

Nolan's smile iced over. "No one ever paid *you* twelve million for a painting either." He scanned the painting again, then turned and faced Vincent squarely. "But you are right. As much as I enjoy my collection for its esthetic merits, I must bear in mind its value as an investment. This painting is worth far, far more than what it cost to revive you. Forgive me if I seem smug, but that was indeed one of my better business decisions."

"It's not for sale."

"On the other hand," continued Marcus, as if he hadn't heard, "the rarity of an artist's work contributes to its value. It is no coincidence that so many great works have become valuable only after their creators died. To the collector, the artist himself becomes a liability. No, I cannot be greedy. This painting, authenticated by the original sketches, will be quite sufficient."

"Don't try to bluff me, Marcus. You can't force me to sell this painting."

"Don't underestimate *me* . . . Vernio. I have no intention of offering you money." He pulled a small metal tube from his jacket. Vincent heard a pop of compressed air, felt the sting of an anesthetic dart. "Nonetheless, my family has controlled your work for five generations. I do not intend to break this tradition." There was no pain, only a patch of spreading numbness. His knees folded and he heard the voice only through the pounding in his ears. "Don't worry about the painting, Vernio. Just think how valuable it will be—when you wake up."

* * *

"The aging process of an oil painting is influenced in two ways," the chemist told Marcus. "First, there is the effect of sunlight, mostly the ultraviolet rays. Second, there is the reaction of the paint with the oxygen in the air. Now, because of Vernio's careful choice of pigments, his works deteriorate very little. Consequently, we can duplicate the effects of time without a lot of telltale chemicals."

"Good. How?"

The chemist showed Marcus a small pressurized chamber. "We'll put it in here. This contains a high-intensity UV light and ozone under pressure. Ozone is a particularly reactive oxygen molecule."

"How long will it take?"

"To age a painting one hundred years? A little over three weeks."

Three weeks later Nolan Marcus opened up the pressure chamber. The painting had crumbled to dust.

Vincent lay in supercooled inertia. He was not frozen this time; the state of the art was deep hibernation. A small computer monitored his vital signs, while a solid-state heat pump kept the temperature constant at twenty-two degrees below zero. Nolan Marcus had ordered the finest hibernaculum money could buy and time-locked it for two hundred years. A loop of laughter circled through Vincent's brain; he wondered when Marcus would find out the truth about his masterpiece. An undercoat of latex rubber was all it took, so simple really. Made a good base, too. But let nature do her stuff and within a decade it would dry out and crack like an old tire left in the desert.

"The finest thing I have ever done. Maybe the finest thing I ever will do. One hundred and twelve years ago it might have been recognized as such. Today it is hardly more than a traveler's check. I do not need posterity to judge me."

He dreamed of Derra. He never even had the chance to say goodbye. But perhaps he would see her work again. At least she mixed her own black.

Introduction to "King of All"

Harry Turtledove contends that he was inspired to write "King of All" by a New Destinies *editorial (Volume IV, Summer 1988). In it I propose legalizing all drugs on the grounds (amongst others), that: a) we are pretty close to a saturated market anyway, b) that the worst effects on society—as opposed to the users—are a result of laws not body chemistry, and c) that if you really want to suppress economic activity you tax it; and you can't tax it until you legalize it.*

Harry follows up with a warning about setting the tax rate too low.

KING OF ALL

Harry Turtledove

During his reign, Darius summoned some Greeks who were present and asked them how much money it would take for them to be willing to eat their fathers after they died. They said they would not do so for any amount of money. Afterwards, while the Greeks were there and listening to what was said through an interpreter, Darius summoned the Indians known as Callatiae, who do *eat their parents' bodies, and asked them how much they would take to cremate them. They set up a great outcry and told him not to talk that way. . . . And so it seems to me that Pindar was right when he said custom was king of all.*

—*Herodotus, III, 38*

By some accident, it was a slow day for the Hawthorne narcotics officers. The police force of the small South Bay city fought the same gain-one-foot-fall-back-two battle against drugs as the cops in any other Los Angeles suburb. Today, though, there seemed to be a truce.

Detective Ralph Sandars was making out an arrest report and listening to his lieutenant tell stories. Joe

Peroni had been a cop for going on thirty years, and seen just about everything. He had a way with a yarn, too.

"This was in the days when I was still riding a black-and-white," he was saying. "My partner and I got an assistance call. Turned out this fat old broad who lived in a little rented cottage way in the back of somebody's yard had tripped over a rug and busted her ankle.

"No way in hell to get the car back there, and I swear the gal musta weighed three hundred pounds easy. We got her up with one arm over each of our shoulders and started hauling her out. God, she was heavy. And just when we get her out the door, my partner, the smartass, turns to me and says, 'I think we're gonna hafta make two trips.' Christ, I laughed so hard I damn near dropped her."

Sandars chuckled. At the desk across from him, Willie Payne broke up so completely that he knocked a half-empty coke onto the floor with his arm. He hunted for a paper towel to use to clean it up.

"Way to go, graceful." Sandars beat three people to the needle. "Call that a sense of rhythm?"

"Up yours, honkie," Payne said without rancor. He looked like a linebacker, a mean one; nobody was ever stupid enough to get cute with him on the street. Beneath the forbidding exterior, though, he was milder than anyone who did not know him would have imagined.

He glanced over at Sandars. "What time you got, man?"

"A quarter to five," the other detective said. "Damn, is it that late already?"

"You better believe it. If things get any deader, they're gonna send us out to write tickets. Finish up that BS you're typing and call it a day."

"Sounds good. I don't remember the last time I worked an eight-hour turn in eight hours." Sandars pounded away, two-fingered, at the cranky old manual, interrupting himself a couple of times to say hello to the evening crew as they drifted in.

Peroni was already gone when he finished the report. He tossed it onto the lieutenant's desk, threw on his jacket, loosened his tie, and went out to the parking lot behind the station. Two uniformed officers just heading out on patrol waved to him as he climbed into his Plymouth.

He went east to Hawthorne Boulevard, turned right to travel south along it, skirting the mall, until he came to El Segundo. He turned left there, drove past the Mexican chicken place called, God help us, Marco Pollo, past the McDonald's that would probably put it out of business one day soon, past Prairie Avenue to Yukon, where he turned right again.

The neighborhood was one of old houses, new condos, and apartment buildings rapidly approaching middle age. Sandars lived in one of the latter, in a one-bedroom place he'd had since his divorce five years before. In that time his rent had gone from $370 a month to $610.

He kept the apartment astringently neat, probably a holdover from his service days, although he had been out of the Army . . . Christ! was it twelve years now? It was indeed, he thought soberly as he hung up his suit and put on a pair of jeans and a T-shirt.

He slapped his belly with more than a little pride. The jeans were the same size he had worn in high school. He plucked his TV off the top of his desk and toted it into the kitchen with him so he could watch the news while he was making dinner. His cooking, like a good deal of the rest of his life, was functional but unexciting. He took a steak out of the refrigerator, dusted it with pepper, salt, and thyme, stuck it in the broiler. A package of frozen peas and carrots went into boiling water on top of the stove. He cracked a can of Bud while he waited for the steak to be ready to turn.

The news was doing a feature on the umpty-ump massage parlors and escort services that operated near the airport. Sweeps month, Sandars thought sourly. Sex brings in the ratings.

He turned down the fire under his vegetables. The

five o'clock news crew got up and left, to be replaced by a new set of pretty faces. For some reason, all the men on the six o'clock news had gray hair—even the weatherman, who couldn't have been over thirty-five.

The lady reporter with them was a blonde. She announced some of the lead stories, then said, "Our special report for this evening"—of course the six o'clock news had a special report different from the one the five o'clock news had done—"will be the first of a three-part series on the newest 'in' drug among the affluent upper middle class." The screen cut to a closeup of plastic bags full of white powder.

Sandars rolled his eyes. His opinion of TV news coverage of drug abuse was, to say the least, unkind. So was almost any cop's.

He perked up when one of the gray-haired newsmen said, "Our feature tonight, Kristin, ties in with one of the day's big stories. Federal agents today seized more than a hundred kilograms of uncut caffeine, with a street value of almost $8,000,000, in a raid on a ship tied up at San Pedro Harbor."

"Hurrah for the good guys," Sandars said, pulling at his beer. He took a bottle of A-1 sauce out of the refrigerator, turned off the broiler and got out his steak, drained the peas and carrots.

When he put dinner on the table, the TV was showing the vessel from which the illegal drugs had been taken. It was a dingy little freighter, with the name *Libertad* stenciled on its side. Men in three-piece suits were walking about on deck.

"In custody are the captain of the *Libertad,* Rafael Ramos; his first mate, Jorge Antonio San Martín; and three more from the crew of seventeen," the newsman said. "Although the *Libertad* is registered in Panama, all the crew members are Colombian citizens."

"What a surprise," Sandars said around a mouthful of steak. Most of the caffeine smuggled into the States came from Colombia.

Sandars finished eating and did the dishes while the consumer reporter talked about how not to be ripped off buying a toaster-oven and the weatherman showed tape of a flood in Utah and said that it would be a couple of degrees warmer tomorrow, with first-stage ozone alerts likely in the San Fernando Valley. Hawthorne, thank God, got the sea breeze and wasn't very smoggy.

The grayhaired sportscaster had a link to Dodger Stadium. He asked the Dodger manager what the team would have to do to break out of its slump. "We gotta start hitting, and we can't afford to keep making as many errors as we have been," said the manager, who looked like a pork roast in a uniform. That much Sandars could have figured out for himself.

After a commercial break, the blonde newswoman said, "And now, as we promised, the first part of our special report on a rapidly growing problem drug—caffeine."

The plastic bags full of white powder reappeared on the screen. A voiceover said, "Caff, the fiend, dust, ups, buzz, sleep-no-more—as with all illegal drugs, caffeine goes under many names. Call it what you will, an estimated 15,000,000 Americans have used it at least once; perhaps a third that many are regular users. Their demand for ever-increasing amounts of the chemical has created an illicit multibillion dollar industry."

The picture shifted to an evergreen bush with shiny leaves. "This is a cafe plant, whose fruit is the principal source of caffeine. Caffheads, as habitual users of caffeine are known, have a legend that the properties of the drug were discovered in the 1880s, when an Arab goatherd named Kaldi saw how frisky his flock became after eating cafe berries and tried them himself."

And that was bullshit too, Sandars thought, a legend surely invented to give a nasty habit a romantic-sounding origin. As for himself, he didn't know where caffeine had been used first, or when. He just wished it hadn't been.

"Although the Arabian peninsula and Ethiopia still grow cafe plants," the correspondent went on, "the biggest supplier of the drug in recent years has been Colombia."

There was a shot of a middle-aged man with a wide-brimmed straw hat and a bushy mustache. He was speaking Spanish; over his voice came that of the interpreter: "Yes, I grow cafe. Why not? They pay me more for it than for any other crop I can raise. I have seven children. They must eat, yes, and my wife?"

Sandars' mouth tightened. This Sr. Valdez might get $300 for a ton of cafe berries. That seemed like a lot of money to him, no doubt, but that ton would yield over a kilo of caffeine, which would eventually sell for nearly $80,000.

Actually, the TV people had their facts surprisingly straight. They went through the pulping, drying, and grinding processes, and the extraction of the caffeine from the fruit with dichloroethylene or trichloroethylene. Colombia winked at the processing labs. Sandars damned the Colombians to hell for that, but understood it—the people who ran them could afford lavish payoffs. A hidden camera got a shot of a huge mountain of discarded ground fruit outside a lab near Bogota.

"Advocates of legalizing caffeine point to what they term its valuable properties," the correspondent said. "It stimulates both the central nervous system and the heart, relaxes bronchial muscles, and acts as a mild diuretic. However, not all its effects are so benign. Here is Dr. Louis Goldman of the UCLA Medical Center."

Dr. Goldman was so bald that he resembled an egg with a big nose. He said, "Perhaps caffeine would be relatively harmless if it were used in doses of fifty to a hundred milligrams. As it is, though, 'caffheads' "—you could hear the quotation marks falling into place—"can go through several grams a day. And caffeine creates both a certain amount of physical dependence and a definite pattern of psychological addiction. The more you take, the more you want."

Wasn't that the sad and sorry truth, Sandars thought. If the word "jitters" hadn't already been in use, someone would have invented it to describe a caffhead coming off his drug.

Dr. Goldman went on, "Against the dubious benefits alleged for it, caffeine has a host of deleterious effects on the system. The most common symptom of caffeine abuse, of course, is insomnia. Because it is a stimulant, it can also create irritability and restlessness. Ringing in the ears has been reported, as have visions of flashing lights. Caffeine administered to an individual with gastric ulcers causes great distress.

"And these are the relative mild syndromes observed. Caffeine constricts blood vessels; even a small dose reduces blood flow to the brain by as much as twenty-five percent. Very large doses, in animals, can cause death from convulsions."

"Have deaths ever been confirmed in human subjects?" the reporter asked.

"Well, no," Goldman admitted reluctantly, "although one does hear stories of smugglers who swallow large amounts in balloons to evade customs, and then have the balloons burst . . . but confirmed, no. However, caffeine is still a dangerous drug. Not only does it have the profound physiological and psychological effects I've mentioned, but laboratory studies—again with animals—suggest that it may be linked to cancer of the pancreas."

"You would not use it yourself, I take it?"

Dr. Goldman's eyebrows rose. "Good heavens, no!"

The picture cut away to the blonde newswoman. "You've seen now the many reasons society frowns on caffeine use. Tomorrow we'll show you some of the people who ignore those reasons, and take a look at why. They—"

Sandars turned the set off in disgust. Just like TV news—sure as hell, they were going to spend the next two days romanticizing caffheads, and in the name of "fairness" destroy whatever good today's presentation had done.

The really infuriating thing was that the medical problems associated with caffeine were only the tip of the iceberg. The underground economy the caffeine trade fostered, the casual disregard for the law caffeine encouraged, the crimes committed by rival dealers and by people who needed money to buy it, those were the real issues. And TV paid no attention to them at all, simply because they were too complex to present in a neat three-minute segment.

The narcotics cop was still fuming at seven thirty, when the Dodger game came on the radio. The Dodgers played errorless ball; their bats came alive, just as the fat manager had hoped—and they lost, 8-7, because their pitching fell apart. Thoroughly annoyed, Sandars took a shower and went to bed.

He woke up the next morning stuck in low gear. He could not stop yawning as he dressed, and he was still doing it when he pulled into the McDonald's parking lot for breakfast.

"Help you, sir?" the girl behind the counter said.

"Yeah. Let me have a Sausage McMuffin, a side of hashbrowns, and a large coke. Gotta get myself going somehow."

"Yes, sir. Is that for here or to go?"

"For here."

"Okay." She handed him a tray, punched buttons on the register. "That'll be $2.24." He gave her a five-dollar bill, and was tucking his wallet back into his hip pocket when she came back with his order. "Here you are, sir. Have a good day."

"Thanks." He grabbed a section of the *Times* off the rack, sat down at one of the little two-person tables. As in a lot of fast-food places, his chair wasn't quite comfortable—they wanted you in and out ASAP. He opened the hunk of paper—it was the sports page, with sarcastic remarks about last night's Dodger game. The Angels had won. That was something.

He only glanced at the headlines. First things first. He picked up his coke and peeled off the foil lid. He raised the little plastic container to his nose, took a deep snort.

Wellbeing flowed through him. "That's more like it," he said out loud. He picked up the paper and started in on his breakfast.

Introduction

This was Robert's favorite story of all the stories he had written. What more need be said?

The Man Who Traveled in Elephants

Robert A. Heinlein

Rain streamed across the bus's window. John Watts peered out at wooded hills, content despite the weather. As long as he was rolling, moving, traveling, the ache of loneliness was somewhat quenched. He could close his eyes and imagine that Martha was seated beside him.

They had always traveled together; they had honeymooned covering his sales territory. In time they had covered the entire country—Route 66, with the Indians' booths by the highway, Route 1, up through the District, the Pennsylvania Turnpike, zipping in and out through the mountain tunnels, himself hunched over the wheel and Martha beside him, handling the maps and figuring the mileage to their next stop.

He recalled one of Martha's friends saying, "But, dear, don't you get tired of it?"

He could hear Martha's bubbly laugh. "With forty-eight wide and wonderful states to see, grow *tired?*

Besides, there is always something new—fairs and expositions and things."

"But when you've seen one fair you've seen them all."

"You think there is no difference between the Santa Barbara Fiesta and the Forth Worth Fat Stock Show? Anyhow," Martha had gone on, "Johnny and I are country cousins; we like to stare at the tall buildings and get freckles on the roofs of our mouths."

"Do be sensible, Martha." The woman had turned to him. "John, isn't it time that you two were settling down and making something out of your lives?"

Such people tired him. "It's for the 'possums," he had told her solemnly. "They like to travel."

"The opossums? What in the world is he talking about, Martha?"

Martha had shot him a private glance, then deadpanned, "Oh, I'm sorry! You see, Johnny raises baby 'possums in his umbilicus."

"I'm equipped for it," he had confirmed, patting his round stomach.

That had settled her hash! He had never been able to stand people who gave advice "for your own good."

Martha had read somewhere that a litter of new-born opposums would no more than fill a teaspoon and that as many as six in a litter were often orphans through lack of facilities in mother 'possum's pouch to take care of them all.

They had immediately formed the Society for the Rescue and Sustenance of the Other Six 'Possums, and Johnny himself had been unanimously selected—by Martha—as the site of Father Johnny's 'Possum Town.

They had had other imaginary pets, too. Martha and he had hoped for children; when none came, their family had filled out with invisible little animals: Mr. Jenkins, the little grey burro who advised them about motels, Chipmink the chattering chipmunk, who lived in the glove compartment, *Mus Followalongus* the traveling mouse, who never said anything but who would bite unexpectedly, especially around Martha's knees.

They were all gone now; they had gradually faded away for lack of Martha's gay, infectious spirit to keep them in health. Even Bindlestiff, who was not invisible, was no longer with him. Bindlestiff was a dog they had picked up beside the road, far out in the desert, given water and succor and received in return his large and uncritical heart. Bindlestiff had traveled with them thereafter, until he, too, had been called away, shortly after Martha.

John Watts wondered about Bindlestiff. Did he roam free in the Dog Star, in a land lush with rabbits and uncovered garbage pails? More likely he was with Martha, sitting on her feet and getting in the way. Johnny hoped so.

He sighed and turned his attention to the passengers. A thin, very elderly woman leaned across the aisle and said, "Going to the Fair, young man?"

He started. It was twenty years since anyone had called him "young man." "Unh? Yes, certainly." They were *all* going to the Fair: the bus was a special.

"You like going to fairs?"

"Very much." He knew that her inane remarks were formal gambits to start a conversation. He did not resent it; lonely old women have need of talk with strangers—and so did he. Besides, he liked perky old women. They seemed the very spirit of America to him, putting him in mind of church sociables and farm kitchens—and covered wagons.

"I like fairs, too," she went on. "I even used to exhibit—quince jelly and my Crossing-the-Jordan pattern."

"Blue ribbons, I'll bet."

"Some," she admitted, "but mostly I just liked to go to them. I'm Mrs. Alma Hill Evans. Mr. Evans was a great one for doings. Take the exposition when they opened the Panama Canal—but you wouldn't remember that."

John Watts admitted that he had not been there.

"It wasn't the best of the lot, anyway. The Fair of '93, there was a fair for you: There'll never be one that'll even be a patch on that one."

"Until this one, perhaps?"

"This one? Pish and tush! Size isn't everything." The All-American Exposition would certainly be the biggest thing yet—and the best. If only Martha were along, it would seem like heaven. The old lady changed the subject. "You're a traveling man, aren't you?"

He hesitated, then answered. "Yes."

"I can always tell. What line are you in, young man?"

He hesitated longer, then said flatly, "I travel in elephants."

She looked at him sharply and he wanted to explain, but loyalty to Martha kept his mouth shut. Martha had insisted that they treat their calling seriously, never explaining, never apologizing. They had taken it up when he had planned to retire; they had been talking of getting an acre of ground and doing something useful with radishes or rabbits, or such. Then, during their final trip over his sales route, Martha had announced after a long silence, "John, you don't want to stop traveling."

"Eh? Don't I? You mean we should keep the territory?"

"No, that's done. But we won't settle down, either."

"What do you want to do? Just gypsy around?"

"Not exactly. I think we need some new line to travel in."

"Hardware? Shoes? Ladies' ready-to-wear?"

"No." She had stopped to think. "We ought to travel in *something*. It gives point to your movements. I think it ought to be something that doesn't turn over too fast, so that we could have a really large territory, say the whole United States."

"Battleships perhaps?"

"Battleships are out of date, but that's close." Then they had passed a barn with a tattered circus poster. "I've got it!" She had shouted. "Elephants! We'll travel in elephants."

"Elephants, eh? Rather hard to carry samples."

"We don't need to. Everybody knows what an elephant looks like. Isn't that right, Mr. Jenkins?" The invisible burro had agreed with Martha, as he always did; the matter was settled.

Martha had known just how to go about it. "First we make a survey. We'll have to comb the United States from corner to corner before we'll be ready to take orders."

For ten years they had conducted the survey. It was an excuse to visit every fair, zoo, exposition, stock show, circus, or punkin doings anywhere, for were they not all prospective customers? Even national parks and other natural wonders were included in the survey, for how was one to tell where a pressing need for an elephant might turn up? Martha had treated the matter with a straight face and had kept a dog-eared notebook: "La Brea Tar Pits, Los Angeles—surplus of elephants, obsolete type, in these parts about 25,000 years ago." "Philadelphia—sell at least six to the Union League." "Brookfield Zoo, Chicago—African elephants, rare." "Gallup, New Mexico—stone elephants east of town, very beautiful." "Riverside, California, Elephant Barbershop—brace owner to buy mascot." "Portland, Oregon—query Douglas Fir Association. Recite *Road to Mandalay*. Same for Southern Pine group. N.B. this calls for trip to Gulf Coast as soon as we finish with rodeo in Laramie."

Ten years and they had enjoyed every mile of it. The survey was still unfinished when Martha had been taken. John wondered if she had buttonholed Saint Peter about the elephant situation in the Holy City. He'd bet a nickel she had.

But he could not admit to a stranger that traveling in elephants was just his wife's excuse for traveling around the country they loved.

The old woman did not press the matter. "I knew a man once who sold mongooses," she said cheerfully. "Or is it 'mongeese'? He had been in the exterminator business and—what does that driver think he is doing?"

The big bus had been rolling along easily despite the driving rain. Now it was swerving, skidding. It lurched sickeningly—and crashed.

John Watts banged his head against the seat in front.

He was picking himself up, dazed, not too sure where he was, when Mrs. Evans' thin, confident soprano oriented him. "Nothing to get excited about, folks. I've been expecting this—and you can see it didn't hurt a bit."

John Watts admitted that he himself was unhurt. He peered near-sightedly around, then fumbled on the sloping floor for his glasses. He found them, broken. He shrugged and put them aside; once they arrived he could dig a spare pair out of his bags.

"Now let's see what has happened," Mrs. Evans went on. "Come along, young man." He followed obediently.

The right wheel of the bus leaned drunkenly against the curb of the approach to a bridge. The driver was standing in the rain, dabbing at a cut on his cheek. "I couldn't help it," he was saying. "A dog ran across the road and I tried to avoid it."

"You might have killed us!" a woman complained.

"Don't cry till you're hurt," advised Mrs. Evans. "Now let's get back into the bus while the driver phones for someone to pick us up."

John Watts hung back to peer over the side of the canyon spanned by the bridge. The ground dropped away steeply; almost under him were large, mean-looking rocks. He shivered and got back into the bus.

The relief car came along very promptly, or else he must have dozed. The latter, he decided, for the rain had stopped and the sun was breaking through the clouds. The relief driver thrust his head in the door and shouted, "Come on, folks! Time's a-wastin'! Climb out and climb in." Hurrying, John stumbled as he got aboard. The new driver gave him a hand. " 'Smatter, Pop? Get shaken up?"

"I'm all right, thanks."

"Sure you are. Never better."

He found a seat by Mrs. Evans, who smiled and said, "Isn't it a heavenly day?"

He agreed. It *was* a beautiful day, now that the storm had broken. Great fleecy clouds tumbling up into warm blue sky, a smell of clean wet pavement, drenched fields and green things growing—he lay back and savored it. While he was soaking it up a great double rainbow formed and blazed in the eastern sky. He looked at them and made two wishes, one for himself and one for Martha. The rainbows' colors seemed to be reflected in everything he saw. Even the other passengers seemed younger, happier, better dressed, now that the sun was out. He felt light-hearted, almost free from his aching loneliness.

They were there in jig time; the new driver more than made up the lost minutes. A great arch stretched across the road: THE ALL-AMERICAN CELEBRATION AND EXPOSITION OF ARTS and under it PEACE AND GOOD WILL TO ALL. They drove through and sighed to a stop.

Mrs. Evans hopped up. "Got a date—must run!" She trotted to the door, then called back, "See you on the midway, young man," and disappeared in the crowd.

John Watts got out last and turned to speak to the driver. "Oh, uh, about my baggage. I want to—"

The driver had started his engine again. "Don't worry about your baggage," he called out. "You'll be taken care of." The huge bus moved away.

"But—" John Watts stopped; the bus was gone. All very well—but what was he to do without his glasses?

But there were sounds of carnival behind him, that decided him. After all, he thought, tomorrow will do. If anything is too far away for me to see, I can always walk closer. He joined the queue at the gate and went in.

It was undeniably the greatest show ever assembled for the wonderment of mankind. It was twice as big as all outdoors, brighter than bright lights, newer than new, stupendous, magnificent, breathtaking, awe inspiring, supercolossal, incredible—and a lot of fun. Every community in America had sent its own best to this amazing show. The marvels of P. T. Barnum, of Ripley, and of all Tom Edison's godsons had been gathered in one spot. From up and down a broad continent the riches of a richly endowed land and the products of a clever and industrious people had been assembled, along with their folk festivals, their annual blowouts, their celebrations, and their treasured carnival customs. The result was as American as strawberry shortcake and as gaudy as a Christmas tree, and it all lay there before him, noisy and full of life and crowded with happy, holiday people.

Johnny Watts took a deep breath and plunged into it.

He started with the Fort Worth Southwestern Exposition and Fat Stock Show and spent an hour admiring gentle, white-faced steers, as wide and square as flat-topped desks, scrubbed and curried, with their hair parted neatly from skull to base of spine, then day-old little black lambs on rubbery stalks of legs, too new to know themselves, fat ewes, their broad backs, paddled flatter and flatter by grave-eyed boys intent on blue ribbons. Next door he found the Pomona Fair with solid matronly Percherons and dainty Palominos from the Kellog Ranch.

And harness racing. Martha and he had always loved harness racing. He picked out a likely looking nag of the famous Dan Patch line, bet and won, then moved on, as there was so much more to see. Other county fairs were just beyond, apples from Yakima, the cherry festival from Beaumont and Banning, Georgia's peaches. Somewhere off beyond him a band was batting out, "Ioway, Ioway, that's where the tall corn grows!"

Directly in front of him was a pink cotton candy booth.

Martha had loved the stuff. Whether at Madison Square Garden or at Imperial County's fair grounds she had always headed first for the cotton candy booth. "The big size, honey?" he muttered to himself. He felt that if he were to look around he would see her nodding. "The large size, please," he said to the vendor.

The carnie was elderly, dressed in a frock coat and stiff shirt. He handled the pink gossamer with dignified grace. "Certainly, sir, there is no other size." He twirled the paper cornucopia and presented it. Johnny handed him a half dollar. The man flexed and opened his fingers; the coin disappeared. That appeared to end the matter.

"The candy is fifty cents?" Johnny asked diffidently.

"Not at all, sir." The old showman plucked the coin from Johnny's lapel and handed it back. "On the house—I see you are with it. After all, what is money?"

"Why, thank you, but, uh, I'm not really 'with it,' you know."

The old man shrugged. "If you wish to go incognito, who am I to dispute you? But your money is no good here."

"Uh, if you say so."

"You will see."

He felt something brush against his leg. It was a dog of the same breed, or lack of breed, as Bindlestiff had been. It looked amazingly like Bindlestiff. The dog looked up and waggled its whole body.

"Why, hello, old fellow!" He patted it—then his eyes blurred; it even felt like Bindlestiff. "Are you lost, boy? Well, so am I. Maybe we had better stick together, eh? Are you hungry?"

The dog licked his hand. He turned to the cotton candy man. "Where can I buy hot dogs?"

"Just across the way, sir."

He thanked him, whistled to the dog, and hurried across. "A half dozen hot dogs, please."

"Coming up! Just mustard, or everything on?"

"Oh, I'm sorry. I want them raw, they are for a dog."

"I getcha. Just a sec."

Presently he was handed six wienies, wrapped in paper. "How much are they?"

"Compliments of the house."

"I beg pardon?"

"Every dog has his day. This is his."

"Oh. Well, thank you." He became aware of increased noise and excitement behind him and looked around to see the first of the floats of the Priests of Pallas, from Kansas City, coming down the street. His friend the dog saw it, too, and began to bark.

"Quiet, old fellow." He started to unwrap the meat. Someone whistled across the way; the dog darted between the floats and was gone. Johnny tried to follow, but was told to wait until the parade had passed. Between floats he caught glimpses of the dog, leaping up on a lady across the way. What with the dazzling lights of the floats and his own lack of glasses he could not see her clearly, but it was plain that the dog knew her; he was greeting her with the all-out enthusiasm only a dog can achieve.

He held up the package and tried to shout to her; she waved back, but the band music and the noise of the crowd made it impossible to hear each other. He decided to enjoy the parade, then cross and find the pooch and its mistress as soon as the last float had passed.

It seemed to him the finest Priests of Pallas parade he had ever seen. Come to think about it, there hadn't been a Priests of Pallas parade in a good many years. Must have revived it just for this.

That was like Kansas City—a grand town. He didn't know of any he liked as well. Possibly Seattle. And New Orleans, of course.

And Duluth—Duluth was swell. And so was Memphis. He would like to own a bus someday that ran from Memphis to Saint Joe, from Natchez to Mobile, wherever the wide winds blow.

Mobile—there was a town.

The parade was past now, with a swarm of small boys tagging after it. He hurried across.

The lady was not there, neither she, nor the dog. He looked quite thoroughly. No dog. No lady with a dog.

He wandered off, his eyes alert for marvels, but his thoughts on the dog. It really had been a great deal like Bindlestiff . . . and he wanted to know the lady it belonged to—anyone who could love that sort of a dog must be a pretty good sort herself. Perhaps he could buy her ice cream, or persuade her to go the midway with him. Martha would approve he was sure. Martha would know he wasn't up to anything.

Anyhow, no one ever took a little fat man seriously.

But there was too much going on to worry about it. He found himself at St. Paul's Winter Carnival, marvelously constructed in summer weather through the combined efforts of York and American. For fifty years it had been held in January, yet here it was, rubbing shoulders with the Pendleton Round-Up, the Fresno Raisin Festival, and Colonial Week in Annapolis. He got in at the tail end of the ice show, but in time for one of his favorite acts, the Old Smoothies, out of retirement for the occasion and gliding as perfectly as ever to the strains of *Shine On, Harvest Moon*.

His eyes blurred again and it was not his lack of glasses.

Coming out he passed a large sign: SADIE HAWKINS DAY—STARTING POINT FOR BACHELORS. He was tempted to take part: perhaps the lady with the dog might be among the spinsters. But he was a little tired by now; just ahead there was an outdoor carnival of the pony-ride-and-ferris-wheel sort; a moment later he was on the merry-go-round and was climbing gratefully into one of those swan gondolas so favored by parents. He found a young man already seated there, reading a book.

"Oh, excuse me," said Johnny. "Do you mind?"

"Not at all," the young man answered and put his book down. "Perhaps you are the man I'm looking for."

"You are looking for someone?"

"Yes. You see, I'm a detective. I've always wanted to be one and now I am."

"Indeed?"

"Quite. Everyone rides the merry-go-round eventually, so it saves trouble to wait here. Of course, I hang around Hollywood and Vine, or Times Square, or Canal Street, but here I can sit and read."

"How can you read while watching for someone?"

"Ah, I know what is in the book—" He held it up; it was *The Hunting of the Snark*. "—so that leaves my eyes free for watching."

Johnny began to like this young man. "Are there boojums about?"

"No, for we haven't softly and silently vanished away. But would we notice it if we did? I must think it over. Are you a detective, too?"

"No, I—uh—I travel in elephants."

"A fine profession. But not much for you here. We have giraffes—" He raised his voice above the music of the calliope and let his eyes rove around the carousel. "—camels, two zebras, plenty of horses, but no elephants. Be sure to see the Big Parade; there will be elephants."

"Oh, I wouldn't miss it!"

"You mustn't. It will be the most amazing parade in all time, so long that it will never pass a given point and every mile choked with wonders more stupendous than the last. You're sure you're not the man I'm looking for."

"I don't think so. But see here—how would you go about finding a lady with a dog in this crowd?"

"Well, if she comes here, I'll let you know. Better go down on Canal Street. Yes, I think if I were a lady with a dog I'd be down on Canal Street. Women love to mask; it means they can unmask."

Johnny stood up. "How do I get to Canal Street?"

"Straight through Central City past the opera house, then turn right at the Rose Bowl. Be careful then, for you pass through the Nebraska section with Ak-Sar-Ben in full sway. Anything could happen. After that, Calaveras County—Mind the frogs!—then Canal Street."

"Thank you so much." He followed the directions, keeping an eye out for a lady with a dog. Nevertheless he stared with wonder at the things he saw as he threaded through the gay crowds. He did see a dog, but it was a seeing-eye dog—and that was a great wonder, too, for the live clear eyes of the dog's master could and did see everything that was going on around him, yet the man and the dog traveled together with the man letting the dog direct their way, as if no other way of travel were conceivable, or desired, by either one.

He found himself in Canal Street presently and the illusion was so complete that it was hard to believe that he had not been transported to New Orleans. Carnival was at height; it was Fat Tuesday here; the crowds were masked. He got a mask from a street vendor and went on.

The hunt seemed hopeless. The street was choked by merry-makers watching the parade of the Krewe of Venus. It was hard to breathe, much harder to move and search. He eased into Bourbon Street—the entire French Quarter had been reproduced—when he saw the dog.

He was sure it was the dog. It was wearing a clown suit and a little peaked hat, but it looked like his dog. He corrected himself; it looked like Bindlestiff.

And it accepted one of the frankfurters gratefully. "Where is she, old fellow?" The dog woofed once, then darted away into the crowd. He tried to follow, but could not; he required more clearance. But he was not downhearted; he had found the dog once, he would find him again. Besides, it had been at a masked ball that he had first met Martha, she a graceful Pierrette, he a fat Pierrot. They had watched the dawn come up after the ball and before the sun had set again they had agreed to marry.

He watched the crowd for Pierrettes, sure somehow that the dog's mistress would costume so.

Everything about this fair made him think even more about Martha, if that were possible. How she had traveled his territory with him, how it had been their habit to start out, anywhere, whenever a vacation came along. Chuck the Duncan Hines guide and some bags in the car and be off. Martha . . . sitting beside him with the open highway a broad ribbon before them . . . singing their road song *America the Beautiful* and keeping him on key: "—thine alabaster cities gleam, undimmed by human tears—"

Once she had said to him, while they were bowling along through—where was it? The Black Hills? The Ozarks? The Poconos? No matter. She had said, "Johnny, you'll never be President and I'll never be First Lady, but I'll bet we know more about the United States than any President ever has. Those busy, useful people never have time to *see* it, not really."

"It's a wonderful country, darling."

"It is, it is indeed. I could spend all eternity just traveling around in it—traveling in elephants, Johnny, with you."

He had reached over and patted her knee; he remembered how it felt.

The revellers in the mock French Quarter were thinning out; they had drifted away while he daydreamed. He stopped a red devil. "Where is everyone going?"

"To the parade, of course."

"The Big Parade?"

"Yes, it's forming now." The red devil moved on, he followed.

His own sleeve was plucked. "Did you find her?" It was Mrs. Evans, slightly disguised by a black domino and clinging to the arm of a tall and elderly Uncle Sam.

"Eh? Why, hello, Mrs. Evans! What do you mean?"

"Don't be silly. Did you find her?"

"How did you know I was looking for anyone?"

"Of course you were. Well, keep looking. We must go now." They trailed after the mob.

The Big Parade was already passing by the time he reached its route. It did not matter, there was endlessly more to come. The Holly, Colorado, Boosters were passing; they were followed by the prize Shriner drill team. Then came the Veiled Prophet of Khorassan and his Queen of Love and Beauty, up from their cave in the bottom of the Mississippi . . . the Anniversary Day Parade from Brooklyn, with the school children carrying little American flags . . . the Rose Parade from Pasadena, miles of flower-covered floats . . . the Indian Powwow from Flagstaff, twenty-two nations represented and no buck in the march wearing less than a thousand dollars worth of hand-wrought jewelry. After the indigenous Americans rode Buffalo Bill, goatee jutting out and hat in hand, locks flowing in the breeze. Then was the delegation from Hawaii with King Kamehamela himself playing Alii, Lord of Carnival, with royal abandon, while his subjects in dew-fresh leis pranced behind him, giving aloha to all.

There was no end. Square dancers from Ojai and from upstate New York, dames and gentleman from Annapolis, the Cuero, Texas, Turkey Trot, all the Krewes and marching clubs of old New Orleans, double flambeaux blazing, nobles throwing favors to the crowd—the King of Zulus and his smooth brown court, singing: "Everybody who was anybody doubted it—"

And the Mummers came, "taking a suit up the street" to *Oh Dem Golden Slippers*. Here was something older than the country celebrating it, the shuffling jig of the masquers, a step that was young when mankind was young and first celebrating the birth of spring. First the fancy clubs, whose captains wore capes worth a king's ransom—or a mortgage on a row house—with fifty pages to bear them. Then the Liberty Clowns and the other comics and lastly the ghostly, sweet string bands whose strains bring tears.

Johnny thought back to '44 when he had first seen them march, old men and young boys, because the proper "shooters" were away to war. And of something that should not be on Broad Street in Philadelphia on the first day of January, men riding in the parade because, merciful Heaven forgive us, they could not walk.

He looked and saw that there were indeed automobiles in the line of march—wounded of the last war, and one G.A.R., hat square, hands folded over the head of his cane. Johnny held his breath and waited. When each automobile approached the judges' stand, it stopped short of it, and everyone got out. Somehow, with each other's help, they hobbled or crawled past the judging line, under their own power—and each club's pride was kept intact.

There followed another wonder—they did not get back into the automobiles, but marched on up Broad Street.

Then it was Hollywood Boulevard, disguised as Santa Claus Lane, in a production more stupendous than movieland had ever attempted before. There were baby stars galore and presents and favors and candy for all the children and all the grown up children, too. When, at last, Santa Claus's own float arrived, it was almost too large to be seen, a veritable iceberg, almost the North Pole itself, with John Barrymore and Mickey Mouse riding one on each side of Saint Nicholas.

On the tail end of the great, icy float was a pathetic little figure. Johnny squinted and recognized Mr. Emmett Kelly, dean of all clowns, in his role as Weary Willie. Willie was not merry—oh, no, he was shivering. Johnny did not know whether to laugh or to cry. Mr. Kelly had always affected him that way.

And the elephants came.

Big elephants, little elephants, middle-sized elephants, from pint-sized Wrinkles to mighty Jumbo . . . and with them the bull men. Chester Conklin, P. T. Barnum, Wallie Beery, Mowgli. "This," Johnny said to himself, "must be Mulberry Street."

There was a commotion on the other side of the column; one of the men was shooing something away. Then Johnny saw what it was—the dog. He whistled; the animal seemed confused, then it spotted him, scampered up, and jumped into Johnny's arms. "You stay with me," Johnny told him. "You might have gotten stepped on."

The dog licked his face. He had lost his clown suit, but the little peaked cap hung down under his neck. "What have you been up to?" asked Johnny. "And where is your mistress?"

The last of the elephants were approaching, three abreast, pulling a great carriage. A bugle sounded up front and the procession stopped. "Why are they stopping?" Johnny asked a neighbor.

"Wait a moment. You'll see."

The Grand Marshal of the march came trotting back down the line. He rode a black stallion and was himself brave in villain's boots, white pegged breeches, cutaway, and top hat. He glanced all around.

He stopped immediately in front of Johnny. Johnny held the dog more closely to him. The Grand Marshal dismounted and bowed. Johnny looked around to see who was behind him. The Marshal removed his tall silk hat and caught Johnny's eye. "You, sir, are the Man who Travels in Elephants?" It was more a statement than a question.

"Uh? Yes."

"Greetings, Rex! Serene Majesty, your Queen and your court await you." The man turned slightly, as if to lead the way.

Johnny gulped and gathered Bindlestiff under one arm. The Marshal led him to the elephant-drawn carriage. The dog slipped out of his arms and bounded up into the carriage and into the lap of the lady. She patted it and looked proudly, happily, down at Johnny Watts. "Hello, Johnny! Welcome home, darling!"

"Martha!" he sobbed—and Rex stumbled and climbed into his carriage to embrace his queen.

The sweet voice of a bugle sounded up ahead, the parade started up again, wending its endless way—

Introduction

Science fiction is dedicated to the open-ended proposition "What if." So it seems fitting to wonder what the world might have been like if the field's greatest practitioner had directed his talents toward some other endeavor. One consequence is obvious, of course: science ficiton would have been infinitely the poorer for it. Heinlein thought up everything*!*

But there's another side to the coin. His prodigious talent and unique ability to see to the heart of things would surely have come into play regardless of what he had turned his hand to. Appropriately, what starts out as an appreciation by two well-known scientists becomes a thought-experiment in what if . . .

FAREWELL TO THE MASTER

Dr. Yoji Kondo and Dr. Charles Sheffield

We sincerely wish that this article could have been delayed well into the next century. Robert Heinlein once predicted that by the twenty-first century either the so-called civilization of ours or he would be gone from this planet. He was too great and gentle a soul to want the first option; *he* departed from us instead. It is up to the rest of us to make sure that the still-impending doomsday does not happen.

Robert Anson Heinlein was a multi-dimensional, many-faceted man; a great writer, thinker, and visionary. We were both privileged to know him personally. We felt honored to be included in the "Heinlein list" given in *The Number of the Beast*, and one of us (YK) has an alter-ego in *The Cat Who Walks Through Walls*. However, perhaps no one except his wife Ginny understood and appreciated all his many sides. We saw only one or two aspects of the man, and mostly in a context little

("Farewell To the Master" is the title of a story by Harry Bates that was made into one of the best-ever science fiction movies, The Day The Earth Stood Still. Bates's original title here seems the most appropriate one possible.)

to do with science fiction. In terms of his long life and long science fiction career, our acquaintance was also relatively recent (since 1979), but we were very impressed by what we saw. What follows is our personal and perhaps biased view.

In our minds there is no doubt at all that Heinlein was and is *the* Grand Master of science fiction. What science fiction is today, including its general acceptance within society, came largely through his efforts.

More than anyone else, he gave the field broad readership and *credibility*. He had the mind of a poet, engineer, and scientist, and that combination made it possible for him to create stories of a realistic future which were personally engrossing and technologically fascinating. He had an excellent relationship with working scientists, characterized by mutual respect and appreciation, and since he spoke the language of science, and liked to talk to and listen to scientists, it should be no surprise to find that his stories are always firmly rooted in today's science, and offer rational projections for the science of tomorrow.

His books enthralled millions of readers throughout the world, and inspired them to aim high—including aiming for the stars. Without the enthusiasm for space exploration engendered by Heinlein and others who followed the trail that he blazed, the coming of the space age might have been delayed substantially. It is certain that a number of our professional colleagues would have followed different career paths, had they not in their youth been stimulated by the science fiction of space exploration.

Heinlein is read first for the simple joy of exciting stories. The scientific and technological background, with an art that conceals art, is so skillfully introduced that its arrival is seldom noticed. This, perhaps, is the reason that Heinlein is not usually the name that comes first to mind when people talk about "hard science fiction" writers. However, the hard science is always there. For example, the orbit descriptions given in his early novels could be written only by someone who understood celestial mechanics. And one of Heinlein's lasting legacies is the introduction of the term "free fall." No one else has ever produced a term that describes the physical condition so psychologically precisely and yet so accurately. The common alternative, "weightlessness," is misleading, since people tend (wrongly) to identify weight with mass, and body mass is unchanged during free fall.

The impressions of exciting stories and cleverly-presented science come early. When we re-read Heinlein, we find increasingly that there is much more. His stories are filled with thought-provoking views on the nature of human beings. Since his perspectives are often in conflict with the conventional wisdom of both "liberals" and "conservatives," it is not surprising that Heinlein has been regarded by his critics as both a reactionary and a radical.

His protagonists espouse philosophies fundamental to the continuation of the human species—survive, and thrive—but at the same time his heroes and heroines are always compassionate. Heinlein would never admit as hero a person who was a bully, or truly evil, or apathetic, or mediocre. His love for personal strength of character, combined with societies permitting maximum freedom and independence of the individual, often leads him to be identified with libertarianism. We feel that an attempt to fit him into any sort of *ism* does the man an injustice. He found his fellow humans a constant source of compassion and amusement, and he accepted them as *humans,* not plaster saints or devils. He did not pretend them to be what they are not, although the fashion among ideologues of all sorts tends to take the opposite viewpoint.

The first time we each met Heinlein was in Washington, D.C., in July 1979. He had been testifying to a Joint Session of the Congressional Committees on Aging and on Science and Technology, and we were invited to join him and his wife (separately—we did not at the time know each other) for lunch and for dinner. Our mutual agent, Eleanor Wood, arranged this for CS, and Heinlein arranged it with YK whom he had corresponded and spoken with through the introduction of his brother, retired general Lawrence Heinlein. We had enjoyed Heinlein's fiction for many years, but did not have a clear idea what the man himself would be like. It quickly turned out that the last subject that he wanted to talk about was science fiction, although when one of us (YK) mentioned that he had been spoiled by reading only Heinlein books lately, Heinlein quickly recommended the names of several authors and their books. All the books he recommended were good reading—but not so easy to obtain. It was necessary to wander as far north as Montreal to find all of them.

After some discussion of the aging process, which he had studied far more than we had (he joked that at his age it was a necessity), the talk turned to the manned and unmanned space programs of the world. It was clear that he already knew a surprising (surprising to us then; not now) amount about it. He quizzed one of us (CS) politely but in great detail on the past, present, and probable future of remote sensing of the Earth from space, and put his finger on the key problems that might arise if the U.S. program should be moved to commercial operation. (It was; they did arise, and they have not yet been solved!)

Soon after our first meetings with Heinlein, we were pleased to receive an invitation to join him and Ginny in Annapolis for his 50th class reunion at the Naval Academy. There, amid a group of aging captains and admirals, the conversation concerned itself not at all with science fiction. It was on the nature and function of the modern navy. Heinlein's own naval career had been cut short when he was invalided out in the early 1930s, defined as "totally and permanently disabled" with tuberculosis. However, his interest in naval matters was undiminished. It was fascinating to hear him, long before the Falklands War in 1982, expressing his misgivings about the vulnerability of conventional battleships, even equipped with the most modern defenses, to airborne missiles. He gave very precise reasons for his concern. We had the feeling that a couple of his old naval colleagues didn't care for the direction of his argument, but they could not refute it. Heinlein had, as an old bearded Navy colleague said with a twinkle in his eye at the 55th Reunion of his Academy Class, "the annoying habit of knowing the facts."

That same Annapolis party offered a glimpse of another side of Heinlein's character. He told us that American culture did not allow men to cry, and that since crying is good for the soul, he had to teach himself how to weep. YK pointed out that in Japan, a man is permitted to cry in certain special circumstances; one might cry, for example, at the death of one's mother, or a general might cry at the news of the death of a worthy adversary. Someone present said "That's gallant!", and Heinlein seemed to agree.

It was at the same 55th reunion that Heinlein proved that neither disease nor major brain surgery had affected his mental abilities. He gave a party, and as each new arrival came in he would introduce the newcomer to everyone in the room, by name—and he continued to do this, without error, until there were at least thirty people present. We should point out that these were not people he previously knew; many were guests of other Academy graduates, whom he was meeting for the first time.

Heinlein was also a regular participant at the Citizen's Advisory Council on National Space Policy. He said little, compared with some of the others present, but what he did say carried great weight. More than almost anyone, Heinlein had the property of *gravitas*, which made everyone who came into contact with him take him seriously. And with good reason. He knew a lot, he had thought about what he knew, and he was endlessly inventive.

We found in our subsequent conversations with him that he was at home with all sorts of subjects, and liked to discuss them either in person or over the phone. The topics ranged from contemporary problems of physics and astronomy, to Zen and the classic (2,500 years old) book on strategy by Sung-tsu. He understood the essence, if not always the technical details, of each subject. He was willing to study those details, if necessary, even when they were tedious. However, his intuition and intellect generally took him quickly to the heart of problems, unhampered by superficial or "authoritative" versions that were not logically self-consistent.

In the world of action, Heinlein was a fencing champion and a master marksman while he was a cadet at the Naval Academy. He also took the "rough-and-tumble" hand-to-hand combat course, which combined the essence of several martial arts. He preferred realistic fighting to sports. To him, fighting was a serious business, to be taken seriously. A student of martial arts can tell that the fighting scenes in Heinlein books are written by an author who really knew how a fight must be won. With the recommendation of YK, Robert Heinlein was accorded the honorary rank of a black-belt in aikido on his eightieth birthday, for his embodiment of the spirit and his exceptional understanding of the principles of the martial arts.

Robert Anson Heinlein died two months before his 81st birthday, which would have fallen on July 7th, 1988. His remains were cremated and his ashes strewn at sea with full military honors. It was a fitting farewell to the grand master who was also a gallant warrior.

CODA If Robert Heinlein had chosen some other career, it is hard to believe that he would not have succeeded as well as he did as a writer.

That thought occurred to both of us several times. By one of the world's ironies of timing, a few months ago one of us (CS) had spoken to Gregory Benford on the telephone about an anthology that Benford was editing, entitled "The Great Man." It would be an "alternate universe" set of stories, exploring the ways that the world might be different if some great man had never lived, or had chosen a different path in life.

Sitting in CS's computer on the day that he heard of Heinlein's death was a text file, constituting a set of notes and the opening of a story. They are printed here, just as they sit in computer memory.

The rest of the story will never be written. But perhaps the curious thing about it is that no one who met Heinlein more than casually will find this alternate universe at all improbable. We do not think that any other science fiction writer, living or dead, would have Robert Heinlein's credibility as protagonist in such a story.

Title: SHORE JOB

Scene in English Channel, 1944. Describe fog, stealth, non-combatant mission to rescue scientist through French resistance.

RAH was treated with penicillin in one of first uses of drug (Fleming discovers in 1927). Recovers completely from TB, stays in Navy. Now full captain, dedicated to life at sea. Also author of "Sailor Beware: How to survive in the U.S. Navy" —underground classic, no official existence but copy owned by every sailor. (Include excerpts: "Truth may be the first casualty of war, but commonsense is up there with it. Here are a few simple rules for survival.")

RAH responsible for torpedo boat making rescue attempt. Has been told by Admiral Moscheles ("Old Cockle") not to go ashore.

Rescues scientists as directed, but sees German D-day preparations. Decides must take back information, regardless of risk. Goes ashore against orders, tells crew to proceed without him if not back in six hours. Delayed for nearly twelve hours, crew disobey their own orders and wait for him. He brings back details of German plans.

RAH insists court martial appropriate, he disobeyed orders and Navy must run on orders. Offers no defense, but says did not expect to survive to face consequences of action.

Information obtained vital, Navy reluctant to punish. Meets top man of Navy, and is passed up line to President of U.S. He is offered a "shore job" as alternative to court martial. Says doesn't like idea, whole life has been as sailor.

The new job is described to him: RAH will be put in charge of captured rocket equipment and rocket scientists found at German facility called Peenemünde. It will be his task to take them, convert them into a national capability to launch and recover objects in space.

RAH admits—grudgingly—that something just might be doable along those lines.

END

SHORE JOB—First Draft

The move from open ocean to land-girt sea was sudden and unmistakable. Even in the darkness, with the ship creeping forward at less than nine knots, four of five senses caught the change. The steady pitching of the small vessel was replaced by a slow and gentle roll, the slap of waves at the bow vanished, and with it went the smell and taste of salt spindrift.

At five-thirty, daybreak began as a pale glow seeping through the fog. One of the two men on the bridge went forward and stared east, ahead of the ship. Visibility was no more than thirty meters. All that could be seen was water streaming past the bow, dark as liquorice.

He returned to the bridge, pausing on the way by a ventilation pipe and listening to the noises from below.

"Fifth day in a row," he said to the other man, when he was again at his position by the compass. "We're in the Channel all right, but where's the sun?"

"Having a lie-in. Don't blame him." Commander Isaacs stared all around them. Daylight had arrived, and the ship rode in a uniform hemispherical bowl of mist. The boom and wail of lighthouses and foghorns came from a hidden ghost world. "Better wake the Old

Man now," he said to the ensign. "He'll want to be here when we check our position."

"He's awake, sir. I heard him coughing his guts up when I went forward. This fog's killing him."

"He's getting it out of his system. He won't let himself cough on deck. Take him a mug of coffee."

"Yes, sir."

The man who followed Ensign Hubbard up the companionway five minutes later was in his middle thirties. He adjusted his cap as he climbed, clapping it tight on a close-cropped bullet head, while he tightened a woolen scarf around his neck with the other hand. At quarter to six in the morning he was already clean-shaven. Before coming to the bridge he went across to the rail, leaned there for a few seconds, and sniffed the air.

"In the Channel, Captain," said Isaacs.

The exchange of salutes was the casual one of old colleagues. "No doubt about that, Commander. Position?"

"We've held course east by nor'east since eight bells on the last watch, and we've made a steady eight and a half knots. From dead reckoning, we're four or five miles south of the Scillies, and not far east of Bishop's Rock. I'm not sure we'll get a look at the sun today."

The older man nodded. "We'll not see it. But I think we're farther east than you say. Listen."

The three men stood silent for ten seconds, until a long-drawn hoot, lasting a full four seconds, came through the fog.

"That's Wolf Rock, clear as a bell. We'll hear it every half minute. But I don't hear the Longships—two bangs. You see, we're too far east to hear it."

"You know the English Channel better than I do. But is there a chance the British have silenced the Longships, sir? For security?"

"Possible, but I'd be amazed."

"I heard they took down all their signposts inland, so the Germans wouldn't be able to find their way if they invade."

"Quite true. And now none of the Brits know where the devil they are when they travel. It's a well-observed phenomenon, Commander, that the British are blinking idiots ashore and geniuses at sea. They won't have silenced the Longships." He sniffed the air. "And it *smells* like the Channel. We'll hold our course."

He stood, warming his hands on a cup of coffee but not drinking, until the young ensign had left the bridge. Then he pulled a packet of papers from inside his jacket.

"Sealed orders, Isaacs."

"Yes, sir. The crew suspected it."

"They'd be fools not to, when we dither about in the middle of the Atlantic for three days. Not to be opened until east of the Scillies. I read them this morning. There's some good news, some bad. Good news first. Our man is alive.

END OF FILE

THE WITCH'S DAUGHTERS

Have no truck with the
daughters of Lilith.
Pay no mind to the
red-headed creatures.
Man, be warned by their
sharp, white teeth;
Consider their skulls, and their
other queer features.

They're not of our tribe, with their
flame-colored hair;
They're no sib to us, with their
pale, white skins;
There's no soul behind those
wild green eyes
Man, when you meet one—
walk widdershins!

When they die, they pop,
like burst soap bubble
(Eight hundred years
is their usual span).
Loving such beings
leads only to trouble.
By Heaven, be warned,
you rash young man!

RAH, August 1946